"I see you've slipped into your ice-queen mode," Julian remarked. "You know what happens to ice when it's left too close to a fire."

"And you think you're the fire to melt the ice? You're as arrogant as hell, Mr. Palmer." Pandora pretended not to see the devilish glint in his eyes or the way he purposely wet his lips as if contemplating pressing them to hers.

"Julian," she amended.

"There may be hope for you yet, Pan." He led her back to her seat and then sat across from her and her companion, smiling.

Caught up in the aura surrounding Julian Palmer, Pandora could only stare.

THE FIRES WITHIN

BEVERLY CLARK

Genesis Press, Inc.

Indigo

An imprint of Genesis Press, Inc.
Publishing Company

Genesis Press, Inc.
P.O. Box 101
Columbus, MS 39703

ISBN-13: 978-1-58571-244-1
ISBN-10: 1-58571-244-2

Manufactured in the United States of America

First Edition

Visit us at www.genesis-press.com
or call at 1-888-Indigo-1

DEDICATION

I would like to thank my children:
Catana, Alvin Jr., Dayna, Gloria, Ericca.

My new husband, Levi.

I would like to thank Elston and Sonia Poston for their encouraging words and for lending me their cheerleader spirit when I needed it.

And I would like to thank Terri, Zuolga, Lillian and Vassie for being my friends as well as my fans.

CHAPTER ONE

Standing at the windows of his thirty-fifth floor Park Avenue office suite, Julian Palmer gazed down at the hundreds of workers pouring from the surrounding skyscrapers. It was a little past five, and most were no doubt headed for the subway that would take them home to their families. The sight was a reminder of how much he wanted a family of his own to go home to. Although New York City was an exciting place to work and offered numerous challenges and diversions, at times it could also be cold and lonely. He knew all too well how cold, how lonely.

Once there had been a woman he had loved and who he thought loved him and wanted to share his life and raise a family. As it turned out, he had been dead wrong about her, and she had damn near destroyed him. It would take an exceptional woman for him to travel that road again. Judging from what he had seen of womankind lately, such a paragon did not exist.

The phone rang, drawing Julian back to the present.

"Yes, Paula. Put her on," he said, easing into his chair. "Gramma Edna."

"Don't you Gramma Edna me, Julian Darius Palmer. You promised to come visit and didn't. And when are you going to find a good woman and get married? What you need is a wife and half a dozen kids. They will make you a happy man."

"Now, Gramma Edna, I can't just grab some woman off the street, marry her and start a family."

"Don't you be flippant with me, young man. You haven't even been looking. And if you have, it obviously has not been in the right places. Now, I know that Vanessa Armstrong person did you wrong, but you can't judge all women by her."

"Please, Gramma, let's not go there. Look, I will get back to you real soon about a visit."

"All right. But don't think I'll forget this conversation. I'm not senile."

Julian smiled. "No, ma'am, you certainly are not. When the right woman comes along, I promise to do what comes naturally."

"You need to be out dating, not working at that office until all hours."

"Yes, ma'am, I'll try to do better. Bye now."

Julian returned to the window, feeling vaguely soul-weary. The mere mention of Vanessa's name had revived the bitter memory of betrayal he had suffered at her hands. His distressing visit to that unhappy time ended abruptly when his cousin Drac, his second in command at Palmer and Associates, walked in.

Returning to his desk, Julian asked, "You have the report?"

"Yes, right here," Drac replied, handing him a folder.

Julian took it and began reading its contents.

"You are joking about acquiring PanCo, right?" Drac asked anxiously. "I'm telling you, Jules, Pandora Cooper will never in a million years allow you to pull it off."

Julian looked up perplexed. "Allow? She might not have anything to say about it. But, no, I'm not joking. You know me better than that."

"You are aware of her reputation!" Drac sputtered. "Aren't you even the slightest bit put off by it?"

"No. Oh, I've heard about this reputation of hers, and I'm sure she's not all that," Julian answered, refocusing on the report.

"She *is* all that, and more," Drac said, annoyed that his cousin was treating his concerns so lightly. "You really should take her more seriously. Gaining control of her company is comparable to staking a claim in heaven. I'm telling you, Jules, Pandora Cooper is dangerous. She might be, even as we speak, contemplating taking *us* over. Talk about a shark of the first water. I take that back; she's a barracuda."

Drac's colorful description of the woman amused Julian. "This can't be my cousin, Dracula Palmer, the experienced, quintessential corporate raider talking."

"Experience doesn't enter into the picture when you're dealing with someone like Pandora Cooper," Drac bristled.

"Her being a woman has got nothing to do with it, either. It's that brilliant, shrewd brain of hers you have to watch out for."

"You make her sound invincible."

"Believe me, if that woman has a weakness, I don't know what it could be. How do you think she built her reputation and earned the title Black Widow of Wall Street? It wasn't by batting her eyelashes, I can assure you. She's taken over fifteen companies, and the sixteenth is pending right now, not to mention all the subsidiaries she has brought under the PanCo umbrella. And she has accomplished all that since opening the doors of PanCo eight years ago. Now do you see what I'm trying to get across to you?"

"Fifteen takeovers and one pending, huh?" Julian stroked his chin thoughtfully. "That's roughly two acquisitions per year. Impressive, damned impressive." Julian grinned, ignoring his cousin's exasperated expression. "If I didn't know you, Drac, I'd say you were a little afraid of the lady."

"Lady, nothing; she's a black widow spider."

Julian laughed. "Didn't I just hear you call her a barracuda?"

"This is not funny, Julian."

"Maybe I should make it my business to meet this formidable lady and judge for myself. Find out more about her, and her weaknesses, assuming she has some, and how I might use the information to our advantage."

"I hear she'll be attending the Martin Charity Dinner this evening."

"Then I'll just have to make it my business to be there, won't I?"

"Cassandra, make sure we have the latest report on Phillips Financial Investments before the upcoming stockholders meeting,"

Pandora Cooper instructed her personal assistant. "I want to take it home to study. Oh, and..."

"Yesum. Anything else, Boss? Massa?"

Pandora looked up from checking her calendar and smiled. "All right, I get the message. I just don't want any slipups this late in the game. I want to keep track of Roscoe Phillips's every move. I have him right where I want him, and I don't intend to let him wiggle off the hook."

"Why is gaining control of his company so important to you?" Cassandra asked.

"He's one of my late husband's cronies, and is one of the people who tried to ruin me after Lyman died. He's a die-hard chauvinist who believes that a woman's place is between the sheets, not conducting business in the boardroom. He's married, but did that stop him from coming on to me? Lyman's death was certainly no deterrent. In fact, it wasn't even a full month after his death when that despicable toad tried to get me into his bed. I have a serious score to settle with that man."

"I get it. Phillips Investments is his pride and joy, his baby, so to speak."

"Exactly. He doesn't know that DC Investments is a subsidiary of PanCo. And by the time he does, it'll be too late."

"He's going to have a stroke when he does find out," Cassandra predicted. "I can just see the look on his face. You know, he has even tried to hit on me, and I'm not remotely close to being his type."

Cassandra's employer was definitely his type. She could see why Roscoe Phillips, any man for that matter, would go for her. Pandora Cooper was an inch short of six feet and had a figure to die for. And she had the classic good looks some models would kill for. She wore her long, glossy black hair in a chignon, setting off her rich, flawless, toffee-colored complexion. Her unusual honey-gold eyes were alert and sharp, and they fairly glowed with intelligence. She exuded vitality and a cool shrewdness many a businessman wished he had.

Oblivious to her assistant's scrutiny, Pandora continued thumbing through her calendar. "Oh, damn. That charity dinner Edwin Martin invited me to is tonight! And there's no way I can get out of going. I'll have to leave the office early to find something appropriate to wear. What are you wearing?"

"I really don't want to go," Cassandra said carefully. "Do you mind if I pass on this one?"

"You know the old saying, misery loves company? If I have to suffer through one of these affairs, it is only fair that you suffer right along with me. Be ready to leave the office at four-thirty to go shopping with me. Of course, the company will pick up the tab for your gown and accessories."

Cassandra wanted to offer a stronger protest, but knew when her boss had that do-as-I-say-or-else sound in her voice that it was useless to try changing her mind.

"Don't look as if I handed you a death sentence, Cassandra," Pandora laughed. "Who knows, you might meet Mr. Right tonight."

"Like you, I'm beginning to think he's as extinct as the saber-toothed tiger. Maybe tonight you'll be the one to meet Mr. Right."

Her smile disappearing, Pandora threw Cassandra a look that could freeze water. "I think we should get back to work so we'll be finished in time to go shopping."

Without another word, Cassandra left the room. The subject had most definitely been closed.

Pandora watched Cassandra leave, regretting having snapped at her. But as far as she was concerned, Mr. Right didn't exist. Her husband had cured her of that particular fantasy years ago. Oh, she had dated occasionally since his death, but a permanent relationship was out of the question.

Pandora pulled a copy of *Financial Weekly* from the stack of financial publications on her desk. She read them all religiously. A picture of Julian Palmer graced the cover this week. She could tell from that smug, arrogant grin on his face that he thought he was king of the financial world, and God's gift to women, too, probably. As far as looks went, he looked like a taller, more sensuously attractive version of the actor Blair Underwood.

She flipped to the feature article on his company, which touted him as *the* man to watch in the future. Pandora was impressed by what she read about the company's track record. Palmer and Associates had under its umbrella way more subsidiaries than her company. But then they had been in business years longer than PanCo. Acquiring Palmer and Associates would be quite a coup if she could pull it off. All companies had their weaknesses.

Returning to the front cover, she wondered if Julian Palmer's apparent arrogance could perhaps be Palmer and Associates. Wresting control of a company from a man like him would be the ultimate challenge.

Pandora buzzed Cassandra on the intercom. "Add Palmer and Associates to your research list of future acquisitions."

Pandora had just finished applying her makeup when her daughter, Destinee, opened her bedroom door and poked her head in. Pandora smiled at this miracle she had helped to create. Her thirteen-year-old daughter was the center of her universe, the only thing in her life she could truly say belonged to her.

"May I come in and watch you get ready?" Destinee asked.

"Yes, come on in, honey. Maybe you can give me a few pointers."

"You don't need me to show you anything. You're beautiful, Mama, and you know it."

"How old are you?" Pandora teased. "Thirteen? Or going on thirty? It's hard to tell sometimes."

"Oh, Mom," she laughed, hugging her mother. Then the dress hanging on the closet door caught her attention. She walked over and picked up its hem, rubbing the fabric between her fingers. "I think this dress is the bomb."

"Thank you, Desi. What shoes do you think I should wear with it?"

Her head tilted to one side, Destinee studied the stunning black crepe dress, appreciating how the crystal-beaded bell design woven into the fabric spilled down the left side.

"I think your silver sandals would set it off perfectly."

Pandora agreed. Her daughter had a keen eye for fashion and had informed her a few months ago that she wanted to be a fashion designer/coordinator. Pandora responded that she would probably change her mind a dozen times before deciding on a career. Destinee had adamantly insisted that she would not. But she had seen evidence of her daughter's eye for style and was beginning to take her seriously.

"Is Neil going to take you to this charity thing tonight?"

"Yes, he is," Pandora answered, dabbing perfume behind her ears.

"Do you like him, Mama? I mean really like him?"

"He's a nice guy," Pandora conceded, fitting her diamond earrings into her earlobes.

"Is that all? Just nice? Not special?"

"Yes." Pandora looked at her curiously. "Why are you asking me that?"

"I thought maybe he was special enough that you would consider marrying him, then I would have a father and we could be a family."

"Whoa! You had a father, Desi."

"I know, but he's dead, and anyway I never really got to know him. He was always too busy to spend any time with me. I want a father I can do things with, one who will make us a family like most of my friends have."

Pandora hated denying her daughter the one thing she wanted so badly. But how could she explain to her child why marriage for her mother was out of the question without telling her the truth about the relationship between her parents?

"We don't need a man in our lives to be a family, honey. We are a family, just the two of us. You and me against the world. Remember?"

Destinee's expression said she didn't agree with her mother. Pandora empathized with her daughter. She herself had missed having a relationship with her own father when she was growing up.

Destinee had an uncle, but he had never shown any sign of wanting to fill that void in his niece's life. In fact, Monroe Cooper despised his brother's widow so much so he could barely tolerate being in his niece's presence because of her strong resemblance to her mother.

She walked over to the closet and removed her new dress from its hanger. She always wore black in public. She had been dubbed the black widow shortly after her husband's death. The Wall Street part of the nickname had been tacked on after her fourth corporate takeover, and had evolved into an even broader meaning over the years.

Pandora slipped the dress over her head and tugged it down her slender curves. She was one of those rare women who don't have to worry about their weight but still worked out three times a week to keep her muscles toned.

Pleased with the fit of the dress, Pandora then slipped on the silver sandals.

"Mama, you look good in black," Destinee said, "But I think it is past time for you to start wearing other colors."

Before Pandora could respond, Destinee quickly moved on to another subject.

"You need something else to complete the look."

"What do you think that might be?"

Destinee searched through the walk-in closet until she came to a clear plastic garment bag containing a silver ranch mink stole; she took it out and handed it to her mother.

Pandora was not pleased. It was a present from her late husband. She had told him that she was against wearing real animal fur, but he had insisted that she accept and wear it, anyway.

"What's wrong, Mama?" Destinee asked, sensing her mother's ambivalence.

"Nothing's wrong, honey."

She didn't believe her and was about to say so when the doorbell rang.

Pandora was relieved. "Rachel's not back from church, so you're going to have to go down and answer the door. It's probably Neil. Tell him I'll be down in a minute."

When her daughter had gone, Pandora returned the stole to its bag and hung it back up. Glaring at the stole balefully, she told herself she should have gotten rid of it long ago.

Then why haven't you, girlfriend?

Because it was a symbolic reminder of how manipulative and cruel men could be and how she could never completely trust one. She should donate it to a charity sale, but knew she wouldn't. Under no circumstances would she ever allow herself to forget what it stood for.

CHAPTER TWO

Julian shifted his gaze to the Martin Hotel's automatic brass and glass double doors each time they swished open. He had an unobstructed view of the foyer from his vantage point, several feet to the right of the concierges' desk. As he took a sip of his drink, he couldn't help doubting if the person he anticipated seeing would make an appearance.

"She may not even show up, Jules," Drac said, walking up behind his cousin.

"She?" Julian raised an inquiring brow.

"Come on, Jules, we both know the only reason you came here tonight was to check out Pandora Cooper. Speak the black widow's name, and the formidable lady appears."

Julian swung around and openly stared at the man and two women standing just inside the double doors. He had seen pictures of Pandora Cooper, and been inundated with news media hype about her business acumen, but none of that had prepared him for the stunning vision in the flowing black gown. He barely glanced at the other woman. He had eyes only for Pandora.

He'd read that Pandora's mother was East Indian. The blending of her African and Indian heritages lent her skin a warm, bronzed tint. And it complimented perfectly her beautiful hair, which was black as the deepest tar pit. She wore this glorious mane swept back from her classic features in a clever twist on top of her head. Her eyes were an unusual shade of brown or even gold, but from where he stood he couldn't be sure. His eyes traveled down her body, moving from her straight nose to the sensual fullness of her lips and on to the proud tilt of her chin.

His gaze lingered on the provocative jut of her high breasts, and then dropped lower to her slim waist, her softly curving hips, her sleek thighs, and finally to her long, shapely legs. Then his eyes journeyed back up her body, stopping at her ripe, kissable lips.

She was an exotically interesting woman, but the sight of a lush body had never rocked him like this. But it wasn't just her body that intrigued him. It was also the you-can-look-but-don't-touch warning on her lovely face when she caught him studying her.

Drac nudged Julian. "Your mouth is hanging open, man."

"What?" Julian answered absently, his eyes riveted on the woman sending barbed arrows his way.

"Beware of the black widow's bite; it has proven to be lethal."

It took Julian a moment to recover from Pandora Cooper's unexpected assault on his senses.

"Who are the people with her?" he finally asked Drac.

"Like you care. What you really mean is that you want to know who the man is, right? His name is Neil Parker. He and the black widow have been dating for a few months, which is surprising. She's kept him around longer than most. She usually drops them as quickly as a black widow spider disposes of her...."

"Don't say it, Drac; I think the lady just hasn't met the right man."

"Or that one fatal victim," Drac muttered under his breath. "You obviously think you're the man to take her in hand?"

"Maybe."

"Vanessa was also beautiful and sexy on top of being an astute businesswoman. You were just as attracted to her when you first met. I'm sure you haven't forgotten what she did."

"No, I haven't," Julian said, gritting his teeth. It was an effort to keep a tight rein on his temper because what his cousin so pointedly reminded him of, he was damned determined to forget. "Who is the other woman with them?"

"Cassie...I mean, Cassandra Jones."

"You know the lady, don't you?" Julian guessed. "I would say quite well, if your expression is anything to go by." Julian looked Cassandra over, observing how her chic gold silk dress and matching wrap complimented her black, artfully arranged braided hair, cocoa brown skin and dark eyes. "She is a very attractive woman," Julian remarked. "You managed to seduce her yet?"

Drac shot him a withering look.

Julian ignored it. "Ms. Jones is the source you used when I asked you to collect info on PanCo, isn't she?"

"One of them, yes," Drac spat out, looking guilty.

"Don't tell me you've actually fallen for the lady?"

Drac turned to face Julian. "That's none of your business."

"Oh, it's like that?" Julian grinned. "Go on with your bad self."

"Julian!"

"You don't have to explain anything to me. Right now my attention is focused on one lady in particular." He handed his drink to his cousin and discreetly trailed the trio into the huge formal dining room.

From the moment Pandora and her companions entered the foyer, she had the uneasy feeling she was being watched. After removing her wrap, she looked around and her eyes collided with an over-heated masculine presence that seemed intent on stripping her naked with his eyes. She knew her instincts had been right on target. She recognized Julian Palmer from his pictures in the financial magazines. He kept staring at her. How dare he look at her as if she were an all-day sucker he wanted to lick.

"Are you all right, Pandora?" Neil asked, noticing her annoyed expression.

"Yes, I'm fine."

"Amen to that."

As soon as they entered the dining room their host, Kerwin Martin, came over to greet them.

"Pandora, I'm so glad you could make it tonight. You, too, Neil, Cassandra," he added, graciously shaking their hands.

Kerwin guided Pandora and her party to their table. He was about to leave when Julian Palmer walked up.

"Julian," Kerwin smiled, "have you met Pandora Cooper?"

"No, I haven't had the pleasure."

"Then allow me to do the honors. Pandora Cooper, Julian Palmer."

"Ms. Cooper." Julian took her hand and brought it to his lips.

Pandora jerked her hand back as if she had been burned by an actual fire.

Julian grinned knowingly, and then said, "Where have you been all my life?"

"Out of your reach," Pandora shot back tartly, turning to her host. "By the way, Kerwin, where is Ingrid?"

"Oh, my wife is around here someplace. I'll see if I can locate her for you." He looked at Julian. "I haven't introduced you to Pandora's PA, Cassandra Jones, and their escort, Neil Parker."

Julian smiled at Cassandra. "Pleased to meet you, Ms. Jones." He glanced at Neil. "Parker," he said coolly.

"Palmer," Neil murmured tightly.

When Drac joined them, Kerwin introduced him to everyone. Cassandra smiled at him and said, "Drac, I didn't know you were going to be here tonight."

"Well, I hadn't planned to, but at the last minute I decided to come with my cousin. Now I'm glad I did."

"Since you've all been properly introduced, I'll leave you to get better acquainted," Kerwin said smoothly, backing away.

Pandora saw how anxious their host was to escape the awkwardness that Julian Palmer and his cousin had generated. She was relieved when the band began to play.

"Care to dance, Pandora?" Neil asked.

"Yes, I would love to."

"Save one for me," Julian said suggestively. When Pandora stopped, he added, "I'm putting my request in early because I know your dance card will fill up pretty quickly."

Pandora wanted to say she didn't want to save him a dance in this century or the next, but said instead, "It would be the polite thing to do." Neil guided her to the dance floor before she could say anything more.

Julian heard Drac ask Cassandra to dance, but wasn't really paying attention when they left. He was watching Pandora and Neil dance. After a few moments, he looked around and, seeing a lady he knew, strolled over to her.

"You really didn't want to come here tonight, did you?" Neil asked Pandora.

"No, but I'm here now," Pandora said. "I'll survive."

For some perverse reason she found herself searching for Julian Palmer. When she finally saw him, he was standing by the windows talking and laughing with a stunningly attractive woman who seemed totally entranced by him, apparently hanging on to his every word. Pandora scolded herself. Why should she care? Why was she letting it bother her one way or the other?

"If looks could kill, Julian Palmer should be a dead man," Neil teased.

Pandora frowned. "What are you trying to say?"

"Nothing. Really."

Still dancing with Neil, Pandora resumed her appraisal of Julian Palmer. He suddenly looked in her direction and those dark, glittering eyes of his caught and held hers captive. His smoldering smile disconcerted her. Tall, dark and handsome didn't begin to cover his sex appeal and animal magnetism.

He reminded her of a lion, the fiercest, and most formidable, of felines. The lion was a patient animal when stalking prey or courting a mate. Julian Palmer was definitely in the same category as that dangerous predator. Those amazing eyes held her in a kind of paralysis she couldn't break free of. She could tell by his smile and manner that he was confident of his ability to conquer the opposite sex, her particularly. He finally released her from his mesmerizing gaze and returned his attention to his companion.

Seeing how intently Drac was watching his cousin and Pandora, Cassandra said, "I don't think there is anything you can do."

"What do you mean?"

"You know what I mean."

"No, I don't."

"Come on, Drac. They are two very attractive, dynamic people. You saw their initial reaction to each other; they practically scorched the atmosphere around them."

"And? It doesn't necessarily follow that they…you make it sound as if the outcome is a foregone conclusion."

"You think so, too. Why else would you be so worried? What you should be doing is concentrating on our relationship, if that's what were having, and leave them to theirs. Well, is it a relationship, Drac? Considering all the questions you've been asking about PanCo, I wouldn't like to believe you were just using me to get the lowdown on my boss."

He smiled. "You know me better than that, Cassie."

"I hope I do."

"I'm just concerned about my cousin."

Cassandra looked at Drac and wondered if it was a good idea to continue seeing him. He was tall and handsome, with intense dark brown eyes that seemed to continuously analyze every person and every situation. Despite that, she was entranced by him.

When the music ended, Pandora and Neil came back to the table. She saw Julian heading to their table and nearly croaked when he sat down across from her.

Pandora was about to tell him that he was at the wrong table when he turned the place card around and his name was printed on it.

"What a pleasant coincidence that my cousin and I have been seated at the same table as you and Cassandra, Pan," he said, purposely excluding Neil.

Pandora glared at him suspiciously, wondering if he hadn't somehow arranged to be seated at her table. Damn him.

"The name is Pandora, Mr. Palmer."

"I know. It's Greek, and means all-gifted. I have to say the name fits you. Personally, I feel more comfortable using the shortened version."

So I intend to use it whether you like it or not was the silent finish he didn't need to say. The nerve of the man.

Pandora fumed.

"Mr. Palmer..."

"Call me Julian, Pan. Or Jules. My friends and people close to me do," he said, suggesting an intimacy that did not exist between them.

Pandora suppressed the impulse to call him an unprintable name. Instead she smiled sweetly and turned to Neil, completely ignoring Julian.

"I'm starved. I wonder when dinner will be served."

"You must be psychic," Julian answered. "The maitre d is signaling to his people to begin serving."

As they waited to be served, Julian studied Pandora, trying to figure out where she was coming from, but he was unable to home in on her particular frequency and it bothered the hell out of him. He never had trouble reading women; well, almost never. Vanessa Armstrong crossed his mind for a second and then was gone.

Julian sensed that Pandora Cooper was different. There was something about her that set her apart from other women, something beyond her great beauty, something elusive he couldn't quite describe.

The appetizer was shrimp cocktail. When Pandora sank her perfect white teeth into the succulent pink crustacean, Julian swallowed hard, practically salivating when her lips closed over the fork. What was the matter with him? He suddenly realized that he was losing sight of his reason for coming here tonight. And what made it so killing was that he was letting his libido govern his behavior.

Pandora picked up on what she assumed was frustration on Julian's face when he looked at her. He was probably used to women falling at his feet on sight. The arrogant rake. Rake? Now where did that word come from? They called men like him womanizers these days. Although rake was an old-fashioned word, it fit Julian Palmer to a tee. Aggressive, most assuredly fit. Perhaps rogue should be included on the list. She couldn't believe she was thinking these things.

For reasons that confounded her, Pandora found herself continuing to study this impossible man. She had to admit that Julian Palmer had a body many weight trainers would like to take credit for helping to build. He was muscular but not muscle-bound. He was drop-dead gorgeous in his tux. His smile was charming, but no less dangerous for all that. A woman could easily find herself succumbing to the enveloping spell he cast.

Pandora knew very well the effect a man like Julian Palmer could have on a woman. Her late husband came to mind, reinforcing her resolve to exclude intimate relationships from her life. Men had their uses. They were useful as escorts, but she had promised herself she would never get involved with one long-term ever again. And that was one promise she intended to keep.

Still, there was something about Julian Palmer. She watched the way his long slender fingers caressed the stem of his wine glass, and for a split second, imagined what they would feel like on her skin. She suddenly recalled how she had felt when her husband had touched her. Somehow she knew it would be nothing like that with this man. She would be in danger of a different kind. Allowing her mind to veer down that path more than disconcerted her.

"Are you sure you're all right, Pandora?" Neil asked, taking her hand in his. "Your fingers are freezing."

"I-I'm all right."

When the song "Close to You" started to play, Julian rose from his chair and extended his hand. "Ms. Cooper, may I have the pleasure of this dance?"

Pandora was about to refuse, but Julian took her hand and led her to the dance floor.

"Are you always so overbearing, Mr. Palmer?" she asked once they were on the floor.

"Call me Julian, Pan," he said softly.

"Don't call me that."

"Call you what?" he grinned. "Once you get to know me, you'll find I'm a very genial person, or so I've been told."

"I'm sure the majority of people who told you that were female."

"Since you're most definitely female, what do you think?"

"I'm not one of your women, Mr. Palmer, so what I think doesn't really matter."

Julian drew her closer. "The name is Julian."

The heat of his nearness unnerved Pandora, and she placed her hand on his chest to push him away.

But he drew her closer. "What are you afraid of? Surely, not of me."

What was he trying to do to her? She had to put some distance between them, but how could she hope to accomplish it during a slow dance?

"I'm not afraid of anything or anybody, especially not you, Mr. Palmer."

"If you call me that again, I might do something you'll say you don't like but really will."

"Like?"

He gave her a quick, sizzling kiss on the lips.

Pandora stiffened, barely containing the urge to run as fast as she could for the nearest exit. To do so would be cowardly, so she forced herself to remain outwardly calm and unresponsive until the music stopped.

"I see you've slipped into your ice-queen mode," Julian remarked. "You know what happens to ice when it's left too close to a fire."

"And you think you're the fire to melt the ice. You're as arrogant as hell, Mr. Palmer." She pretended not to see the devilish glint in his eyes or the way he purposely wet his lips as if contemplating pressing them to hers. "Julian," she amended.

"There may be hope for you yet, Pan." He led her back to her seat and then sat across from her, smiling.

Caught up in the aura surrounding Julian Palmer, Pandora could only stare.

Then Neil's voice broke her trance-like state. "Pandora. Pandora? Come back."

"What? Oh, I'm sorry, Neil."

"Is anything wrong?"

"No, of course not. Why would you think that?"

"Why do you keep staring at Julian Palmer that way?" he asked in a low voice. "Did he say something to offend you while you were dancing?"

"No," Pandora answered, annoyed by the question because it had touched a nerve. "I've done my duty in coming here and giving Kerwin and Ingrid my support. I'm ready to leave now."

"Don't worry about Cassie," Drac volunteered. "I'll see that she gets home safely."

Pandora got up to leave.

"I'm sorry to see you leave so soon, pretty lady," Julian said in a low, sexy voice.

"Yes, well, I'm a little tired," she replied, yawning to lend credibility to her words. "I've had a busy day."

His amused smile told Pandora he knew the real reason she wanted to leave, and being tired wasn't it.

"It's been interesting," Julian said, "I hope to see more of you in the near future, Ms. Cooper."

Pandora again compared him to a lion pursuing a mate. According to an article she had read in the style section of *The New York Times* he was one of the most eligible bachelors in New York City, hinting that he wanted it to remain that way. But the way he looked her over belied that. Just gazing into his roving dark eyes sent shivers through her. But it didn't matter what he wanted, she definitely wasn't in the market for a lover, and Julian Palmer had better get that through his head. And yet something in that seductive smile of his said she would be wise not to discount any possibilities where he was concerned.

CHAPTER THREE

"Dressed to do your usual damage, I see," Cassandra said, commenting on her boss's outfit as Pandora walked past her desk Monday morning.

"It's always best for a woman to wear her power suit when dealing with men in business. You are taken more seriously," Pandora said, entering her office.

"I doubt if any businessman in this city is stupid enough not to take you seriously, power suit or no," Cassandra remarked, following her inside.

"I know why I keep you around," she said, tossing her briefcase onto her desk. "You're good for my ego, on top of being one of the best personal assistants in New York City. Are we ready to do it?"

"Yes, ma'am."

"You do have the very latest report on Phillips Investments?"

"As you requested."

"Good."

"You're really something, boss lady." And she definitely was that, Cassandra thought. The black pinstripe suit she wore made an I-intend-to-kick-some-serious-butt statement. "We have everything we're going to need," she added.

Board members and stockholders were filing into the conference room when Pandora and Cassandra arrived at Phillips Investments. They hung back until most were seated, and then took chairs near the back of the room.

When Roscoe Phillips brought the meeting to order, Pandora opened her briefcase and took out a folder.

The polling of stockholders soon began.

"Conrad Banker, one share," Roscoe called out.

Pandora Cooper held up a proxy sheet. "I have secured their vote." She saw the look of barely concealed anger in Roscoe Phillips's face when he saw her.

He cleared his throat and continued the polling. Pandora answered three more times at one vote each. Tight-lipped rage gripped Roscoe Philips when it finally dawned on him what was happening.

The buzzing sound of surprise and confusion from the other stockholders and spectators filled the room.

"Monroe Cooper, fifteen shares," Roscoe read, smiling at her nemesis.

Pandora looked smugly confident. She had known her brother-in-law was buying up just enough stock for what he thought would gain him a significant toehold in the company. And so she was always staying several jumps ahead of him.

"Roscoe Phillips, twenty-five shares," Roscoe proudly announced, sending an overconfident smile Pandora's way.

"Brim Con, one share." Julian answered.

Pandora's head jerked up in surprise. She wondered why he had decided to acquire stock in Phillips Investments. The share he held was among the few she had been unable to secure. An uncomfortable feeling bubbled up inside Pandora. What game could he possibly be playing?

Maybe you're the game he's really after, an inner voice whispered.

When Roscoe Phillips gazed at Pandora, he suddenly looked sick and turned the proceedings over to his vice president, Nolan Anderson.

So far, Roscoe and company owned or had under their control forty-six percent of the majority votes and common shares of stocks. Pandora could see that Roscoe was getting anxious because he was now sweating profusely and looked as though he might pass out any minute.

Pandora allowed herself a confident smile. Roscoe should have been more conscientious about securing control of the votes, as well as his stock options, before going public. He had the right idea, but not the shrewdness needed to pull it off. Whenever a company makes stock available to the public, it runs the risk of losing control or being taken over. It had become abundantly clear that Roscoe had not planned properly for either possibility.

Julian watched as Pandora circled her prey like the barracuda his cousin had compared her to. She raised her hand several more times; one proxy at four shares, another at five and yet another at ten. Drac had tried to warn him about her, but he hadn't taken the warning seriously. There was no doubt that when the meeting ended, Pandora would indeed have controlling interest in Phillips Investments.

He glanced at Monroe Cooper and saw his eyes ablaze with hatred when he looked at Pandora. It was obvious there was no love lost between the two, but, judging from the way Pandora glared back at her brother-in-law, he felt there was something deeper, much deeper, to their relationship. What was the history behind those barbed looks passing between them? Could they have once been lovers at some point? Or even as recently as a few days before this meeting?

"DC Investments, twenty shares," Nolan Anderson announced.

Pandora answered, relishing the shocked look on Roscoe Phillips's face when he realized she owned DC Investments.

"Jeremy Kendricks, Sharp Securities, three proxy votes."

"I have his proxy," Julian answered.

"Lloyd Whitman, five shares," Nolan Anderson continued.

Pandora answered. "I have secured his proxy."

The room suddenly grew quiet enough to hear a cotton ball drop. It was down to crunch time. So far Pandora owned forty-eight percent of the company's shares and proxy votes and needed only three more to win control.

Pandora smiled. It was exhilarating to be so close to gaining control of Roscoe Phillips's company and getting one over on her brother-in-law. She glared at the two men who had tried to either seduce or threaten her into submission. She had screwed the top down on them quite nicely and was now primed for the final strike.

Julian had played along with Monroe Cooper's clever little game because he was curious to know what was going on and, of course, to see Pandora in action. Watching her was worth dealing with the likes of Monroe Cooper and Roscoe Phillips.

"Seaboard Corporation, three shares."

Monroe and Roscoe smiled at each other and looked around for Charles Healey, the broker for Seaboard Corporation. Pandora knew from their smug expressions that they felt secure in the knowledge that the vote was safely theirs and victory was only moments away.

"I have secured his proxy," Pandora replied triumphantly, holding up the document.

"But that's impossible," Roscoe shouted over the din in the room.

"No, it's not. Seaboard signed their shares over to me last night. It's all perfectly legal, I can assure you."

"Ms. Pandora Cooper now owns fifty-one percent of Phillips Investments by outright shares and proxy votes," Anderson reluctantly conceded.

Julian had never seen such a triumphant look on a female's face, but he was sure that the one he saw in Pandora Cooper's couldn't be matched.

It began to dawn on him why Pandora took over companies with such vengeance and relish. They were all headed by powerful men. She obviously had little or no respect for them. He wondered if she felt that way about all men. He knew he should be wary of, and be turned off by, what he had discovered. Instead, he was more intrigued than ever by this phenomenal woman. He stood and left the room through a side exit. Drac was right on target; Pandora Cooper *was* dangerous. He knew he would have to be cautious in his dealings with her. It wasn't going to be easy, because he was intensely attracted to her.

Pandora looked around for Julian. When she didn't find him, she felt an unwelcome sense of disappointment.

A newsman from a television station pushed a microphone into Pandora's face as she exited the stockholders meeting.

"Any challenges left, Ms. Cooper?"

"There will always be other challenges."

Monroe Cooper stepped in front of her. "You're going to get a taste of your own medicine one day, Pandora," he jeered. "And I want to be there to see you choke on the bitter dregs, Ms. Black Widow of Wall Street."

Before she could reply, Monroe stalked away.

"Any comment on that, Ms. Cooper?" a reporter from another station asked.

"No," Pandora answered. "I've won the day as I had intended." After learning how badly Monroe had wanted those shares, her strategy had been to start discreetly securing small numbers of them over the last year and a half. She was proud of how well this tactic had worked.

"You think you've done something great today, don't you?" Roscoe shouted as he approached Pandora.

"I have controlling interest of your company. I'd have to say it feels great. You can expect a very different agenda in the future. You're getting exactly what you deserve, you arrogant bastard."

"It's all because I dared try to get the untouchable black widow in my bed, isn't it?" he asked viciously.

"It's not just that. You're married, for one thing, and for another, you dared to forget with whom you're dealing. I'm not your average lady. In fact, I think I'm more than you, or any man, will ever know what to do with. I know the one thing you won't forget is what happened here today, will you?" With that, she walked away.

"You really are a black widow spider, aren't you, Ms. High and Mighty Bitch? You called the damned media, didn't you?" he yelled after her. "What did you offer Healey for those shares? What you wouldn't give to me?" he said nastily. "You're going to pay for what you've done to me. I won't rest until I see it happen. If it's the last thing I ever do, I'm going to bring you down," he said, pushing his way through the crowd of reporters and cameramen.

"I'd say you've made a dangerous enemy, Pan. If I were you, I would watch my back from now on," Julian said, standing at the bottom of the stairs of the Phillips building as Pandora rushed to escape the media.

"Thanks for the advice, Mr. Palmer. And just how did you happen to come by that stock and those proxy votes? And why would you want to buy them? Or were you really interested in Phillips Financial Investments?"

"Oh, I had my own reasons for acquiring them."

"And you're not going to tell me what they are, are you? In gaining control, have I also made you my enemy?"

Julian grinned. "No, you haven't, at least not yet, anyway. I foresee a quite different kind of relationship springing up between us, lady."

"Dream on."

"Oh, I can assure you that what I envision will be more than a dream, Pan. And you'll enjoy the reality of it as much as I will."

"Why you…"

"If you call me a name, I'll…"

Pandora moved back a step.

He smiled. "Retreat can be the better part of valor. You can run, but you cannot hide. Another time, Pan. Until then, *hasta la vista*, baby."

Having overheard the exchange, and seeing the harried look on Pandora's face, Cassandra asked, "Are you all right?"

"No, I'm not all right. I want you to find out everything there is to know about Julian Palmer. And, no, I won't be all right until I've taken Palmer and Associates out from under its arrogant owner's nose."

"I think maybe you should forget about that. You may just be out of your depth."

"We'll see about that."

"How did the meeting go, Jules?" Drac asked his cousin when he returned to the office.

"Pretty much as you predicted. You were right, by the way; Pandora Cooper is all that and more. I never thought, never imagined, things would actually turn out the way they did."

"So she's gained controlling interest in Phillips Investments," Drac commented matter of factly. "It's no big deal, Jules."

"Even after having seen her in action, I can hardly believe what I saw," Julian said, looking awestruck.

"So what is your next move?"

"I haven't decided on a precise game plan. I need to find out what makes this woman tick. The file you compiled is superficial. I want to know about her personal life."

Julian poured himself a cup of coffee. "Do you intend to go on seeing her personal assistant? Cassandra, is it?"

"Yes, but..."

"There is vital information only she can provide."

Drac stirred nervously. "Look, Julian..."

"Don't sweat it, Drac. I'm not going to use the information to get her in trouble. Although I'm not yet sure how I intend using the information once I have it. I've never met a woman quite like Ms. Cooper. Achieving my goal will be a real challenge every step of the way."

"What exactly is your goal? I'm not sure I know what it is anymore. I thought you were just interested in obtaining her company."

"I was, I mean, I am."

"It seems to me you're more interested in the woman than her company. Can't you see the similarities between her and Vanessa? That woman put you through hell, Julian. Surely, you're not eager to go that route again." When Julian didn't answer, Drac shook his head. "I think you're obsessed with Pandora Cooper. And I can't for the life of me understand why."

"You wouldn't, because you only see her as a black widow spider. I see more than that. There's something about her—I can't explain it—but you know how I love solving puzzles."

"She's more than just a puzzle, Jules."

"Probably, but if she can be put together, I want to be the one to assemble the pieces."

"Now, Jules."

"You stick with Cassandra and leave Pandora Cooper to me."

CHAPTER FOUR

"Do you think it's wise to..." Cassandra began.

Pandora cut her off. "I know what I'm doing, Cassandra. Julian Palmer needs to learn that my being a woman doesn't mean he can dismiss me as a force to be reckoned with."

"I doubt if he does. He seemed genuinely interested in you as an attractive woman at the charity dinner, and again when he approached you last week after the stockholders meeting at Phillips Investments."

"He probably has his sights set on my company and thinks he can seduce me into a relationship with him. And as a thank you gift, I should hand my business over to him. I've got news for him, it ain't gonna happen."

"You really believe PanCo is all he's interested in?"

"I'm not so sure he isn't using his cousin to get to me through you."

Cassandra opened her mouth to speak, then closed it, her expression troubled.

"I'm sorry, Cassandra. I know how you feel about him, but it is a possibility."

"I know. I've wondered the same thing since we started seriously seeing each other."

"It's just another reason to go ahead with my plan. Has Joshua Brewer called?"

"No, not yet. He said as soon as he has accomplished his mission he will get in touch with us."

"I know he did. It's just that I'm anxious to know if he was successful without alerting Julian Palmer to our game plan."

"If he's anything like Drac described him, you won't be able to pull it off."

"You make him sound—he's just a man like any other, Cassandra, not God."

Just then Joshua Brewer strode in.

Pandora smiled. "Josh, what do you have for me?"

"You'll have to figure out another way to gain control of Palmer and Associates. His mother and grandmother each own twenty percent of the available stock in the company. As for the rest of the shareholders, Palmer has an option clause with them."

"What kind of option clause?"

"Before they can sell to any outsiders, he is to be informed and allowed to make a counter-offer. And not only that, he has the right of first refusal, which means..."

"He has the right to approve or disapprove any buyers that he feels do not have the best interest of the company in mind with their offer? We can forget about the forty percent his mother and grandmother own. They certainly wouldn't consider selling to us."

"I'm sorry, Pandora. I tried to warn you. The shareholders I've spoken to will no doubt alert Palmer to the fact that I approached them with an offer to buy them out."

"There has to be another way."

"If there is, I'm not aware of it," Josh answered. "If you didn't have a similar clause..."

"He could raze PanCo," she finished. "He's been one step ahead of me all the way. That doesn't happen very often. Julian Palmer is a more formidable rival than I thought. I should have listened when Cassandra suggested reconsidering any aspirations I had of gaining a toehold in his company. There is no other way to get into Palmer and Associates unless he allows it, is there?"

"You know the answer to that. Why are you so obsessed with acquiring Palmer and Associates? There are other companies just as lucrative, and much easier to obtain."

"There's no challenge in just acquiring unless—you wouldn't understand, Josh. Well, it's over for now."

"You mean you *still* haven't given up completely on the idea?" Josh asked, incredulously.

"Oh, no. This is only a temporary setback—temporary being the operative word."

Cassandra could see that Josh was still in awe of Pandora after years of doing business with her. Josh was an independent broker Pandora sometimes used as a blind to prevent companies from finding out her interest in taking them over. She knew it frustrated him no end when Pandora tenaciously insisted on doing it her way, completely ignoring his advice.

After Josh left her office, Pandora started pacing before the bank of windows. She wondered what Julian Palmer would do once he found out what she had tried to do. Using his sources, she knew it wouldn't take him very long. He had said they weren't enemies, hinting at unfinished business between them. If he really felt that way, what would he do next? He wasn't the kind of man to let something like this ride.

"What did I tell you?" Handing Julian a report, Drac shot his cousin an I-told-you-so look.

After he had finished looking it over, Julian muttered, "It's a good thing I covered my butt. If I hadn't, you might very well have the formidable Ms. Cooper for your new boss. The woman is shrewd. It was all in a days work using Joshua Brewer to do her scouting. Evidently, she'll stop at nothing to get what she wants. I have to admit I admire that about her."

"You certainly didn't admire that quality in Vanessa when she used it against you. As I recall, you said she was an unprincipled bitch."

"That was different."

"How do you figure? Vanessa may have gone about it differently, but the results were the same. If you don't stay alert, Ms. Pandora Cooper will end up outmaneuvering you, too. You saw for yourself how determined she can be. Do you really want to chance taking another viper to your bed?"

Julian became contemplative. He now knew that Pandora had this thing about triumphing over men in business. An image of Vanessa the day he discovered how thoroughly she had betrayed him popped into his head. She had been all smiles and sexy words when she delivered the final *coup de grace*. It was just days before their wedding, and they had just finished making love.

"You're fantastic in bed, Jules," Vanessa said sultrily.

"It's because I love you so much." He kissed her neck and then her breasts.

She eased off the bed.

"Where are you going? I'm not nearly finished with you."

"But I am with you," she said picking up her clothes from the chair where she had flung them in her haste to have her way with him.

"It's only an appetizer. I may not let you out of my sight for at least a month after we're married," he said, getting up and grabbing her.

"I said I was finished with you, and I meant it. I had to have a taste of your wildfire passion just one more time before…"

Julian tensed. "Before what?"

Vanessa started dressing.

"Before what, Vanessa?"

"My father's company is solidly back on its feet, thanks to your expertise, your connections and your money."

He reached for her. "You know I didn't mind helping you. I love you and was more than glad to do it. But what does that have to do with what you just said? I don't understand."

"I'll make it clear to you. I've found somebody else."

Julian hauled Vanessa to his chest. "What the hell do you mean, you've found somebody else?"

"Just that. Elton Powell is the new man in my life."

"Is this some kind of sick joke and I'm slow getting the punch line? We're going to be married in a matter of days."

"I'm sorry, but it's not going to happen."

"Now that I've practically depleted the cash flow in my own company to help you, you no longer have any use for me? Is that what you're telling me, Vanessa?" he asked, shoving her away from him.

"There's no need for you to get violent. We can still be lovers."

"You're wrong; we can't. You knew I wanted you for my wife and that I wanted to raise a family with you."

"The wife part I could have handled, but I definitely don't want any squalling brats tugging on my skirts."

"That wasn't what you told me when we discussed having children." He shook his head to clear it. "So I was just a steppingstone to richer pickings. I know Elton, and he has quite a reputation with women. He'll never marry you." Julian strode over to Vanessa's purse on the dresser and threw it at her. "Hurry up and get the hell out."

"If you change your mind about being my lover..."

"I won't. I'm not that hard up for sex. As far as I'm concerned you no longer exist."

Vanessa had not only torn his heart to shreds but had also wormed millions of dollars out of him. He had come close, much too close, to compromising the family business because of her. That was something he could never forget or forgive. He would be damned if he would allow history to repeat itself. Still, he desired Pandora Cooper like crazy.

"Pandora isn't Vanessa," Julian said, returning to the conversation with his cousin. "After seeing the clever way she handles takeovers, I've come to the conclusion that she's almost as good at what I do as I am. Despite what I already know about her, hell, I'm still no closer to finding out anything useful about her. But I sure intend to keep on trying until I do."

"Don't forget that although the black widow's web may look as fragile as gossamer, its entangling threads are like cables of steel, Julian," Drac warned. "You will do well not to forget that."

"Whereas I gave stock to my mother and grandmother, she has thirty-five percent of her stock in a trust portfolio account in her daughter's name. And, of course, she's the broker. She's left no loose ends dangling where her company or her daughter's security is concerned."

"Did you even hear what I said, Jules?"

"I heard you, all right, Drac. And I'm not about to forget how dangerous Pandora can be. I can handle it, don't worry."

"Then you don't plan to stay away from her, do you?"

When Julian didn't answer, Drac knew there was cause for concern. "Jules!"

Julian just smiled mysteriously. He may have won the first round with Pandora, but he had a feeling it was just the beginning.

"Mr. Monroe Cooper is here to see you," Cassandra informed Pandora over the intercom.

She grimaced. "Send him in."

Monroe strode into Pandora's office looking like a proud warrior surveying the property of an enemy he intends to annihilate. Monroe Cooper was a handsome black man in his early forties with salt and pepper hair. His good looks, however, did little to conceal his hard, abrasive ways. He was seven years younger than her late husband. Lyman had been fifteen years older than Pandora. Mere days after his death, she learned that Monroe and his brother were more alike than she had imagined. She had seen the same cruel streak shining in Monroe's eyes and oozing from his arrogant manner as in his brother's.

"All right, Monroe, why are you here?"

"I still make you uneasy, don't I, despite your winning performance at the stockholders meeting."

"Snakes always have that effect on me. Now get to the point of your visit."

He gazed at her insolently. "You're all business, right? I knew you first, Pandora, but when you met my wealthy older brother you decided to marry him instead. I tried to warn you that you were making a mistake, but you wouldn't listen. I would have appreciated you much more than he ever could. But then, my brother had more money than I did, didn't he?"

"I didn't marry him for his money, and you know it."

"Right. You were a poor but brilliant waif who had the misfortune to fall for and marry a father figure. Today you are no longer a waif but still brilliant, and don't forget wealthy, thanks to my brother's money."

"If you want to think that. Now if you came here just to harass and insult me…"

"I didn't. It's time for our yearly meeting to discuss my niece's welfare, per my brother's instructions in his will."

Pandora had forgotten it was that time again. How she hated Lyman for arranging things this way. Although she might hate it, she knew she had no choice but to accept his terms. Having to deal with Monroe about things concerning Destinee was her husband's ultimate revenge. She had learned early in the marriage how jealous and controlling he could be. It wasn't your usual jealousy; he believed that her instincts in business surpassed his. That was a definite no-no for a woman to do that to a proud, chauvinistic man like Lyman Cooper. But he had found a way to control her from the grave; using her love for her daughter and her dislike of dealing with his brother as the licking stick.

The self-satisfied smirk on Monroe's face said he was reveling in his power and her discomfort at having to deal with him.

"You could have called and made an appointment, Monroe."

"And give you time to reinforce your defenses? I love needling you, Pandora. You may be a genius in business, but underneath you're as human as the rest of us mere mortals. Maybe more so."

"Monroe," she said impatiently, "let's get on with the meeting. I do have other business that requires my attention."

"Destinee will be starting high school in the fall. I have a list of the best schools for you to consider."

"Destinee and I have already chosen a school, thank you."

"Since I share guardianship with you, you could have had the common decency to ask my advice."

"I didn't think we needed to, Monroe. It's not as if you really care. According to the guardianship papers, your position is not absolute. What I do regarding my daughter is my business, and you only have a say if you believe, or can prove, I'm not acting in her best interest. I'm above reproach on that score, and I always will be."

"And you'd better stay that way. You're so smug, aren't you, Pandora? If I find anything the slightest bit questionable or improper in your care of my niece, I'll jump on you with hobnailed boots. If you had married me in the first place, you could have saved yourself..."

"I wouldn't have married you because I didn't love you, Monroe."

"But you loved my brother, right?"

"Whether you believe it or not, I did."

"So much for love. Take one step wrong, Pandora, and I'll move to get custody of Destinee so fast you won't know what hit you."

"You're worse than a rattlesnake, Monroe."

"Don't forget how poisonous they are, and that just one bite could prove fatal."

"Are you threatening me?"

"No, of course not. I'm just making sure you know where I'm coming from, that's all. I think we should get on with the meeting, don't you?"

Pandora was mentally battered and emotionally drained by the time Monroe left her office. She knew the reason he was so resentful of her, but there was nothing she could do to change the past. Why couldn't he accept that? He had been in top form today. How could any one man be so obnoxious? Pandora glared at the check he had left on the desk. He knew she didn't need, or want, it. Instead of depositing the money in an account for Destinee, Monroe had chosen to give it to her in person, rubbing her nose in the fact that he had a say in her daughter's welfare.

Pandora deposited the yearly profits due her daughter from the Cooper Corporation into a trust fund, separate from the stocks Pandora had set up in the company in her daughter's name. Through her father, Destinee also had percentages in several of the Cooper family's other businesses. When she reached the age of twenty-five, she would be an extremely wealthy young woman.

Monroe liked to remind Pandora that Lyman had left sixty percent of one of the major family businesses to him and their sister, Sasha. Rather than continue working at the Cooper Corporation, Pandora had sold her stock in the company. Then she had resigned, using the profits from the sale to start her own investment business.

When Monroe found out what she had been up to, he was more than a little pissed off and vowed to make her pay for not selling her interest to him. He had bought back most of the stock, but at a much higher price. She knew he would never stop hating her for that. Since then he had tried every conceivable scheme under the sun to trip her up. He couldn't get back at her in business, so he used his position as Destinee's co-guardian to insinuate himself into her life.

She was tired of fighting with him and enduring Sasha's rudeness and malicious remarks. Had she thought it would have kept them from treating her like dirt, she would have sold her share in the business to Monroe, but she knew better. Sasha was jealous, and Monroe Cooper wanted not only to possess her but also to punish her for choosing his brother over him.

This fixation of Monroe's wasn't about love or marriage anymore, or even the business; it was about power, greed and revenge, not necessarily in that order.

"You look like you could use a cup of coffee right about now," Cassandra said, coming in with a pot of coffee and a cup on a tray.

"You're a lifesaver, Cassandra. It's exactly what I need. Was Mr. Cooper his usual sweet self?"

"What else? He mentioned marriage and me and him in the same sentence. I would rather have married Godzilla."

Cassandra laughed. "I think Godzilla is kind of cute."

"You would, but then you're weird. You and Drac Palmer are perfect for each other," she said wryly, taking a sip of coffee. Cassandra had told her how Drac's father's obsession with horror flicks had led him to name his sons Dracula and Frankenstein, respectively.

"Your sister-in-law called to remind you about the Cooper family's annual summer party."

"I wish I could avoid contact with the entire Cooper clan, but since they are my daughter's only other family, I can't. I wish I had brothers and sisters. At six months old, my father was left at an orphanage; he never knew his father or his mother. My mother's sister, the only relative my mother had left, died when I was twelve. Monroe, Sasha and her children are the only close family Destinee has got."

"With hardly any family you must have had a lonely childhood."

"I did. I barely remember my father. He was always away on some story or other. He was a freelance photojournalist on assignment in India when he met and married my mother and brought her to the States. It had to have been a complete culture shock for her. When I was eight, he died in a plane crash en route to an assignment."

"Your mother must have been a strong woman to raise a child alone in a country with a culture so different from her own."

"She had become a citizen only a little over a year before my father was killed."

"How did you and your mother live?"

"She was a talented seamstress and did intricate needle work. She was hired by one of the exclusive fashion houses in the garment district. We didn't have much money, but we managed. I promised myself when I grew up I would take care of her. But she died from pneumonia when I was eighteen, and I never got the chance to make her life easier."

"You were left on your own at a young, vulnerable age, weren't you?"

"I graduated from high school at fifteen and got a scholarship through the gifted program with the government to go to New York University. I was a year away from graduating when my mother died."

"You graduated from college at nineteen! I knew you were a genius, but…"

Pandora laughed. "Don't spread it around, okay? I don't see myself as being very smart. I married Lyman Cooper, didn't I? The only good thing to come from my marriage was Destinee. I can never regret having her."

CHAPTER FIVE

"I don't see why we can't skip going to Aunt Sasha's party just this once," Destinee whined, getting into the car.

"Now, Desi, let's not go there, okay?"

"I would love to not go there. Uncle Monroe will be there, and you know I can't stand him."

"Destinee!"

"Well, it's true. He's all for show every time I see him. I know he doesn't like me, and neither does Aunt Sasha."

Pandora cringed. What could she say? They had to go. She wasn't giving Monroe ammunition to use against her. If she didn't go, he could convince a judge she was deliberately keeping Destinee from her family.

"I thought you liked being with your cousins."

"I do most of the time. If it wasn't for Aunt Sasha..."

"Maybe it won't be so bad this time."

Her expression said not. Pandora understood her daughter's aversion to being around her aunt and uncle. Pandora always felt uncomfortable in her sister-in-laws company. When the house came into view after she had turned her car onto the road leading to it, Pandora frowned. It was a beautiful country estate and it had once belonged to Lyman. He'd left it to his sister because he knew how much Pandora had loved the place. Each time she came here since his death was yet another slap in the face. Her husband had been the ultimate control freak. Just because she hadn't asked how high when he said jump, he had done this malicious act to get back at her.

Destinee had been a baby when they came here and didn't remember how it was, but her mother would never forget. Since her husband spent the majority his time in New York City and rarely at their country home, it had been her haven, her escape from the everyday New York City rat race. She would take her daughter there on weekends the first few years of their marriage. But Lyman had taken even that simple pleasure away from her. He couldn't stand seeing her happy.

As they were getting out of the car her sister-in-law came through the front door. Sasha had her usual exaggerated sweet smile pasted on her thin brown face. She wore her black hair in a short afro style. Although not a pretty woman, she might have been more attractive if not for her sarcastic, catty attitude. Pandora steeled herself against the deep dislike she had for the woman.

"Pandora, you're right on time," Sasha said, smiling at her niece. "Destinee, what a cute outfit. Miranda has been worrying me to death about when you were going to get here. She and the other kids are down by the pool. I hope you brought your swimsuit. Go on down and join them while your mother and I have a little chat."

The look Destinee gave her mother seemed to ask, *Do you really want me to leave you alone with Aunt Sasha?*

"Go ahead, honey," Pandora urged, taking her daughter's sport bag from off the back seat and handing it to her. "Enjoy yourself. I'll be along in a little while."

"You really should give me and Monroe custody of her, Pandora," Sasha said as soon as Destinee was out of earshot. "We are her family."

"I'm her mother, Sasha, not you. I'm all the family she needs and wants. She belongs with me, and that's where she's going to stay. End of discussion."

"I'll never understand what Lyman saw in you," Sasha laughed. "Then again, maybe I do," she said, looking Pandora up and down. "I guess it's the reason most older men marry much younger women."

"Sasha, can't you at least pretend to be civilized?"

Sasha's face darkened. "I think we should join the rest of the guests."

Pandora hated these little confrontations with her sister-in-law. It was as though Lyman was somehow instructing his sister on ways to ruin her life. But she refused to give him or Sasha the satisfaction of caving.

Pandora's stomach lurched at what she saw when she reached the patio. Lyman may have failed to drive her completely crazy, but his brother was giving it his best. Monroe walked up to greet her, but he wasn't what caught her eye; it was Roscoe Phillips following a few steps behind him. The smirk on his face said how much he was enjoying her reaction to seeing him there.

"If it isn't my company's major stockholder," Roscoe said snidely, urging the woman behind him forward. "Janice, I'd like you to meet the formidable Ms. Pandora Cooper, the Black Widow of Wall Street, in all her poisonous glory."

Janice extended her hand to Pandora. "Pleased to meet you, Ms. Cooper."

Monroe wore a deceptively friendly smile. "Don't be so formal, Janice. You can call her Pandora." He turned to Pandora. "If it's all right with you. Is it?"

"Of course." Pandora seethed with anger at Monroe and Roscoe's latest attempt to unnerve her.

"If you'll excuse us," Monroe said to Roscoe and his wife, putting his hand beneath Pandora's elbow and leading her away.

Pandora jerked her arm away.

"Why did you invite Roscoe Phillips here?" she demanded.

"He's only the tip of the iceberg, my dear sister-in-law. Julian," he called out.

Pandora turned and saw Julian Palmer at the bar, a drink in his hand. He lifted his glass and saluted her. She glared at him, and then at her brother-in-law.

"I would introduce you, but I think you two already know each other, don't you?" Monroe asked sarcastically. "You did, after all, try to take over his company."

Julian walked over. "Yes, we do know each other, but not as well as I would like."

"Now that you're here, Pandora, it evens out the numbers.

I'll leave you two to get better acquainted while I mingle with my other guests," Monroe said, flashing a nasty imitation of a smile.

Julian's face was a study in amused curiosity. "I have to say I like the way fate keeps throwing us together."

"If that's what you want to call it. If you'll excuse me." Pandora tried to walk past Julian.

He caught her wrist, stopping her cold. "Not so fast, Pan, I want to get to know you better."

"Mr. Palmer, I haven't got time for this."

He pulled her toward him. "You could make time, couldn't you?" He led her toward a white lattice gazebo a few feet away.

Pandora tried to pull her wrist free, but he wouldn't let go. She felt like screaming, but when she saw interested eyes watching them, she let him lead her into the gazebo.

"Sit down, Pan."

"Would you please stop calling me that!"

"Why? Does it really bother you so much? If so, is it because it suggests an intimacy between us you're afraid to acknowledge?"

"What an ego. There is no intimacy between us, and you know it. I don't want an intimate relationship with you, or any other kind for that matter."

"Or any man, right? What a shame. All that fire and passion going to waste."

She moved to leave the gazebo. Julian put a hand on her arm, preventing her departure once again.

"Is it just me, or all men? I can understand your attitude toward Roscoe and Monroe; they are real bastards."

"And you're not? Let my arm go. Please."

"Or what? You'll scream?" He let her go. "Sit down, Pandora. Please." Although he said it in a soft voice, an insistent tone underlined his words. "That's better. I'm beginning to think your reputation is a deliberate fabrication. The question is why did you feel you had to build it in the first place?"

"I don't know what you're talking about."

"Oh, you know all right." He grinned, moving closer to her.

She inched away. "What are you trying to prove by this?"

"I'm not trying to prove anything, Pan. I'm just trying to understand you."

"Don't bother."

"Because you're not interested, right? I think you are, but you would never admit it to me or to yourself. You're a lady of contradictions, aren't you, Pandora Cooper?"

She was jarred by his keen perception and inched even farther away.

"Too close for comfort, huh? You really do intrigue me, lady. And when that happens, I get curious and feel compelled to investigate."

"Haven't you heard that curiosity killed the cat?"

"And haven't you heard that satisfaction brought him back?"

"I don't want or need a man in my life, certainly not one like you."

"I believe you do. You're only saying that because you haven't found a man who even begins to know what to do with you—one who knows how to stoke the fires within."

"And you think you're that man? Julian, there is no fire to stoke."

"I beg to differ."

"You would never beg a woman for anything."

Julian grinned. "Oh, I don't know. Where you're concerned, I might consider making an exception."

Pandora rose and headed for the gazebo gate. "I doubt it. Not after..."

"Your, ah, aborted attempt to take over my company?" He smiled. "Oh, I'm willing to overlook your little transgression this time."

"How magnanimous of you."

"I think so. I can be a very forgiving man on occasion."

"I think we should be getting back to the party."

Julian watched Pandora as she walked away. There was something about her that made him feel oddly protective of her. Why he should when she was spitting at him like a riled up lioness, he didn't know. He knew it was crazy. Drac would say the black widow can take care of herself and that Julian should worry about his own skin. Julian surmised that the woman he had just gotten a glimpse of was more vulnerable than the average woman. Her defensive barriers were higher and stronger, but not so high they couldn't be scaled or so strong they couldn't be torn down.

Pandora went to the pool and stood watching Destinee, her cousins, and the other kids play water volleyball.

"You see how happy she is here," Sasha said, walking up behind Pandora.

"Won't you ever give up? That doesn't mean you should have custody of my child. She's happiest with me. And that's as it should be. I'm her mother, not you."

"You think you're so tough, don't you, Pandora? You'll never get another man fool enough to marry you. Count yourself lucky that my brother did you the honor."

"You would like to think that, wouldn't you, Sasha? As for having another man in my life, I don't need or want one telling me what to do and how to do it the way your husband and Monroe do you."

Sasha shot Pandora a hateful look and stalked off.

"You can be deadly when you want to be," Julian teased Pandora.

She just glared at him and headed for the buffet table a few yards away.

"I'm hungry, too. I think I'll join you."

"Can't you take a hint and just go away?"

"Now, Pan, you know you wouldn't want me to do that. Who else would you have to spray your venom on?"

"Does anything ever faze you?"

"You do more than faze me; you fascinate me, Pandora Cooper."

"If that's true then you had better get over it."

"And if I can't?"

Pandora ignored him, taking a plate and filling it. Undaunted, Julian did the same and followed her to a cluster of lawn chairs.

When Pandora raised a barbecued chicken leg to her mouth,

Julian saw the strained look on her face and traced her line of vision to the cause: Monroe Cooper and Roscoe Phillips. He looked back at her and, for a fleeting moment, he thought he saw a trace of fear laced with disgust in her honey-colored eyes, but it was gone too quickly for him to be certain.

Pandora rose from her chair, threw her plate into a nearby trashcan and walked toward the pool.

Julian didn't follow. He saw that Monroe had been watching them and noted the satisfied smirk on his face. Julian felt a rush of anger. The bastard was threatening Pandora in some way. Considering her triumph over him at the stockholders meeting, he wasn't surprised. Even so, there seemed to be more involved than he knew about. He vowed that he would know more sooner rather than later.

The yard lights came on, and on Sasha's cue, the kids left the water and went to the pool house to dress. The adults began gathering around a raised platform.

Pandora had to admit her in-laws had gone all out this year. They had hired a well-known jazz band to perform. Sipping her wine cooler, she sat down to enjoy the music.

"They're very good, aren't they? Almost as good as you."

Pandora pretended not to hear Roscoe Phillips.

"Do I make you nervous, Pandora? I hope so. It's only the beginning in my campaign to bring you down. One day I'm going to have you beneath me, writhing and moaning, begging..."

"Roscoe, give it up? The only place that will ever happen is in your dreams. Besides, what would your wife say?"

"You are a real bitch. I can't wait to see you get what you deserve..."

"You won't be the one to deliver the *coup de grace*."

"I wouldn't be too sure about that."

Long after Roscoe Phillips had walked away, his threat lingered in the air. She shivered.

"Surely you can't be cold on a night like this," Julian said, taking a seat next to Pandora. "If you're cold, allow me to warm you."

Pandora shot up from her chair. "I think it's time my daughter and I left."

"I seem to have a knack for making you leave places before you're really ready to go."

"Don't flatter yourself."

"I'd love to flatter you, if you would let me." He stood and came up behind her. "Will you let me, Pan?"

When she felt his warm breath on the back of her neck, Pandora closed her eyes and willed the tingle of awareness making her heart pound so furiously go away.

"You're a very desirable woman, Pandora Cooper. And I'm not saying it just to flatter you; it's the truth."

"I-I've got to go," she said, barely above a whisper.

He put his hands on both sides of her neck. "There's a special chemistry working between us, Pan."

"No, there isn't."

"You can deny it all you want to, but it doesn't change the fact that it exists."

Pandora turned her head. "I have to go."

Julian touched her cheek. "All right, but it won't do you any good to try and avoid me, Pan." He stepped back and watched her walk away.

CHAPTER SIX

"Cassie tells me Pandora Cooper and her daughter, Destinee, go to Central Park every Saturday afternoon," Drac said, relaying his latest tidbit to Julian. "Remember how you, me and Frank used to do that when we were kids?"

"Yes, I do. People used to call us the black musketeers—one for all and all for whatever we could get into. Ah, those were some good times, weren't they?" Julian laughed.

"Yes, they were," Drac agreed, smiling fondly. "I guess Pandora and her daughter have a similar ritual."

Julian came around to the front of his desk and perched on a corner of it, "Her daughter is thirteen, about the same age as my niece, right? You know how close Talaya and I are. I know she likes Mary J. Blige, Usher and Beyoncé, to name a few pop stars she admires. Destinee Cooper probably likes them, too."

"Your point is?" Drac asked, curious. "Why the sudden interest in Pandora Cooper's daughter? Surely you're not thinking of robbing the cradle."

"No, smart-ass. I've decided the best way to get to the mother is to make friends with her daughter."

"How are you going to do that?"

"Don't worry, I have it covered."

"You could be right on target there," Drac said thoughtfully. "From what I've been able to gather, Pandora Cooper doesn't really have a private life. She attends a lot of social functions, but they're mostly connected to business. The woman eats, drinks and breathes business. I would go so far as to say she is obsessed with getting over on men."

Julian quirked his brows. "I agree. I also think she purposely promotes the black widow image to deflect unwanted attentions from men. The question is, why?"

"Are you sure you want to find out? The lady is complicated, Julian. Maybe you should back off."

"Don't worry about me, Drac. I've been taking care of myself for thirty-six years."

"I know, but I keep remembering how close Vanessa came to destroying you. It should have made you leery of ever getting that close to another businesswoman even remotely like her. Family means everything to you, Jules, and that woman took your dream away without a qualm. Do you really want to risk going through that again? The black widow could…Are you even listening to me?"

"I am leery, I have to admit, Drac. But please give it a rest. Just tell me what else Ms. Jones told you about Pandora."

"She has a cabin in the Catskills where she and her daughter spend three weeks every summer."

"I want you to find a place nearby to rent."

"Julian."

"School is out, so you don't have a lot of time, Drac. I'll need to clear my calendar and delegate before I can take an early vacation."

"You intend to go the whole nine with this no matter what I say, don't you?"

"You know me when something or someone interests me."

"You can be single-minded, that's for sure."

"Don't worry, I know what I'm doing, Drac." Julian laughed at the doubt clouding his cousin's face.

"Mickey seems to be mad at Goofy," Destinee said, pointing. "See how they're fighting over the crusts of bread I tossed to them."

Julian laughed. "I should hope not."

Pandora took a step toward him. "Julian, I really don't..."

He shrugged off her attempt to blow him off and kept his attention on Destinee.

"Have you heard of the song, 'You Are My Destiny?' "

"No. You mean there's really a song with my name in the title?"

"Oh, yes. In fact, I own the CD."

"You do?" Her eyes were sparkling.

"Maybe your mother will bring you over to my place so you can listen to it."

"That would be so cool!"

Pandora nearly choked. "Julian..."

"It's all right, Pan. I'll call you later in the week to set up a day and time. Look, I've got another mile to jog before heading home. Bye, Pan, Destinee."

"Bye, Mr. Palmer."

"Julian," Pandora called after him. He turned, but all he did was wink and smile at her before jogging away.

The gall of the man, Pandora fumed. Was it coincidence he was jogging in the park when she and her daughter just happened to be here? She doubted it. If all he wanted was PanCo, then why was he seeking her and her daughter out?

"Where do you know him from, Mama?"

"We met at the Martin Charity Dinner, then again at Sasha's party."

"Oh, yeah," she said, "I remember seeing him now." Destinee sighed dreamily. "He sure is fine."

Pandora had to agree with her daughter's assessment; he was that, all right, in his Hilfiger jogging suit. Her husband had been a charmer, too, and good-looking as well, but...

"Do you like him?"

"Like who?" Pandora asked.

"Mr. Palmer, Mama," Destinee answered impatiently.

"I guess he's all right."

"Typical males," Pandora said to herself, watching two male ducks fiercely pecking each other in the pond. She was a bit amused by her daughter's recent obsession with the Disney cartoon characters. She owned at least ten T-shirts with images of Mickey, Goofy and other cartoon characters on them. Pandora figured it was a passing teenage fad.

"Look, Mama, aren't the baby ducks cute?"

"Yes, they are."

"I wish we had a baby."

"You can always visit your cousins."

"It's not the same. I get so lonely sometimes. Besides, Aunt Sasha doesn't want me playing with Calvin Jr. because she doesn't like me."

"What makes you think that?"

"It's just a feeling. She's not mean or anything, but…"

"But what?"

"She says things like, 'you're just like your mother,' as though it was some kind of disease or something. Or Lyman wouldn't stand for the way your mother is raising you. Stuff like that."

Pandora was taken aback. It was hardly a secret her sister-in-law loathed her, but she had never imagined that Sasha would deliberately hurt Destinee. At least she hadn't wanted to believe it.

"Mama, when are you going to get married again so I can have my own baby brother or sister?"

"Desi, I…"

"Pan. I'm surprised to see you here."

"Julian!"

"In the flesh, pretty lady." Smiling at Destinee, he asked, "And who might this lovely young lady be?"

"Destinee Cooper," she said blushing. "Who are you?"

"Julian Palmer at your service, ma'am." He gave her a mock bow.

Destinee giggled. "You're funny."

"I don't know if I should consider that a compliment or an insult."

"I didn't mean you were that kind of funny." Destinee let her wrist go limp.

"He's more than all right, Mama. He's gorgeous."

"Unless you want to be late for the first park concert of the season I think we'd better get going."

"You hardly touched your food. Are you feeling all right, Pandora?" Rachel Hodges asked her employer, crinkling her graying brows in concern one evening after dinner.

"Oh, I'm fine, Rachel, just thoughtful, that's all." Rachel had begun working for her two weeks before she became Lyman Cooper's wife fourteen years ago. Pandora didn't know what she would do without this tall, outspoken woman.

"I would say it was more than that."

Pandora smiled. "You mean you want it to be more than that, don't you?"

"Eight years a widow is way too long. You're only thirty-four years old. You need the love of a good man."

"Having a man in your life isn't the cure-all for a woman's ills anymore, Rachel."

"I'm not saying it is for every woman, but for you..."

"Rachel," she said in a warning tone.

"I know you had a rough time of it with your husband, but all men aren't bastards."

"Just most of them."

Long ago memories of exactly what kind of bastard Lyman Cooper was sent revulsion surging through her. Destinee was the only positive thing to come from their marriage.

"You've got to get on with living, Pandora."

"I'm doing that, Rachel."

"No, you're not. You're just existing." She pointed to the papers spread out on the coffee table. "You call burying yourself in work every night living?"

"It's the only way of living I can deal with, Rachel. I don't want to talk about this anymore."

Rachel shook her head. "Sticking your head in the sand ain't gonna make the situation any better. Destinee wants and needs a father."

"She's thirteen, Rachel, not five. She'll be grown in a few years."

"It doesn't make her need of a father and a real family now any less important."

"You just want me to go out and snatch a man off the street and marry him so Destinee can have a father? Rachel, please."

"When I hear you talk like that, I want to go dig Lyman Cooper up and kill him for making you so bitter."

"You'd only find worms after all this time, Rachel," Pandora laughed.

"Probably wouldn't even find them there. His body is no doubt still intact. Even worms wouldn't want any part of him. I'm going to my room. Is there anything I can get for you?"

"No, you go ahead, Rachel. See you in the morning." Pandora put aside the file she had been studying, got up and walked over to the entertainment center and chose Vanessa Williams CD "Next". She wondered what was next for her.

She felt uneasy and didn't know why. She had her daughter. She was a successful businesswoman. Their financial future was secure and yet…

Pandora sat down on the couch and picked up the report she had abandoned earlier. She read and then re-read the first paragraph. For some reason, she couldn't keep her mind on her work. More troubling, it had lost some of its excitement.

Her mind wandered restlessly. She did want more from life, but she did not want a full-blown relationship. The truth is that she didn't know what she wanted anymore. Julian Palmer was responsible for making her doubt her lifestyle and question her feelings. Damn him.

"Mama, are you busy?"

Pandora looked up from her papers. "I'm never too busy for you, honey. Why?"

"You remember the hunk in the park?"

"You mean Julian Palmer? Yes, I remember." As if she could ever forget that arrogant man.

"Did he ever call?"

"Destinee, I..."

The doorbell rang. Pandora wondered who could be calling without telephoning first.

"I'll get it," Destinee said, heading for the door.

She returned moments later carrying two boxes.

"A deliveryman left these. One is for me," she said excitedly, handing the long box to her mother.

Pandora was at a loss as to who might have sent it. It couldn't have been Neil, she reasoned, as she had told him several weeks ago they could never be anything more than friends. She opened the box and found an assortment of early- summer flowers. The inside card read:

For a lady with as many changeable moods as the different color flowers in this arrangement.

—Julian.

"Mama, look what Mr. Palmer sent me." Holding up a CD, Destinee read her card aloud:

Here is your own copy of You Are My Destiny. *I hope you enjoy listening to it.*

—Julian Palmer

"Mama, it's the CD he promised to play for me if we ever went to his place. Wasn't that sweet of him to send it to me instead?"

"Yes, it was."

"Do you like the flowers he sent you?"

"They're very pretty."

Destinee went to the phone and dialed the number on the card.

"Mr. Palmer, this is Destinee Cooper. I got the CD and Mama the flowers. I wanted to thank you for sending them to us. Yes, she's standing right here. First, I wanted to invite you to have dinner with us on Sunday. Can you make it?"

"Destinee!" Pandora hissed, reaching for the receiver.

Destinee danced around, keeping just out of her mother's reach, and waited for Julian's answer. "Yes!" Her face broke into a delighted smile. "We eat at six o'clock. Is that all right with you?"

Smiling triumphantly, Destinee handed the receiver to her mother.

"Julian, I'm sorry if my daughter…"

"No problem, pretty lady. I'll be there at six sharp. See you then."

"Julian, you don't have to…" Pandora heard the hum of the dial tone in her ear. She hung up the receiver and turned to her daughter. "You just don't invite a total stranger over for Sunday dinner, young lady," she admonished.

"You said you knew him already, Mama, so that doesn't exactly make him a total stranger. He's so fine. Don't you think so?"

"He's a little old for you, don't you think?"

"For me, yes, but he's just the right age for you…and to be my future father."

"Destinee Isabella Danielle Cooper!"

"Lighten up, Mama. I can hardly wait until Sunday. We have to go shopping for something really hot for you to wear. You can't wear black. I think you would look good in red. What do you think?"

"Desi, please."

"Don't worry, I'll help you pick out just the right dress."

Destinee went to the entertainment center and popped "You Are My Destiny" into the CD player.

Damn you, Julian Palmer. What are you up to? Pandora had not heard this duet version of the song, and she had to smile as it's haunting melody filled the room. She knew that Julian had plans where she was concerned, just not what they included. She had a feeling that he wouldn't stop pursuing her until he had gotten whatever he was after.

CHAPTER SEVEN

Drac plopped down into a chair in Julian's office. "I can't believe you've actually been invited into the black widow's web?"

"Drac! I've told you not to refer to her that way."

"Sorry. Anyway, I'm dying to know how you managed to pull it off."

Julian was clearly pleased with his coup. "I would like to take all the credit, but I couldn't have accomplished it without the help of a young lady by the name of Destinee Cooper. She was the one who really did the inviting, not her mother."

"Gramma Edna always said you could charm females from one to eighty. I'm beginning to believe her," Drac laughed. "I'm surprised the formidable Ms. Cooper let her daughter get away with it."

"Believe me, it was *a fait accompli*. You have to meet Miss Destinee Cooper to appreciate her. She didn't give her mother any choice. She's one determined young lady."

"She no doubt inherited that particular trait from her mother, which is another reason you should avoid getting involved with them. The mother just might chew you up and spit you out."

"You're being paranoid, Drac."

"Don't ever say you weren't warned."

"Over and over and over again. You're like the TV bunny whose battery never runs down."

Drac threw his hands up. "All right, Jules. I'm through."

"Mama, will you stop pulling your dress down. You have legs that look better than Tina Turner's. You should be proud to show them off."

"I'm not anything like her, Destinee. This dress is kind of short, don't you think? Maybe I should go change."

"Uh-uh, you look perfect. Relax. Mr. Palmer will be here any minute."

The doorbell rang.

"Too late," Pandora mumbled to herself.

Rachel came into the room with a smile lighting her plump, round face, and Julian Palmer following close behind.

The man could probably charm a dead woman out of her grave, Pandora thought cynically.

Destinee walked over to Julian. He presented her with a bottle of Martinelli sparkling apple cider that was wrapped to look like champagne.

"For a very special young lady. You're not old enough for champagne, but this is the closest I could come to it."

He turned to Pandora. "And this is for you, Pan." Julian said, handing her a single, long-stemmed red rose.

His fingers brushed against hers when she reached for it. The way he looked at her made her heart race. She tried hard to appear unaffected, but knew she hadn't fooled him. Why was she reacting to him like this? Why couldn't she just tolerate him the way she did all the others?

Destinee smiled at Julian. "We're glad you could come. Aren't we, Mama?"

Pandora ignored her daughter, politely saying to Julian, "We hope it wasn't too short a notice for you."

"It wasn't, but I do have one complaint. I've been trying with no success to reach you all week to arrange for both you and your lovely daughter to spend next Saturday evening with me."

"Have you? I'm sorry," Pandora answered, not sounding the least bit contrite.

Destinee frowned. "I'm sorry, too. Me and Mama have been waiting to hear from you, haven't we?"

Pandora had the grace to look guilty.

"Let me know when you're ready for dinner to be served," Rachel said to Pandora before excusing herself.

Julian noticed that Pandora hadn't actually agreed with her daughter. Maybe she was beginning to know what it felt like not to be completely in control of every situation. With Destinee's help, he was going to make her realize there was more to life than takeovers and mergers, that there were other, more pleasurable, pursuits.

During dinner, Pandora could feel Julian's eyes on her and purposely did not look at him. Instead she zoomed in on her daughter's adoring glances at Julian, and she found herself resenting the natural rapport blossoming between them. It would make ousting him from their lives all the more difficult. For God's sake, why did he have to be so charming, so fine, so gallant? Now where did that word come from?

Julian saw bewilderment on Pandora's face and guessed that she wasn't too pleased with the way the evening was going. But he knew he had a potentially powerful ally in her daughter.

He also noticed how attentive and affectionate the housekeeper was, and saw in her another ally in his campaign to win over Ms. Pandora Cooper. Rachel obviously cared deeply for both mother and daughter. What was it about Pandora that commanded such staunch loyalty? To hear Drac tell it, Cassandra Jones would do anything for her employer.

Julian knew from experience that Pandora could be shrewd in her business dealings. Shrewd, yes, but he had never heard it said that she used underhanded tactics. He was assuming she didn't need to resort to that; all she had to do was use that superior brain of hers to thwart all comers.

Pandora was relieved when they finished eating. She could send Julian Palmer on his way and that would be that.

"Do you like strawberry shortcake?" Destinee asked Julian.

"It's one of my favorites. You didn't bake me one, did you?"

"Me, bake?" Destinee giggled. "No, but Rachel did. Hers is to die for. It's one of Mama's favorite desserts, too."

"Is it?" Julian trained the warming rays of his smile on Pandora. "At least we have that in common, Pan."

The message he conveyed said he believed they had more in common and that he intended to find out what.

Pandora wanted to strangle her daughter. How was she going to make her understand that she didn't want Julian Palmer involved in their lives? She didn't trust him or his motives. And why this continuing pursuit?

When Julian licked whipped cream off his bottom lip, Pandora felt a sensual connection flowing between them. The thought that she was more than a little attracted to him frightened her.

Julian watched Pandora's eyes change from soft and warm to hard and cold. Something was wrong. It was as though she had suddenly become afraid of him. He could see there was much about her that he had yet to discover or understand.

After dessert, the three returned to the living room.

"We really enjoyed your company, Mr. Palmer," Destinee said, smiling brightly.

"Call me Julian, Destinee."

"I don't think it is proper for a young girl to call a grown-up by his first name," Pandora interjected.

"It's all right, Pan. I don't mind; in fact, I insist. After all, we're friends now, aren't we?"

"When will we see you again, Julian?" Destinee asked.

"That's up to your mother. I'll make time for the two loveliest ladies in New York. I'm ready anytime you can fit me into your busy schedule."

"I'll walk you to the door, Julian," Pandora said with an overly sweet smile.

Julian saw the sparkle in Destinee's eyes as he and her mother left the room. He knew he could count on her to not let her mother "forget" to call him.

"I don't know what your game is, Julian Palmer," Pandora said as soon as they were out of earshot of her daughter. "But whatever it is..."

Julian hauled Pandora into his arms and lowered his mouth to hers. The shock of his unexpected move wore off almost immediately, and she began to struggle.

Pandora tried to turn her head to end the kiss, but Julian wouldn't allow it. He deepened the kiss and tightened his embrace until his hard, lean body was intimately connected to the soft contours of her body.

A faint moan of pleasure escaped her throat. What was he doing to her? She meant to tell him to stay out of their lives, but here she was melting in his arms. She somehow found the strength to pull away.

Julian's breathing was ragged with desire. No other woman had ever affected him like this, had ever made him come so close to losing control.

"I think you had better leave, Julian."

"You enjoyed what we just shared. Don't try to deny it."

"If it's what you want to believe."

"It's the truth, Pan, and you know it."

"Stop calling me that ridiculous name."

"The word stop is not in my vocabulary when it comes to getting what I want. And make no mistake, lady, I do want you."

"Well, you can't have me."

The look in his eyes said, *Oh, can't I?*

"Please, just go."

"I'll go, but what's between us ain't hardly over. It hasn't even begun." With that, he opened the door and walked out.

The taste of him lingered on Pandora's lips. As she slowly closed the door, reality hit hard. This man was extremely dangerous! More dangerous than she ever could have imagined.

"I knew you liked him," Destinee said.

"What?"

"You like Julian or else you wouldn't have let him kiss you like that. I think he's perfect for you, Mama."

"Destinee, I hardly know him. A kiss from a man like him doesn't mean anything. He probably has dozens of women standing in line waiting their turn."

"I doubt it. I bet he's particular about whom he gets involved with."

"How would you know something like that?"

"It's just a feeling I have. I can't wait until he takes us out for a day of fun. I know it'll be cool. He makes me feel—I don't know how to explain it—like he would be the kind of father I've always dreamed about."

"Don't get any ideas," she warned her daughter.

"I'm not gonna let you forget to call him," she promised. "He's special, Mama, really special."

"I think she's right, Pandora," Rachel chimed, entering the living room.

"Not you, too," Pandora grumbled. "What is this, the headquarters of the Julian Palmer Fan Club?"

"We won't mind if you become a member, Mama," Destinee said mischievously.

Preparing for bed later that night, Pandora mentally replayed the evening. Julian Palmer seemed sincere and genuinely interested talking with her daughter. But if all he was interested in was going to bed with the mother, then why was he going out of his way to charm the daughter? She was inclined to believe there was much more behind what she had seen so far.

Pandora was leery of Julian Palmer—all men, for that matter. She remembered how charming Lyman could be when he wanted to be. He had charmed her into marrying him. But it had been all designed to totally possess her, and she had discovered that too late, much too late.

"Why did you marry me, Lyman? I thought you loved me," Pandora had asked him one night after they came back from having dinner with his family.

"I married you because you needed a man to point you in the right direction. I made you my personal project, Pandora, my protégée, my creation. All you needed was molding."

"What you're saying is that you are a control freak. I'm not some lump of clay, Lyman. I'm a human being with feelings, ambitions, hopes and dreams."

"You're also my wife, don't forget."

"There's not much chance of that since you remind me of it every waking moment of every day."

He had slapped her. "Don't you ever talk to me like that."

"You're my husband, not my father."

"In a way, I'm like a father to you. I knew when I met you that you saw me that way. I couldn't let my brother have you. You're beautiful, Pandora, but like all women, you need someone to keep you in line. I'm just the man to do it. I want you; take off your clothes."

"I don't want you touching me."

"I said get naked. If you don't, I'll tear that fancy dress off you. You will do everything I tell you. Do you understand me?"

"I understand, all right. I understand that I made a huge mistake in marrying you. Your pretty words were all lies. There are other women who would have loved for you to order their lives for them. Why didn't you pick one of them?"

"You are a financial phenomenon, my dear Pandora. You were all of nineteen when you applied for a job at Cooper Corps. And even then I saw your potential. I knew if I kept it in the family, you would make me an even wealthier man."

"What if I hadn't wanted to fall in with your plans?"

"Oh, I knew you would. You see, I knew you were hungry for what I offered you. In exchange for a chance, all I required of you was to be my loving wife. You thought it would be a piece of cake, didn't you?"

"I never saw our relationship in those terms. I married you because..."

"You loved me, right? You were a naive fool to buy into that fantasy. You just fell into lust. I knew exactly what to do with you."

"Yes, you did. You twisted what I felt for you into something ugly and repulsive. Well, I've had enough."

"You think so?"

She had struggled to escape him, but he was too strong for her. She blanked out what happened next. It was an act of possession, pure and simple. From that day on, their relationship had headed downhill. In the weeks following, he had pushed her to the breaking point. Only after she discovered she was pregnant did she have the strength and willpower to seek counseling, which saved her sanity and her life.

After what she had gone through with her dead husband, she wasn't eager to jump into another relationship. She had learned hard lessons about men from the examples in her life. First, from a father she could never rely on. Then from a husband who taught her that men could never be trusted with something as vulnerable as your heart. She never intended to give hers to another man ever again.

Sipping a brandy, Julian gazed out the living-room window of his plush, ultra-modern penthouse apartment. He was restless and sexually excited after his encounter with Pandora. She was even more woman than he had fantasized. There were fires hidden deep inside her. God, how he longed to coax them into a scorching blaze.

He started out coveting her company, but now he wanted her more than he could ever want her company. And it wasn't only about sex.

It wasn't about sex with Vanessa at first, either, an inner voice reminded him.

He shook his head, trying to rid it of such reminders. He had to banish these lingering doubts, to stop making comparisons between Vanessa and Pandora. Pandora was different.

Is she really different, or is it what you want to believe?

She's not in dire straits as Vanessa had been. Pandora Cooper was successful and financially secure. And she was as knowledgeable about business as he was. She loved children and had a daughter she obviously adored. And that daughter might help further his cause, as might the housekeeper. But he needed to show Pandora that he was genuinely interested in her and that she could trust him.

And how are you going to accomplish that miracle?

He didn't know, but Destinee could be the key. If he could only convince her stubborn mother to give him a chance.

He would have to draw on every bit of patience he had in pursuing Pandora. He didn't want to move too fast and frighten her away. He was curious to know how her husband had treated her. Was he responsible for her intense distrust of men? Whatever it was, he intended to knock down those walls she had built around her emotions and free the woman hiding behind them.

CHAPTER EIGHT

"Is Destinee looking forward to starting high school?" Cassandra asked Pandora the following morning at the office.

"Oh, she is, but at the moment her most recent kick is to see her mother matched up with Julian Palmer."

"What?"

"Oh, that's right, you don't know the latest. Destinee invited the man over for Sunday dinner. Know what? He accepted and came."

"But I didn't think you were interested in him."

"I'm not, but Destinee is interested in him enough for the both of us. I'm going to have to do something about it."

"Why would you want to do anything short of falling into his arms? You have to admit that Julian Palmer is fine to the bone, Pandora."

"Now don't you start. Rachel's already climbed aboard the Julian Palmer bandwagon."

"If he's anything like his cousin, you had better not let him get away."

"I don't want to catch him, or any other man. I don't want to discuss Julian Palmer, period."

"If you say so, but I think you protest too much."

"Cassandra!"

"All right, all right. I'm done."

"Mama?" Destinee called from the doorway.

Pandora looked up from the computer screen. "What are you doing here?"

"Aren't you glad to see me?"

Pandora smiled. "I'm always glad to see you, honey. I'm just surprised to see you here at the office, that's all."

"I didn't have anything to do, so I thought I would invite my mother to have burgers and fries with me."

"I thought you were going to Coney Island with Kayla and her sister."

"I was, but I decided I didn't want to go. Do you have time to go out to lunch with me?"

"I'll make time for you, Desi. You know that. Just give me ten minutes to wrap this up, okay? So where do you want to go?"

"The Gyp Joint," they said in unison, laughing.

Pandora and Destinee were halfway through their lunch at the Gyp Joint when Julian and a young girl Destinee's age walked through the door. Pandora groaned when she saw him steering the girl in their direction.

"We have to stop meeting like this, Pan. I'd like you and Destinee to meet my niece. Talaya Andrews, Mrs. Pandora Cooper and her daughter Destinee. Talaya and I have lunch once or twice a month, and we usually eat here. It's a lucky coincidence our coming here the same time as you two. Or is it fate?"

"I would go with coincidence," Pandora said dryly.

"Whatever," Destinee said. "I'm just glad to see you, Julian."

"Talaya is starting high school in September."

"Me, too," Destinee said.

Julian looked surprised. "I thought you were only thirteen?"

"I am."

"You must have inherited your mother's genius." Julian grinned. "Right?"

The question in Pandora's eyes asked, *How do you know unless you've been digging around in my personal life?*

"I wouldn't exactly say that," Destinee answered. "I just got skipped a grade. It's not a big deal."

"Uncle Julian helped me pick a high school," Talaya confided, her light brown eyes sparkling. "East Shore High is the same school he and my mother attended."

"That's the high school my mother and I decided on. This is just too cool."

"I think so, too," Talaya piped up.

"Why don't you two talk about it in that booth over there? I want to talk with Destinee's mother."

"Destinee and I are almost ready to…" Pandora began.

Interrupting, Julian said, "Let them go. They probably have a lot in common to talk about."

"More than we do," Pandora groused.

Julian took her hand. "I wouldn't say that."

"I would." She said, taking her hand back. "You've been investigating me, haven't you? Just what are you up to, Julian Palmer?"

"Lighten up, sweetheart. By the way, why haven't you called me? Or returned any of my calls? I'm anxious to spend time with you and Destinee. I can bring Talaya along, and we can make it a foursome."

"Look, Julian…"

"Hey, why don't you stop fighting it?"

"Yeah, Mama," an eavesdropping Destinee said.

Pandora felt ambushed, put on the spot. To question suspicions of Julian's motives would make her the bad guy, especially in front of his niece. Her daughter and Talaya resumed their chattering while an exasperated Pandora glared at Julian.

"If looks could kill," he laughed. "What day and where do you want to go for this outing? How about Saturday? A picnic in the country. What do you say?"

"What can I say? I should tell you I have a thing about being bulldozed into anything."

"I'm not doing that. It's only a simple invitation."

"I have a feeling that nothing having to do with you is ever simple."

"If you like complications, Pan, I can be as complicated as you want me to be."

"Ooh, you're impossible."

"I've heard that said about me a time or two."

"Julian, what do you really want? What are you really after?"

"The pleasure of your company and that of your lovely daughter, especially yours." He gave her a smoldering look filled with the promise of things to come.

Destinee and Talaya came back to the booth acting like old friends.

"We know some of the same people from junior high, Mama," Destinee said delightedly. "I think we're going to be good friends. Don't you, Talaya?"

"Yeah."

Pandora checked the time. "I hate to cut this short, but I really do have to get back to the office."

Turning to Destinee, Julian said, "Your mother has agreed to a picnic next Saturday."

"Yes! Where are we going to have it?" Destinee asked.

"We could go to Connecticut to the park near Gramma Edna's house in the country, Uncle Julian," Talaya suggested.

"It's exactly the place I had in mind," he answered. "I can pick you up at eight Saturday morning. That sound good?"

"Mama?" Destinee pleaded.

"All right, all right. I'll have Rachel pack a picnic lunch for us. Now, I really do have to get back to the office. I have a ton of work to finish before I go home."

Julian and Destinee shared conspiratorial glances, which Pandora didn't miss, didn't know if she liked and wasn't sure how to interpret.

CHAPTER NINE

Pandora remained apprehensive about the outing, even as she helped Rachel pack the picnic basket Saturday morning. During what seemed like a week without end she had tried to find plausible excuses to get out of going on the picnic. To her dismay, she found none that would hold water.

"I'm glad you're beginning to get a life, Pandora," Rachel said approvingly.

"Now, Rachel…"

"I know, mind my own business. You are my business, dear."

"Just don't put too much stock in today's outing. Okay?"

"Even when you're preparing to relax and enjoy yourself, you manage to work the word stock into it."

Pandora laughed. "All right, Rachel, I get your point about all work and no play."

"I sure hope you do. Mr. Palmer is exactly what you need at this point in your life. Destinee agrees with me."

"She would. She thinks the man can walk on water."

"It's a good thing she can relate to him so easily. He's not a man you can run over or control, that's for sure."

Pandora agreed. It was exactly why she didn't want to get involved with him. She had to be in control of her life. Julian Palmer was a man used to having things his own way. But at least he didn't seem harsh or cruel. Julian wasn't anything like her late husband, but he was still a take-charge kind of man. How would she deal with that if she and Julian were to…What was she thinking? There was no she and Julian.

Yet.

Today, Pandora resolved she and her daughter would enjoy this outing with Julian and his niece, and that would be the end of it. She will give him no reason to read more into it than what it was—an outing without strings or promise.

"Is Destinee up?" Pandora asked Rachel.

"She's up, all right. She woke me at the crack of dawn to help her pick out just the right outfit to wear."

"What? Not our resident fashion coordinator."

"This picnic means a lot to her, Pandora. I haven't seen her this excited about anything in a long while."

Pandora grimaced. Was it already too late to keep Julian at bay? She was so afraid her daughter's expectations were already too high where he was concerned. She hated to disappoint Destinee, but there was no way she was going to let Julian Palmer be a permanent fixture in their lives. One picnic did not a relationship make.

"Mama, you're not gonna wear black, are you?" Destinee asked from the kitchen doorway.

"What's wrong with my wearing black?"

"It's depressing. I thought you agreed to start wearing brighter colors."

"I did. But, Destinee, I can't just throw my entire wardrobe away."

"It's all you have, then? Were definitely gonna have to make some serious changes in your wardrobe."

Pandora looked down at her black silk shirt and black designer jeans. She didn't see anything wrong with what she had on.

"Well, I guess it can't be helped today," Destinee said, giving up. "I can hardly wait until Julian and Talaya get here. When I talked to her yesterday, she said her great-grandmother was really looking forward to meeting us. I bet she's cool like Julian."

Pandora heard the longing in her daughter's voice and knew how badly she had always wanted to have loving grandparents. Lyman's parents were dead, and so were Pandora's. Julian knew that and somehow knew how much this visit with his grandmother would mean to Destinee. It was an act of kindness for which she was grateful, no matter how much she dreaded the outing itself.

"Mama, please don't wear your hair in that tight bun, let it hang free for once." Destinee pulled the pins from her mother's hair and watched as her hair fell in soft waves below her shoulders. "See how pretty it looks down. Don't you think so, Rachel?"

"I can't wear it like this; it'll tangle."

Destinee took the rubber band off the morning paper and smoothed Pandora's hair into a ponytail at the nape of her neck.

"That's much better. You look younger."

"I'm glad you approve," Pandora responded wryly.

Rachel smiled. "I think Destinee is right."

They were all waiting in the living room for Julian and Talaya when, at last, a midnight-blue Escalade pulled up at the curb.

"They're here!" Destinee screeched excitedly.

Destinee opened the front door and gave Julian a big hug. The bond between the two seemed a little stronger each time they met, despite her mother's apprehensions. Pandora had to admit he was having an effect on her, as well.

Julian saw the tension leave Pandora's face. Was he making headway at last? Maybe his campaign had a chance, after all.

"I like your outfit," Talaya told Destinee.

"Thanks. I like yours, too. You look good in yellow."

"She would know," Pandora said. "She's interested in fashion design."

"Me, too!" Talaya exclaimed. "Uncle Julian says if I'm still interested by the time I graduate, he'll help me get into the best college for design."

"So did my mother!"

"I think we had better get started for Connecticut," Julian said, smiling at the girl's infectious excitement.

"Yes, let's do," Pandora agreed, suddenly aware she was now almost as eager as her daughter to go on this picnic. And that was more than a little unsettling.

Destinee and Talaya chattered away in the back, but Julian and Pandora were silent in the front. Julian glanced at Pandora now and then and even tried to strike up a conversation a few times. She would respond briefly and then fall silent again. He guessed she was trying to keep her distance because of what she was probably beginning to feel for him. She just didn't know that he had no intention of letting her keep her distance for long.

Pandora saw determination in his occasional glances. She realized she had unwittingly issued a challenge to him by not going along with the program. Was there no way to discourage him?

"The P.T. Barnum Festival just happens to kick off this weekend," Julian said, breaking another stretch of silence.

"Me and Mama used to go to them when I was younger," Destinee recalled fondly. "My father was always too busy to come with us, but we used to have a good time, anyway. Just the two of us, didn't we, Mama?"

"Yes, we did. Those were some special times."

"Well, there's no reason you can't have a special time today," Julian said gently. "But first we stop by Gramma Edna's. If I know her, she has something special cooked for us to take on our picnic."

"It really wasn't necessary for her to go to that trouble."

"You don't know Gramma Edna, Mrs. Cooper," Talaya said. "When she sets her mind to do something, there isn't anybody short of God who can get her to change it, so we've learned to just go along with her."

Pandora suspected she was as impossible as her grandson in that respect. Julian's grandmother lived on the outskirts of Bridgeport, Connecticut, in an imposing old colonial-style house. The beauty of the surrounding woodland took her breath away. She imagined how it would look in the fall—clear blue skies, crisp cool air, and trees with red, brown and orange leaves. Today, everything was green, the air was warm and the sun shone brightly.

As he drove up the winding road to the house, Julian asked Pandora, "How do you like it?"

"I like it just fine."

"What about you, Destinee?"

"It's great. It reminds me of the Catskills, where me and Mama spend time every summer, but this is even better. It feels more homey."

"Maybe we can bring you back here in the fall when the leaves change," Julian suggested.

"Julian, I don't think she can come," Pandora objected.

"The invitation includes you too, Pan."

"Why do you call my mother that?" Destinee asked Julian.

"No particular reason. I just like it."

"Me, too. It sounds so personal. It makes us seem closer, more like a family, don't you think, Julian?"

He grinned at Pandora and answered Destinee's question.

"Yes, I do. I want us to become that kind of close."

Pandora wanted to say something, but didn't know quite what. The nerve of the man. His ego had to be made of marble. Then again, maybe it wasn't ego at all; maybe he was genuinely interested in her and her daughter.

"There's Gramma Edna," Talaya cried delightedly.

Pandora saw a white-haired woman sitting in a rocking chair on the front porch. Julian got out of the Escalade and ran up on the porch. His grandmother stood up and Julian swept her into his arms and whirled her around.

"Be careful of these old bones, Jules," she warned sternly in one breath, then broke into happy peals of laughter in the next. "Put me down, you rascal. You're just like your father and grandfather." When Julian gently set her down, Edna turned to Pandora and Destinee. "I see you have the two ladies you told me you were bringing. You neglected to mention how pretty they were, though."

"What about me, Gramma Edna?" Talaya pouted.

"You're a Palmer."

Gramma Edna said those words as if they were all the explanation needed. These Palmers were something else, Pandora thought.

"This is my grandmother, Edna Palmer," Julian said. "And Gramma, this is Pandora Cooper and her daughter, Destinee."

"Pandora," Edna said slowly, as if trying the name on for size. "How unusual, but I like it." Then she smiled at Destinee. "There is a song called 'You Are My Destiny.' Did you know that, young lady?"

"I do. Julian gave me the CD as a present," Destinee said proudly, beaming at him.

The family matriarch looked from Pandora to Julian, then back again. It wasn't a good sign, not a good sign at all. This woman was probably as shrewd as her grandson, Pandora thought, and she could tell she was linking the two of them together romantically.

"You can call me Gramma Edna, too, if you like," she told mother and daughter.

"Can we really?" Destinee asked in an awed voice.

"Yes, really. Come into the house. I barbecued a couple of slabs of ribs and some chicken early this morning."

"You shouldn't have gone to so much trouble, Mrs. Palmer—Gramma Edna," Pandora said.

"Oh, shoot, it was my pleasure, child."

A sense of family could be felt as soon as they stepped into Gramma Edna's parlor, an old-fashioned word, but the only one that seemed to fit, Pandora thought. It was like stepping back in time to colonial Connecticut. The fireplace was made of natural rocks found in the area, she'd venture to guess. Pictures of the family were on the mantle. More pictures were arranged on the beautiful mahogany grand piano, which dominated an entire section of the room.

Talaya and Destinee sat down at the piano and started playing chopsticks.

Pandora observed how completely at ease her daughter was, blending in and acting as if she belonged here and had always been a member of this family. Pandora herself was being drawn in by the inviting atmosphere in the comfortable old house. She wandered over to the mantle to get a closer look at the photographs.

"Over here is a picture of Julian's grandfather," Gramma Edna told her. "Julian looks just like him, don't you think?"

"Great-granddaddy was fine when he was young," Talaya offered.

"He was fine when he was old," Gramma Edna corrected, picking up a more recent picture of her husband and showing it to Pandora.

"Yes, he certainly was," Pandora answered, studying the picture and seeing a definite family resemblance between Julian and his grandfather. She wondered if the grandfather, too, had been a lion in business in his time—as his grandson was today.

"I've been trying to convince Jules to get married and start a family of his own. Except for that one time he came close, with Vanessa Armstrong, he hasn't been interested until now."

Julian gave his grandmother a warning look.

Pandora was intrigued—and curious. *Except for one time with Vanessa Armstrong*. Who was this Vanessa? How long ago was this? The marriage never happened, so what was his grandmother hinting at? Surely, she didn't seriously think she and Julian were...But it was crystal clear that this was exactly what she was thinking because he had brought her here. What had he been telling his grandmother about their relationship? Relationship? But they didn't have a relationship, at least not a serious one.

Julian saw the panic on Pandora's face. He would have to go slow; he didn't intend to lose any ground with her. What he needed was time. All he needed was time.

"It's time we left for the picnic so we'll have time to go to the Barnum Festival. You coming with us, Gramma Edna?"

"Oh, no, child. I'll leave it to you young people."

"You are young, Gramma Edna," Julian countered.

She laughed. "You flatterer, go on with you."

Pandora couldn't help envying the easy affection between Edna Palmer and her grandson. She had missed that kind of warmth since her mother's death.

They said their good-byes to Gramma Edna and went on their way. Julian had picked the perfect place for a picnic. Only a few miles from

Gramma Edna's house, the park, Julian told them, had been named after an important chief of the Niantic Indians. It was being scrupulously kept up; the grass was closely cut and the benches and tables freshly painted.

"Destinee, I want to show you a special place I found," Talaya said. "There are some really cool Indian statues and monuments you've just got to see."

"Okay."

"Don't stay too long," Pandora called after them. "We'll have the food ready in a little while."

"Take your time," Julian said, adding, "I'd like to talk with Pan alone."

"Okay, Uncle Julian," Talaya answered. Before Pandora could say anything, the girls practically flew away.

"I promise not to eat you, Little Red Riding Hood."

"Very funny."

"I like your hair that way. You look almost as young as your daughter."

"I guess I should thank you for the compliment."

"I was only being truthful; no flattery intended. Come on, loosen up, Pan."

How could he expect her to do that when he was so close? The attraction between them was slowly drawing her in, and she was fighting it. Was it Julian or herself she was fighting?

"Let me help you spread out this feast."

"Tell me about yourself, Julian."

"You've had me investigated. I'm sure there's nothing I can tell you that you don't already know."

"I don't know anything personal about you. For instance, what color you like, your favorite sport, things like that."

"My favorite color is gold," he smiled. "Like the color of your eyes. My favorite sport is sailing. Grandfather taught me everything he knew about boats. He and my father and I went sailing every summer. Sometimes we would take Drac and his brother, Frank, with us, but not Uncle Howland. He gets seasick just watching the waves lap against the dock," Julian laughed.

Pandora laughed, too.

"I like it when you laugh. Your face lights up."

She cleared her throat. "There's enough food here to feed a small army," Pandora said nervously, taking out several huge Ziploc bags of barbecue.

"We can eat the sandwiches now and save the barbecue for our dinner. Gramma Edna's ribs are sensational."

"Are you always so practical? You seem to have an answer for everything."

"Not quite everything."

"Meaning?"

"Meaning you fascinate me, Pandora Cooper, and I don't understand what makes you tick."

"And that bothers you?"

"What do you think?" He took one of her hands and brought it to his lips.

His lips on her skin sent sizzling sensations to Pandora's brain, and she closed her eyes for a moment.

Julian moved closer, and then pulled her into his arms.

"You're so beautiful, Pan. I want you, girl. Oh, how I want you."

His words lifted the fog clouding Pandora's judgment and she pulled away.

"Don't fight it, Pan. I know you want me as much as I want you. Why don't you just go with the flow?"

"There is no flow."

He wanted to show her how mistaken she was, but he saw the girls heading back.

"Later, Pan."

"I wouldn't go overboard about it, Julian."

"I'm a risk-taker. I'll follow my instincts where you're concerned."

"Your instincts had better help you understand what the word no means."

"Are you telling me no?" he asked softly.

"Is this some kind of game, Julian? Because if it is..."

"What?"

"Never mind."

During lunch, Julian's eyes kept returning to Pandora. He sensed her fear of him on some level. Or was it something else entirely making her react to him the way she had? Had her husband abused her?

Pandora was aware of the intense looks Julian kept casting her way. What was it about her that challenged him so? She had done nothing to encourage him. Nevertheless, he seemed prepared to go to any lengths to impress her.

Julian took note of her questioning eyes. Didn't she know that any red-blooded male would desire her? He had to do some serious breaking through with this hard-case lady. But he was a very patient man when he had to be.

"Time to clean up," Pandora said. She had expected an argument from the girls, but they offered none. In no time they were on their way to the P.T. Barnum Festival.

They arrived back at Pandora's house late in the evening. Rachel fixed a salad and iced tea to go with the barbecue. Pandora asked her to join them for dinner.

"Oh, Julian, I had a wonderful time," Destinee said.

"Didn't you, Mama?"

"Yes, I did," she answered truthfully. She hadn't had that kind of fun in a very long time.

Julian watched Pandora and decided he had made some progress, and his instincts told him not to push his luck. "It's getting late, Talaya. We should be going."

"I'll talk to you tomorrow, Destinee," Talaya promised.

As they were leaving, Julian's lingering look at Pandora suggested more fun times, as well as serious ones, soon.

CHAPTER TEN

"PanCo. Cassandra speaking."

"Cassie."

"Drac, hi. You're not calling to bail on lunch, are you?"

"No, I'm looking forward to it more than you are."

"I doubt that. So what's up?"

"I want to know what's going on between my cousin and your boss."

"Why don't you ask him?"

"I have, and for once, he won't tell me anything."

"Everything must be going all right, then. Pandora was a little subdued and thoughtful when she came into the office this morning. I'd say your cousin is making headway with her."

"Why do you think that?" Drac sounded worried.

"They spent Saturday together."

"Alone?"

"No, Destinee and his niece, Talaya, were with them."

"Talaya? Listen, we can talk about this over lunch. See you then."

Cassandra cradled the phone and sat wondering what that was all about when the phone rang. She quickly answered.

"Drac?"

"No, sorry to disappoint you."

"Mr. Palmer! How may I help you?"

"Call me Julian. What does your boss's schedule look like this afternoon?"

Cassandra flipped through the calendar. "Her last appointment should be over at four."

"Do you think you can fit me in at, say, 4:30?"

"Mr. Palmer…I mean, Julian, I really don't think…"

"Why not tell her the owner of Advance Securities requests an urgent conference with her."

"Julian, I can't lie to her."

"You wouldn't be lying. Do you have the latest issue of *Financial Weekly*? If you do, you'll see I now own the company."

Cassandra found the magazine among the stack on her desk and flipped to the article describing Julian as the new head of Advance Securities.

"Yes, I see it."

"You had better hide this issue from Pandora."

"When she finds out you own the company, she's going to…"

"Have a fit?"

"You know it's one of the companies she was interested in."

"Yes, I know. Don't worry, just leave everything to me. Okay? All I need you to do is get me in to see her."

"Okay, but…"

"Trust me, Cassandra."

She had just shoved the magazine into her desk drawer when Pandora walked out of her office and stopped at Cassandra's desk.

"George Dorsey is my last appointment today, isn't he?" Pandora asked distractedly.

"Not quite. You have one with the head of Advance Securities at 4:30. He made it sound urgent."

Pandora knitted her brows. "But I thought…Advance Securities? That would be Jerry Thorpe. I wonder what he wants. Maybe he's decided to reconsider my offer to buy his company. Yes, that must be it."

"Yes, it must be." Cassandra wisely kept her eyes glued to the computer screen.

Pandora sat on the edge of her desk, her arms folded across her chest. She couldn't concentrate on work. Her mind kept going back to the day she and her daughter had spent with Julian Palmer. Why did he have to be so devastatingly good-looking? Why did he have to be so rousingly sexy? Why did he have to seem so different from other men? Why did she have to find him so irresistibly intriguing?

Pandora returned to her chair and swiveled so she could look out the window. But her mind wasn't on the view of Central Park; it kept going back to Julian Palmer. Why did her daughter have to see him as perfect father material? And why, Pandora chided herself, did she see him as a potential lover? She must be losing her mind. Julian Palmer was driving her stone crazy.

It was lunchtime already, and she had gotten little done. She decided to eat in the cafeteria today because she just didn't feel up to going out. She got her purse and headed out.

"Cassandra, I'm going to the—Oh, I'm sorry, Mr. Palmer! Drac, isn't it?"

"How are you, Ms. Cooper?" Drac asked.

"You can call me Pandora."

"Were going out to lunch. Why don't you join us?" Cassandra asked.

"I don't think so, but thanks for inviting me. I'll see you when you get back."

Drac turned to Cassandra after Pandora left the office.

"I wonder how she feels about me. Do you know?"

"She's not that bad, Drac," she said, evading his question. "I'm ready to go. Just let me alert the answering service that Pandora and I will both be out of the office."

Julian walked into Cassandra's office at exactly 4:28 that afternoon.

"I think you'd better make yourself scarce," he said to Cassandra. "I don't want you to get caught in the crossfire for helping me."

"The bad side of Pandora Cooper is definitely not a place I want to find myself, that's for sure."

Julian smiled warmly at her. "It'll be all right, Cassandra. I'm wondering why you decided to go along with me on this. I know how loyal you are to Pandora."

"I think it's about time she had a man in her life, one she can't intimidate or control. I think she needs you, Julian."

"So do I," he grinned. Squaring his shoulders, he walked over to Pandora's office door. "The thing is convincing her of that. Wish me luck."

"You got it."

"Tell that cousin of mine I think he's one hell of a lucky man to have you." Julian didn't knock on Pandora's door; he just opened it and walked in. Once inside, he turned the lock.

At the sound of the click, Pandora looked up from her Advance Securities file.

"Julian! What? How?" Her eyes narrowed. "Cassandra!" She reached for the intercom button.

"She's gone for the day."

"You're responsible, aren't you?" she demanded. "What are you doing here, Julian?"

"I came to see you, of course." He flashed that killer grin.

"But Jerry Thorpe is the head of Advance Securities."

"Not anymore. I bought the company from him the end of last week."

"Why haven't I heard or read anything about this?"

"The story just came out in the financial magazines."

"I wondered why Cassandra hadn't brought in the latest magazines. I just assumed she had been too busy. All this time..."

"Now don't be upset with her. She only did that because she cares about you. Besides, you know you wanted to see me as much as I wanted to see you."

He took a couple of steps closer to Pandora's desk.

"Julian, I think you'd better leave before..."

"Before what?" He took another step. Then another. "I'm not ready to go."

Pandora felt conflicting urges—to take flight or wait for him to reach her.

Correctly sensing her conflicts, he said, "There's nothing wrong with you, Pan. You're a normal, passionate woman."

"How do you know that about me?"

"I can't give you a pat answer. I just know it's true. Have dinner with me."

The phone rang, giving her a much needed reprieve. Cassandra had gone for the day, so Pandora had to take the call herself. She switched on the speakerphone.

"Mama, Talaya and her mother want me to have dinner with them. May I please?"

"Destinee!"

"You can talk to Talaya's mother. I have her on three-way."

Pandora and Julian heard the phone click over.

"Mrs. Cooper, this is Selena Andrews, Talaya's mother. May I call you Pandora?"

Pandora glanced suspiciously at Julian. "Yes, of course."

"Your daughter and mine have become as thick as thieves these days. Is it all right for her to have dinner with us? I promise to pick her up and bring her back home early."

"I don't know..."

"Come on and say yes, Mama, please."

"Oh, all right. But next time..."

"I know. Thanks, Mama. I love you."

"I love you too, honey."

"Pandora, we can talk when I bring her home," Selena said. "It'll probably be around eight. Is that all right?"

"Yes. I'll see you then, Selena."

Pandora hung up and stared at Julian, who had inched even closer to her.

"I suppose you planned that, too?" she asked tilting her head toward the phone.

Julian held up his right hand. "Sorry, I can't take the credit for that. I'm only responsible for getting in to see you today."

"You want me to believe it was just a coincidence your sister and niece conveniently inviting my daughter to dinner this evening?"

"Believe what you want to about that. I've already said all I intend to on the subject. You have no excuse for not agreeing to have dinner with me now, do you?"

"Maybe I had other plans."

Julian sat on the edge of her desk, and leaning forward took her chin between his thumb and forefinger. Then he lowered his lips to within inches of hers.

Pandora's heart began to race at the feel of his fingers on her skin, the close proximity of his lips to hers. For some reason, she didn't draw away from him. She couldn't, and didn't want to.

He planted a gentle yet firm kiss on her lips. Its aim was to make her respond, and she did.

"Now was that so bad? Come on and have dinner with me."

As if in a daze, Pandora slid all the way back in her chair, not sure if she should accept his invitation.

"You don't really have any dinner plans, do you?" Julian asked her.

Without thinking, she answered, "Of course not. I mean…"

Julian smiled. "I know what you meant, and I also know what you need, Ms. Cooper." He leaned forward to kiss her again.

Pandora pushed her chair back and rose to her feet. "All right, Julian."

"Is that a yes to my dinner invitation?"

When she nodded, he shouted, "Hallelujah."

"Now don't overreact, okay? It's only dinner. *Only* being the operative word."

"Oh, Pan, you're priceless. Don't you know there's dinner, and there's dinner with me?"

Pandora stood studying him, wondering what he meant by those words. What did he really have in mind for the evening? She wasn't sure she liked the hungry-wolf gleam in his eyes. It made her feel like one of the three little pigs. She had to laugh at her analogy, because she knew the look in his eyes signified the kind of hunger an aroused male has for a female.

Pandora retrieved her purse from her bottom desk drawer. By now, her eyes had taken on an uneasy look.

"It's too late to change your mind," Julian said. "Let's go."

"Are you always so…"

"Whatever you were going to say, the answer is yes, and then some. Now." He held out his hand.

Pandora hesitated.

"If we stay here alone for very much longer, I won't be responsible for my actions."

"You're impossible."

His smile said he knew it, and she wouldn't want him to be any other way.

With a shrug she put her hand in his and let him escort her from the office.

CHAPTER ELEVEN

A chauffeured limousine was waiting in front of her office building, prompting Pandora to stare at Julian accusingly. "You were so sure I would accept. Of all the..."

"You're here, aren't you?"

"Of all the..."

"You're beginning to sound like a remix, Pan. Please, would you just get into the car so we can go have our dinner?"

Pandora wanted to say more, but killed the impulse. Inside the limo, she leaned back against the soft leather cushions and a feeling of sheer contentment enfolded her.

"You need to lighten up and relax, Pan. Haven't you heard the old saying that all work and no play makes Jill a dull girl?"

"I thought it was Jack."

"That refers to men, and you're definitely not one of those."

"Where are we going for dinner?"

"Let it be a surprise."

Seeing that it would do no good to press further, Pandora closed her eyes and enjoyed the air-conditioned comfort of the limousine.

Julian became aroused just watching her closed eyes and relaxed body. He imagined their naked bodies in his bed making love. Afterward, she would be mellow—like now. The thought caused him to harden even more. His pants suddenly felt uncomfortably tight across his lap. He tried to adjust his position, but it did no good. He groaned.

Pandora opened her eyes and asked, "Are you all right, Julian?"

"Yes," he lied. "We'll be at the restaurant in a few minutes."

"I didn't realize how tired I was until now."

"You work too hard. Tonight you're going to relax and enjoy yourself."

"Is that an order, sir?" she challenged.

"One of these days, woman..."

"What?"

His answer was to flash her a devastatingly sexy smile.

Butterflies fluttered in Pandora's stomach and her mouth felt dry. What was it about him? She had seen plenty of handsome men, but none of them had come close to affecting her like this.

Julian saw the puzzled look in her eyes. He could tell she was having doubts about her decision to have dinner with him. But there was still hope for their relationship. She would probably laugh if he told her that was exactly what they were having. *You're in for a treat this evening, Ms. Cooper,* he said to himself.

Pandora sat up straight when the driver eased the limousine through the gates of what appeared to be a huge estate. What was this place Julian had taken her to?

Minutes later, he escorted Pandora to the front door. A man dressed like an English butler admitted them inside.

He smiled and said in a crisp British accent, "Welcome to The Drawing Room, sir, madam."

As they stepped farther inside, Pandora's mouth fell open. The entrance hall led into an authentic recreation of an old-fashioned English drawing room. Several overstuffed couches, love seats and lounge chairs were scattered around the room. An antique-looking television surrounded by easy chairs and end tables with bowls of nuts was in one corner. The television was one of the few signs of modern technology in the room.

Reading lamps were at both ends of the couches. A bookshelf along one wall held an amazing assortment of popular books. Current editions of a variety of magazines were on wooden magazine racks.

The atmosphere was easy and unhurried. It made one feel like taking off ones shoes and walking barefoot in the deep pile of the chocolate-brown Sherwood carpet.

"Your table will be ready in a few minutes, Mr. Palmer, sir. Make yourselves comfortable; someone will be here momentarily to take care of you."

A waiter dressed in authentic footman's livery appeared to take their order. Pandora was impressed. It was the equivalent of stepping back in time to the Victorian era. As a teenager, Pandora had often wondered what it would feel like to be waited on hand and foot and have a whole staff of servants at her beck and call as if she were royalty.

Perhaps guessing her thoughts, Julian said, "You will be royalty this evening, Princess Pandora."

Pandora was in awe of this man. How could he read her so accurately? Was she that transparent?

"Would you like a drink while we wait?" Julian asked.

"Mineral water with a twist of lemon," she told the waiter. Minutes later, he returned with their drinks and guided them over to a green velvet love seat beneath the soft lighting of a Waterford crystal chandelier.

"So what do you think of The Drawing Room?" Julian smiled.

"It's wonderful," Pandora admitted. "I didn't know a place like this existed in New York City."

"That's because you never go out and have a good time for the sake of having a good time. But, starting this evening, you're going to learn how to let go."

"Is that another order?"

Amused but clearly serious, he grinned. "No, just think of it as a tempting suggestion."

Soon afterwards, a hostess came to show them to their table. The enormous room was sectioned off into ten, individual mini- settings resembling English drawing rooms. A stairway led to another level with more dining units. As Pandora and Julian were being shown to their own setting, the melodious strains of the Moonlight Sonata filled the room.

Their drawing room had a picture window, which afforded a breathtaking view of a garden. It also had a love seat facing an artificially lighted fireplace that looked like the real thing. A lace-covered, perfectly set table had been placed before the window. A candle in a crystal holder and a rose in a matching vase graced the center of the table.

Julian pulled out a chair for Pandora and then sat across from her.

Pandora looked around at the other people dining in their individual settings and smiled. "This is a fabulous concept, Julian."

"Are you beginning to relax?"

"Oh, yes. How could I not in an atmosphere like this?"

"I'm glad to hear it." He grinned. "Now if you could just loosen up around me."

How did he know she still felt uneasy around him? She didn't think she had given away that much.

"Julian."

"You're one tightly wound lady, but I intend to remedy the situation."

"How?"

"That's for me to know and you to find out."

Looking exasperated, she rolled her eyes upward.

A wine steward came to the table with his list, followed shortly by a waiter carrying lace-trimmed menus.

Julian ordered dry rosé aperitifs.

Pandora had a sudden thought. "There isn't pigeon pie or anything like that on the menu, is there? Because that's where I draw the line."

Julian and the waiter exchanged amused glances.

"No, there isn't. Actually, the smoked salmon is more what I had in mind. You can always order chicken if you're in the mood for eating a bird."

"Smoked salmon will do just fine, thank you," she said, looking anywhere but at Julian or the waiter.

"In that case," he said to the wine steward, "we'll also have Alsace Riesling to go with our meal."

"What shall we talk about while we wait?" Julian asked. "Anything having to do with business is off-limits this evening."

"What else is there to talk about?"

"Pan, Pan."

"What?"

"You really don't know how to enjoy yourself, do you? When was the last time you went out dancing? I'm not referring to affairs like the Martin Charity Dinner. I mean really gone out somewhere to let it all hang out."

"I don't have time for things like that."

"Because work and more work is all you ever have on your mind. Pan, you give a new meaning to lighten up."

"Julian."

"Well, it's true."

"Going out and having fun is nice, but…"

He took her hand in his. "You need someone to enjoy yourself with."

"And you think you're that someone?"

"I can be if you'll let me." He kissed the back of her hand. "Will you let me, Pan?"

Pandora eased her hand from his. "Here comes the waiter with our dinner."

Julian was pleased that Pandora was beginning to take him seriously, beginning to recognize that he wasn't going to just go away. What he had to do now was make her understand why he had no intention of giving up on her.

They enjoyed their dinner in companionable silence for a short while. Then Pandora ventured a comment.

"I've read and heard quite a few things about you, but for all that, you're still a mystery man, Julian Palmer. You have a way of eliciting confidences without revealing anything about yourself."

"There's not much to tell. I grew up in Brooklyn, and after graduating high school, I went to college. When I finished, I took over my father's business. I've lived a pretty ordinary bachelor existence ever since."

"Ordinary? I don't think so. You have a zest for life that truly amazes me. Does anything ever faze you?"

"No, because I refuse to let it. My father taught me to never consider anything a failure, because it can be turned inside out and made into a success."

"What an interesting philosophy," she murmured. Julian was such a positive man. More than that, actually. He was special, and she was beginning to see him in an entirely different light, not as the control freak she first assumed him to be. He was just a forceful man with compassion mixed in. And don't forget sexy, gorgeous and a few other assets. Realizing she was staring, Pandora glanced away.

Julian saw her looking at the dance floor in the center of the room, so he strode over to the orchestra leader. Returning a few minutes later, he took Pandora's hand and guided her onto the dance floor as the band began playing "Unchained Melody."

It was as though they were in another world, one far removed from the daily rat race of New York City. It was the perfect escape. To Pandora, it was heaven not having to worry about the next takeover or merger. Or the latest attempt by her in-laws and their cohorts to make her life hell. She was out with an attractive man who seemed genuinely interested in her as a woman.

Julian felt the tension leave Pandora's body and breathed a sigh of relief. Her body was soft yet firm and completely feminine. The sensuous fragrance she wore enveloped his senses. He brushed his cheek against the smooth silkiness of her jet black hair and breathed in its delicately arousing scent.

Pandora didn't resist when he drew her closer. What was he doing to her?

He's doing what you want him to, girl, an inner voice insisted.

She gazed up into his dark eyes, and the spellbinding effect he had on her grew stronger. Her body began to respond. She felt her breasts peak and swell, aching to be caressed. When he nuzzled her neck with his lips she trembled, closing her eyes and letting herself drift along on a sea of sheer bliss.

Julian saw the impassioned glaze in her honey-gold eyes and smiled when they darkened to an even deeper golden color as her desire began to build. When he touched his thigh to hers, he felt both pleasure and pain surge upward into his groin. He closed his eyes, reveling in the feeling.

The song finally ended, awakening them to their surroundings. And like a slow-lifting English fog, the highly charged moment slipped away, and Julian led Pandora back to their table.

"I've really enjoyed this evening, Julian. I can't remember being this relaxed in I don't know how long. Thank you."

"My pleasure, madam," he said in his best English accent.

"You're crazy, you know that?"

"A good kind of crazy, I hope."

"Very good," she smiled.

Julian's insides shifted. Her smile had completely devastated his senses. He wondered if he could control his ardor long enough to woo her slowly, because at this very moment he wanted her so badly his whole body ached.

When she saw the raw desire glittering in his eyes, Pandora glanced at her watch. "I really think we should be going. Your sister and niece will be bringing Destinee home in a little while."

"You and my sister should hit it off. But one thing I don't want you to do is listen to and believe any of her horror stories about me."

Pandora laughed. "Horror stories, huh? You mean I'm going to get the opportunity to hear the real low-down on you, and you want me to pass it up?"

"Just remember she's my sister, and her opinion might be a little warped."

"You mean dead on, don't you? I bet you were something else when you were growing up, Julian Palmer."

"To hear my mother and Gramma Edna tell it, I was."

"And they wouldn't lie, would they?"

"I plead the fifth on that one. Since you enjoyed this evening, you won't say no when I ask you out again, will you?"

"Julian, I don't know."

The waiter walked up. "Would you like coffee, sir, madam?"

"No, I don't think so."

"None for me."

"Are you ready to leave, Pan?" Julian asked, reaching for his credit card. When she nodded, he handed the card to the waiter.

"I'll prepare your check, sir. It'll just be a moment."

Julian turned to Pandora. "Will you go out dancing with me Saturday night at Club Cloud Nine?"

"Julian, you have to know going to clubs is hardly my thing. You're really into trying to change me, aren't you?"

"No, I'm not exactly trying to change you, Pan, I'm just into helping you learn to…"

"Relax. I remember. Do I really look that stressed out to you?"

When he didn't answer the question and just hunched his shoulders, the gesture was answer enough.

Minutes later, in the limo, Julian turned to Pandora.

"About my invitation. You never gave me an answer."

"I'll have to get back to you."

"Uh-uh, now."

She saw the look of implacable determination on his face and gave in. "Oh, all right, you win, you bully."

"I'm not being a bully, Pan, I just want to spend time with you."

She had heard words like that before, but not delivered in quite so impassioned a way. Julian had style, she had to give him that. It began to sink in that he was serious, dead serious, about his intentions toward her. The realization made her uncomfortable. Lyman had seemed just as serious at first, but later he had shown his true colors.

Julian saw fleeting suspicion and fear in her eyes.

Surely she wasn't afraid of him. No, that wasn't it. More than likely she was afraid of herself and her response to him. Being this close to a man in any intimate sense was evidently not in her recent memory, which raised serious questions about her relationship with her late husband. Whatever the problem, he intended to help her with it.

CHAPTER TWELVE

When Pandora got out of the limo in front of her condo, Julian followed her. She held up her hand to stop him.

"It's not necessary to come in with me."

"I want to, all right? Now give me your keys like a good girl."

"I'm not a child, Julian."

His eyes roved appreciatively over her body. "Believe me, I know that. You're definitely all woman."

Pandora felt her face heating up. Surrendering she handed her keys to him. He opened the door and stepped aside to let her enter first.

"I thought I heard you come—oh, Mr. Palmer!" Rachel sounded surprised, but her expression said she was delighted to see him. "Would you two like some coffee?"

"I don't think…" Pandora began, but Julian jumped in, saying, "I'd like that very much, Rachel. If it isn't too much trouble."

Rachel grinned. "Oh, it's no trouble at all, sir."

"None of that 'sir' business. Please, call me Julian."

A smile lit the housekeepers face as she left the room.

"Do you always have that effect on women?"

"What effect is that?"

"You know very well what."

"Whatever it is, it doesn't seem to be having an effect on a certain woman I know," he said, his tone heavy with unspoken meaning.

"Oh, it's having one, all right."

"If that's true, I'm afraid to ask what kind."

"No, you're not. You're not afraid of anything, Julian, and you know it. My guess is that you're enjoying all of this."

"I'll confess to enjoying being with you, Pan," he said, pulling her into his arms and kissing her. Releasing her, he murmured, "I think you've enjoyed being with me this evening, too?"

"Yes, I have to admit I have. Satisfied?"

"Not hardly, sweetheart. But it's a step in the right direction."

"By right direction, you mean in your direction?"

His expression was as intimate as a kiss when he said, "Something like that."

Rachel returned with the coffee. "I'll leave you two alone."

Pandora shot her an annoyed look, which she ignored.

"Mutiny," Pandora muttered under her breath, watching Rachel's retreating figure.

Julian laughed. "What did you say?"

She flashed him a look that said, As if you didn't hear. But she said, "Let me pour you a cup of coffee."

"All right. Just don't sweeten it with arsenic, okay?"

Pandora had to laugh. "Don't worry, I won't. My daughter and Rachel would kill me. You've managed to weave a spell over both of them."

"That should tell you something."

"And just what should it be telling me?"

"That I'm worth all their adoration."

"What an ego. Your modesty overwhelms me."

"Ah, but I wish that were true, then maybe you'll let me overwhelm you in certain other ways."

Finding it harder and harder to come up with answers, Pandora was relieved when Destinee, Talaya and Selena walked in. Destinee ran into Julian's open arms, and he hugged her affectionately.

"I'm so glad to see you, Julian."

"I'm glad to see you, too, sweetheart." He sent a they- all-love-me-what-can-I-say look Pandora's way.

"Pandora Cooper, this is my little sister Selena Andrews—Talaya you've already met."

Selena walked over to Pandora. "I'm his only sister. I should warn you that this brother of mine has that effect on every female between the ages of one and eighty."

"I guessed as much," Pandora responded.

"Maybe I should stay around to defend myself."

"Bye, Julian," Selena said in a slightly mocking tone.

His eyes narrowed.

"Don't worry; I won't say anything bad about you, my brother."

"Since I don't have anything to worry about, I guess I'll be going."

"Can't he stay, Mama? Please?" Destinee pleaded.

"Another time, Destinee," Julian answered. "You can call me later and fill me in on all the gory details. Deal?"

Destinee laughed, adding a comrade-in-arms wink. "Deal."

"I'll talk to you later," Julian said to his sister on his way out. When he reached the door, he turned and looked at Pandora. "I'll pick you up at eight Saturday evening."

As soon as the door closed behind Julian, Destinee exclaimed, "You're really going out on a date with him, Mama?"

"Now, don't get the wrong idea."

"Come on, Mama, you know you like Julian."

"I like him, but…"

"No buts about it. You do, I can tell." Destinee turned to Talaya and asked, "What do you think?"

"I like the idea. The more they see of each other, the closer they'll get, and the more fun well end up having."

"You're probably right," she answered wishfully.

Pandora turned to find Selena studying her. Just what had she gotten herself into by getting involved with this family? Selena was a feminine version of her brother, though her skin was several shades lighter. She was petite and feisty. Talaya resembled her mother, but her eyes were lighter brown, and where her mother was petite, her daughter was not.

"We're not all bad, Pandora," Selena said.

Talaya laughed. "I don't know, Mom. She hasn't met Uncle Howland yet."

"He's Drac's father," Selena explained.

Pandora thought about the names the man had given his sons. "You don't need to explain. I've heard about his fixation with the otherworldly, even when it came to names for his children."

"That's a nice way of putting it," Talaya allowed. "I wonder what he would have named them if they had been girls."

"I'm sure he would have thought of something just as bizarre and crazy," Selena laughed. "I don't know why Aunt Macy let him get away with it. I take that back; it was probably because she worshipped the ground he walked on and thought his mouth was a prayer book."

"Selena, you're bad," Pandora laughed.

"Julian says that, too. Getting back to the subject of my brother, what's going on between you two?"

"Nothing."

"Yet," Destinee tossed in. "And that's because Mama won't let it happen."

"I strongly suggest you and Talaya go up to your room," Pandora said, "so the grown-ups can talk without comments from the peanut gallery."

"Oh, Mama, I'm only telling the truth."

"Destinee!"

"Yes, ma'am. Let's go to my room, Talaya. Grown-ups," she said, throwing her hands up.

"Yeah," Talaya agreed, following Destinee.

"Now, getting back to my brother. You are interested in him, aren't you, Pandora?"

"He won't let me be anything else."

"I see," Selena grinned. "It's like that, huh?"

"Now don't *you* start."

"What? Getting the wrong idea? I don't think I am. I could see from the way he looked at you that Julian is more than a little interested in you, girlfriend." She pursed her lips. "But for some reason you're afraid of getting involved with him, aren't you? Why is that?"

"It's a long story."

"Isn't it always? You want to talk about it?"

"Although we've only just met, I feel I can talk to you about almost anything..."

"But not about my brother, right?"

"Look, Selena..."

"You don't have to justify yourself to me, Pandora. If you're not ready to talk about him, you're just not ready. When you are, I want you to know I'll be a friend and listen and not pass judgment. Okay?"

"Okay." Pandora said, giving her new friend a grateful look.

"May I come in?" Destinee asked from the doorway of her mother's bedroom later that night.

"Yeah, come on in, honey." Pandora put the book she was reading down and prepared herself for an interrogation.

Destinee plopped down on the side of her mother's bed.

"Mama, we really need to go shopping for some new clothes for you. Every time I mention the subject you conveniently forget or can't find the time. Now that you've started going out with Julian, you're going to need some really hot things to wear."

"One date doesn't mean it'll become a habit."

"Oh, right."

"Desi!"

"Dating Julian is like eating potato chips, Mama; you can't stop with just one. What day are we going to go shopping?"

"You're relentless, Destinee Cooper. How about tomorrow afternoon at one? Since you have a pupil-free day, come to my office."

"Perfect. I'll be there." She hugged and kissed her mother before hopping off the bed and leaving the room.

Pandora picked up her book and turned to the page she had marked. Seconds later, she closed it again and put it on the nightstand. There was no way she could go back to reading tonight; her mind was too occupied with Julian and their upcoming date.

She had rarely dated before she met Lyman. After his death, she had occasionally gone out, but had never let any of her relationships with men evolve beyond the platonic. None of the men she had gone out with had ever come close to making her consider a steady arrangement—until now.

Julian Palmer made her feel alive again. Could it grow into—no, she wouldn't think along those lines. She restlessly swept the covers back and padded over to her walk-in closet and examined its contents. Destinee was right, she did need a more colorful wardrobe. It was time she stopped wearing widow's weeds. It wasn't as though she was still in mourning for her late husband. She never had been. Considering the way he had treated her throughout their marriage, all she had felt was relief when he died.

Okay, she will go shopping with her daughter. Julian Palmer had inspired her at least that much. Maybe he was what she needed in her life right now. At The Drawing Room she had been completely relaxed, and by evening she had felt quite comfortable with Julian. She had to admit she was looking forward to going out with him again.

"You're smiling this morning," Cassandra said to Pandora as she came through the outer-office door. "What's up?"

"Does anything have to be up? Oh, all right. I've agreed to go out with Julian Palmer Saturday. I have you to thank, I believe."

"You do? I thought you would be angry with me for sneaking Julian in to see you."

"On the contrary."

"Then I'm glad I did it, but I can't help wondering why you agreed. You said you weren't interested."

"It's a woman's prerogative to change her mind, isn't it?" she said mysteriously.

"Wait til Drac hears about this. I can hardly wait to tell him."

Pandora frowned. "He doesn't like me very much, does he?"

"I don't think it's so much that he doesn't like you. It's just that he's protective of his cousin. He told me that when they were growing up, Julian used to take up for him when the other kids teased him about his name. They're almost like brothers, so you see why Drac acts the way he does. He's also afraid you'll end up hurting Julian."

"I was right about the vibes I felt coming from him when he was here yesterday. He really does see me as the original black widow spider." She bit the inside of her cheek. "Well, I have given the world that impression. I can't complain now because they've taken it seriously, can I?" Pandora said philosophically.

"You're really beginning to come out of your she'll. I'm grateful to Julian for doing that."

"Pandora, I need to have a talk with you." The all-too-familiar voice of her brother-in-law came from the doorway.

Her happy mood vanished at the sight of Monroe Cooper.

"Monroe, why are you here? As I recall, we covered everything concerning Destinee in our last meeting."

"Oh, we did, but this is about an entirely different matter."

"All right," she said in a sharp-edged voice, then turned to Cassandra. "Hold all my calls for the next five minutes."

Monroe followed Pandora into her office and closed the door, taking a seat in front of her desk.

"All right, get to the point of your visit, Monroe. I have a lot of work to do."

"You're a very attractive woman, Pandora, and you become even more so with the passing of time. A lot of men would agree with that, including Julian Palmer."

"What are you trying to say?" she asked impatiently.

"Just that any man would desire you. Haven't you wondered why he came to Sasha's annual summer party? He's never come to anything I've invited him to. You've caught his eye, and he wants you in his bed."

"You really believe that?"

"I know it. Wake up, Pandora. Can't you see it's your company he's salivating over? And he's planning to use sex to get it."

"And you haven't been trying to do the same thing?" she shot back.

He shrugged. "But unlike me, Julian Palmer is more experienced at going after and getting what he wants when it comes to women."

"Your point being?"

"The first step toward achieving his goal was to observe you up-close and personal at the stockholders meeting, then again at the party. He was getting to know you so he could plan his strategy for getting you into his bedroom, later gaining control of your company via the boardroom."

"Monroe, please. If that's all you came here to say, you can leave right now."

"I have to warn you that going out with him does have its disadvantages."

She wondered how he knew about that. "Disadvantages? What are you talking about?"

"I saw the two of you at The Drawing Room last night. You were so fascinated by him you didn't even see me, Sasha or Calvin."

"Have you enlisted Sasha and her husband to spy on me now?" she asked in a tight, angry voice.

"No, but we are keeping track of your every move. If you do anything questionable, I'll petition the court for custody so fast it'll leave your head spinning for days."

"There's nothing wrong with me going out with whomever I please."

"No, there isn't, but if your conduct is—shall we say—the least bit risqué…" He left his threat hanging in the air. Grinning, he added, "I see you understand."

"I understand that by throwing him at my head you thought you would be putting temptation in my path. I'm not going to let you rule my personal life. I'll see whomever I want to see and go out with whomever I choose."

"You had better take a little good advice seriously. What you do can have adverse consequences if you're not careful." Monroe got up from his chair. "You can get serious about Julian Palmer if you want to, but remember if you do anything that can be seen as an unhealthy influence on my niece, I'll take you to court and sue for custody. Do I make myself clear?" He smiled. "I thought so. I'll be seeing you round, Pandora." With that, he left her office.

Pandora sat immobile in her chair long after Monroe had gone, angry tremors quaking through her. God, the man was devious. How dare he come here and practically admit setting her up, then turning around and threatening her like that just because she had gone out with Julian Palmer.

She once again cursed her late husband for putting that provision about their daughter in his will. Monroe knew nothing about raising a teenage girl, or any child for that matter. He had never been married, and he had never been close to any of Sasha's children, either.

As for her sister-in-law, Sasha just plain hated her. Pandora had never been able to figure out why. Sasha had a husband, children and supposedly a happy family life—all the things Pandora yearned for, but did not expect to ever have. If it wasn't for Destinee, Pandora didn't know what she would do. There was no center to her universe without her daughter.

The thought of anyone trying to take her child away terrified her. She had always kept her conduct above reproach. There was no way Monroe could prove she was unfit just because she went out with Julian or any other man, for that matter. He was just trying to intimidate her. Well, she had no intention of letting him get away with it.

CHAPTER THIRTEEN

"This dress is really you, Mama. You've just got to get it."

Pandora agreed with her daughter's opinion of the jade green sheath dress. Made of silk, it was long and figure-hugging, with slits that stopped just above the knee on either side. The vivid, gold-trimmed dragon emblazoned on the front of the bodice gleamed back at her as she stood before the mirror. The gold in the dress picked up the gold in her eyes, giving Pandora an even more exotic look.

"It's perfect for your date with Julian, Mama. All you need to set it off is a pair of gold high-heeled sandals. Julian is tall so you don't have to worry about towering over him."

"Destinee!"

"You are a tall woman, Mama." She looked at herself. "And me, too. I'll probably look just like you one day," she said proudly. "At least that's what Aunt Sasha says."

The mention of Sasha's name brought to mind her conversation with Monroe. She wished that both Monroe and Sasha would stay the hell out of her personal life. Thanks to her dead husband, they would be in her life until Destinee turned eighteen.

"What's wrong, Mama? Don't you like the dress?"

"I like it just fine. I was thinking about something else, that's all. I should be getting back to the office." Pandora stepped out of the dress and back into her black linen suit. This would be the last time she wore black to the office unless she was attending board meetings or other business functions.

She and Destinee had chosen five suits for her to wear to the office: one in maize, one cream, another in sky blue, and the last two in royal purple and teal. For casual wear, they had selected five equally colorful pantsuits and a pair of red jeans. Not bad for a start, her daughter had told her.

Pandora was beginning to like the idea of wearing bright, happy colors again. They made her feel freer and more relaxed. This thing about relaxing was really working. And she had Julian to thank for that.

"We made the right decision getting this dress, Mama. You look fantastic," Destinee said to her mother in her bedroom the evening of Pandora's date with Julian. "You're going to make Julian's eyes pop right out of his head."

"You really think he'll like it?"

"He'll more than like it, Mama. Trust me, he'll love it, so stop worrying."

They heard the doorbell.

"That'll be Julian," Destinee announced excitedly. To see her reaction, you would think Destinee was the one going out with Julian. But Pandora had to admit that she, too, was a little eager, more than a little excited. She felt as nervous as a teenager on her first date. She had so much confidence when it came to facing down men in business, but none when it came to personal interactions—like going out on a date with a man like Julian Palmer. She was baffled by this.

"I'll go downstairs and open the door," Destinee said. Heading out of the room, she gave her mother last-minute advice. "Wait a few minutes before you come down."

Her daughter was growing up so fast Pandora was beginning to wonder who was the parent and who was the child.

Julian stood stock-still when he saw Pandora descending the stairs. He had thought Pandora was lovely before, but tonight she took his breath away. He was delighted she had decided to wear her glorious, silky black hair down. Her rich brown skin seemed to glow, and her luscious full lips seemed to be beckoning to him.

"You see, Mama, Julian is speechless because you look so beautiful. Right, Julian?"

"Absolutely," he answered huskily. "Ready to depart, Your Royal Highness?"

"Julian."

"You look like royalty to me. Your carriage awaits, my princess."

"Carriage, huh? Will it turn into a pumpkin at the stroke of midnight?" she asked under her breath. Would she be like Cinderella and revert to her old ways at evenings end?

Pandora gazed at Julian. Fine was the only word that could accurately describe him. The beige summer suit he was wearing did wonderful things for his dark, deeply bronzed skin. The way those wicked midnight eyes of his glittered and his arousing habit of wetting his full bottom lip when he looked at her made her heart beat a little faster.

Only a little, girlfriend?

Okay, a lot.

Julian flashed one of his killer smiles, then wrapped her arm around his. The courtly gesture caused Pandora to giggle girlishly. The pleased look on Destinee's face did not escape her notice.

"The two of you look like you we're made for each other, Mama," said Destinee. "I hope you have a great time."

"Oh, we will, Desi. I intend to make sure of that," Julian vowed.

"Mama calls me Desi sometimes, too," she said approvingly.

When Pandora and Julian stepped inside Club Cloud Nine, a hostess dressed in a short white costume with a pair of small, glittering wings on the back walked up to greet them.

"Somehow I can't picture an angel looking anything like that," Pandora whispered to Julian.

"Me, either. But as an earthling on a scale of one to ten, I'd say she is an eight. She does have great legs."

"Julian!"

"You have nothing to worry about on that score, Pan. Your legs are a ten."

"Only a ten?" she laughed.

"I love to hear you laugh. You need to do it more often, and in the future, I plan to see that you do."

"The future, huh?"

"Oh, yes, were going to have one, sweetheart. And what a future it promises to be."

The hostess showed them to one of the many tables with painted wallboards resembling clouds behind the chairs as a back-drop. Stars were painted on the midnight blue walls and ceiling. In the center of the room, a giant moon-shaped strobe light suspended from the ceiling twirled continuously. Dancers were doing various interpretations of the tango to Kenny G's "Havana."

A waiter in a white suit came to take their order.

"We'll both have the cloud nine number one," Julian told him.

"Cloud nine number one?" Pandora asked.

Julian grinned. "Oh, it's a drink I think you'll like. It's the house special."

"I'm afraid to ask what makes it special."

"Don't worry, it won't kill you."

"I have to tell you that I don't have a very high tolerance for alcohol, Julian."

"No need for you to worry, Pan. You won't be driving."

"Is it that potent?"

"Our drinks are here. I'll let you be the judge."

"By the time I start feeling the effects, it may be too late."

"In any case, I'll take care of you," Julian said in a husky, sexy voice. "I plan to be there if and when you ever need me, lady."

His softly spoken words made her feel cherished and special, something she hadn't felt in she couldn't remember how long. In fact, if she ever had.

After finishing their drinks, Julian asked Pandora to dance.

Luther Vandross's "I Know" started playing. Julian held her close as the ballads story began to unfold.

"Are you enjoying yourself?" Julian nuzzled Pandora's ear as they glided around the dance floor.

"Oh, yes, I really am. I'm glad I let you talk me into coming here tonight."

The song ended, and Julian guided Pandora back to their table.

"The atmosphere is incredible, Julian. I've never felt this free and uninhibited."

"I didn't think you had. I'm glad to be the one to introduce you to that feeling."

"Is that all you plan to introduce me to?"

"What do you mean?" he demanded.

"I've been wondering why you accepted Monroe and Sasha's invitation to their summer party."

"You think my motive was suspect, even sinister? If you must know, I wanted to see you in an informal setting. I had already seen you in action in a business setting; I wasn't convinced that the persona of the black widow you had so carefully cultivated was the real Pandora Cooper. And the other day, and especially tonight, I saw the truth."

"What truth?

"That you aren't what you seem."

"You think not?"

He took her hand in his and kissed it. "I know not."

Pandora looked into his eyes and saw flames of desire that so closely mirrored her own. It scared her.

When Julian leaned forward and gently kissed her lips, Pandora returned the kiss, letting the lingering communion of their mouths revive the tart taste of the cloud nine number one on her tongue.

"I've never felt this way before," Pandora confessed.

Julian kissed her again, but lightly this time. Although he ached to deepen the kiss and plunder its sweetness and tell her how much he wanted her, he decided against it. He didn't want to move too fast and frighten her, but knew it was going to be hell restraining himself. He ended the kiss as "Eastside" by 480 East began to play.

"Let's get up and boogie, Ms. Cooper."

"Boogie? I can't remember the last time I did anything like that."

"Just let the beat take you."

After watching Pandora down her second cloud nine number one, an amused smile hovered at the corners of Julian's lips when he realized the reason she had become so pliant. And why she was letting herself go with the flow of the music on the dance floor.

"You're glowing, lady," Julian whispered in her ear.

"I'm definitely feeling no pain," she said, fanning her hot face with her hand. "Whew, it is warm in here. I haven't danced like this since I was about fourteen."

"Didn't your husband ever take you out for a night on the town?"

"Oh, we went out, but never to a place like this. Lyman was not only fifteen years older than me, but he thought and acted that way—literally. A night like this would never have been a consideration for him, believe me." She stopped abruptly and stared at Julian. "And just how did we get on the subject of my late husband?"

"I don't know, but we don't have to stay on it. I'm much more interested in the woman you are today."

"I'm afraid that's a very dull subject," she said, slurring her words.

Julian chuckled softly. "I think you're a little tipsy, Ms. Cooper."

"If I am, it's all your fault," she said producing a pout that wobbled charmingly.

"I take complete responsibility, princess." He glanced at his watch. "It's almost midnight. Are you going to turn into a pumpkin, Cinderella?"

"I thought her carriage did that."

"You're not so far into your cups after all. You're right, it did, but that definitely won't happen with my carriage. I guarantee you."

"Because you hired a limo. Good foresight, Mr. Palmer."

"Didn't I tell you what I would do to you any time you called me Mr. Palmer?"

"Yes, and I can hardly wait to receive my reprimand." She puckered her lips.

"Oh, Pan." The movement of her lush lips made him groan.

"I'm still waiting," she murmured, flicking her tongue across her lips.

Julian's insides jerked. "I think it's time I took you home, your highness." Julian rang the limo driver from his cell phone. Pandora had told him that she had little tolerance for alcohol. After only two drinks, she had gotten more than a buzz. He was glad he had managed to dissuade her from trying the other cloud nine drinks, which were much stronger. He had been unable to talk her out of ordering her third and fourth cloud nine number ones, though. He had a feeling she would have one hell of a hangover in the morning.

Julian hated to see the evening come to an end, but it was only the first of many. He held Pandora in his arms as they headed back to her condo, but then he decided to have the driver cruise around Central Park. He opened the window and let in the cool night breeze. The effect seemed to somewhat revive his woozy companion.

"Am I drunk, Julian?" Pandora asked him.

"Slightly intoxicated. You weren't kidding when you said you had little tolerance for alcohol, were you?"

"I had a wonderful time. I want you to know that." She squirmed on his lap.

"I think you'd better be still," Julian said thickly, tightening his arms around her waist.

She felt him harden beneath her, and she looked up at him, an awed expression on her face. "Did I do that to you?"

"Yes, you most certainly did. And since you aren't ready or in any shape to do anything about it…" He let his voice trail off.

Pandora stilled immediately and started pretending to have great interest in the passing scenery. Central Park in moonlight was something to behold. Tonight the ducks floated on a moon-silvered pond, giving it an achingly romantic effect.

"I'm not ready to go home yet, Julian," Pandora informed him.

"I would suggest we go to my place, but you know where we would likely end up."

"Yes, I do," she answered, her voice sounding decidedly more sober. "Can't we just ride around a while?"

"Yes, we can do that." Julian studied the vulnerable expression on her face and knew he wanted her in his life always and forever. His cousin, Drac, wouldn't approve of his choice, but he didn't care. Pandora Cooper was an exceptional lady. She was intelligent, beautiful and all woman.

He had heard rumors about her husband's treatment of her. If true, the man had to have been a fool. He wondered how much of what he had heard was true, and how much was just gossip or mere speculation. He would have to wait until she voluntarily confided that information in him.

Then he began thinking about Pandora's daughter. He could tell the child was starved for fatherly love and affection by the way she responded to kindness and attention from him.

Since meeting Pandora, Julian wanted a family of his own more than ever. He wanted Pandora and Destinee to become an integral part of his life. He would do whatever he had to, fight whomever he had to fight, to make it happen. He recalled the tension he had felt between Monroe and Pandora. There definitely had been something between them, he was sure of it, but what? For some reason, Pandora loathed the man. Julian himself never liked or trusted him.

"You're so quiet, Julian. Is anything wrong? Did I embarrass you tonight?"

"No to both questions. I've enjoyed every minute I've shared with you tonight, Pan. I like seeing you have a good time. We'll have to do it again real soon. Can't have you regressing on me, now can I?"

"After tonight, I don't think I will. You've made me aware of a dimension to myself I never realized existed. You've opened a door to my personality that has been kept locked all these years—a carefree side, a side you've made me crave to experience and enjoy again."

Julian slanted his mouth over hers, igniting a fire inside her. The heat spread through her body with amazing speed. Her body throbbed with a need she had never felt before, certainly not with her husband. Pandora eased away from Julian to catch her breath. Things were moving too fast, way too fast.

"Maybe you had better take me home now, Julian."

Julian was so aroused it took a few moments for her words to register. The hard throbbing flesh between his legs took even longer to receive the message and respond. He cleared his throat and took deep calming breaths.

"Yes, I think you're right."

"Julian."

"It's all okay. I'm all right."

Pandora knew he was lying. She could tell he still wanted her very badly, but was exerting astonishing control over himself. It made her realize how much he cared for and respected her. She appreciated that control because she wasn't ready for the kind of relationship he obviously wanted. She wasn't sure if she ever would be. Although she was attracted to Julian, more than attracted actually, something deep inside was preventing her from advancing to the next step.

Julian put his arm around her shoulders. "Pan, you can't run away from what we feel for each other, baby."

"Julian, I..."

He put his finger across her lips. "Shh, don't fight it. We're going to make love. It's inevitable. But the time has to be right for both of us."

Julian signaled to the driver to take them to Pandora's condo. During the ride home, Julian just held Pandora in his arms. Just for tonight, what they had shared was enough.

CHAPTER FOURTEEN

Pandora groaned when she awakened the next morning. How her head ached. She wondered what went into the cloud nine number one. If she ever went back she would be sure to limit herself to just one drink. Julian had tried to warn her, but she hadn't listened, and now she was paying for it.

She remembered Julian helping her up the stairs to her bedroom, and then…She closed her eyes, trying to force herself to recall what had or had not happened. He had kissed her good night, and then he had left. Her face burned when she thought of how she had responded to his kisses. What must he think of her now? She had behaved like some love-starved animal.

Not a love-starved animal, girlfriend. A love-starved woman. There's a difference. All he has to do is touch you and you melt. You more than want him. You might as well admit it.

She did want him and more besides, but…

You're afraid.

What exactly was she afraid of? Was it of Julian or herself?

Destinee burst into the room. "Mama, get up. I want to hear all about your night out with Julian."

Pandora groaned. "Not now, honey."

"Well, when?"

"Later, okay? I need to shower and brush my teeth." Her mouth felt as gritty as desert sand, and the lingering taste of the cloud nine number ones had soured on her tongue.

Pandora felt almost human again after a second cup of coffee. Thankfully, it was Sunday, and she didn't have to face going to the office. She related the highlights of her evening to her daughter and retreated into the study to look over some papers.

After picking up one file after another and promptly discarding each one, she finally conceded the futility of trying to work. Her mind kept detouring back to Julian and the way he had kissed her and the way she had responded. She couldn't forget how he had made her body burn with just a look. The ringing of the phone broke into her reverie, and she picked up the receiver.

"Hello."

"Pan?"

"Julian!"

"You sound surprised to hear from me. I told you, I plan to be around, girl. When are you going to start taking me seriously?" Then he became gently solicitous. "How are you feeling?"

"Except for a slight headache, I'm fine."

"Slight headache? You sure that's all? I did warn you not to be fooled by the cloud nine number ones sweet taste because that didn't necessarily mean it didn't have a huge kick, especially if you drank too many."

"So you did."

"You and Destinee want to go for a ride in the country with me?"

Pandora didn't have to think about it. "I don't know about my daughter, but I'd love to."

"Fantastic. I'll be by to pick you both up in an hour."

"All right." After hanging up, Pandora questioned why she had accepted so readily.

Because it's what you wanted to do, that's why, a niggling voice interjected.

Julian was acting like a man on a mission, but it was unclear where that mission was headed. If, as Monroe had intimated, all Julian was interested in was getting the black widow into his bed and her company under his financial thumb, then why was he as tuned into her daughter's sensibilities as he was to hers?

She had to know the reason. She needed time to assess the situation to make sure she wasn't blind to some hidden motive or self-serving agenda. She had failed to do that when she had gotten involved with Monroe, and later with Lyman. She had been so young and naive. She was fairly certain that Julian wasn't like them, but he was still a man. He was that, all right, she smiled, remembering how his hardened sex had throbbed beneath her buttocks in the limo.

Their ride in the country ended at Julian's mother's house in White Plains.

Julian laughed when he saw Pandora's wary expression turn when he told her where they were.

"My mother won't bite you, Pan."

"I know that." She rolled her eyes, annoyed by his teasing tone.

"Lighten up, Mama," Destinee said. "Julian's grandmother and sister are cool. I'm sure his mother is, too."

Pandora wondered why he had brought her here. Was he really that kind of serious about her? She knew he wanted her, but taking her to meet his mother was maybe a bit much.

Julian could almost see the wheels turning in Pandora's mind. She was forever questioning his motives when it came to her and her daughter. Good thing he didn't let it get to him. On the other hand if she weren't so leery and cautious, he wouldn't admire her so much. She was an intriguing, complex woman.

"Julian, who have you got with you?" Lenora Palmer asked, unlocking her screen door and stepping out on the porch.

"It's a surprise, Mrs. Palmer. Doesn't your one and only son rate a hug?"

His mother laughed, circling her arms around her son's waist. "Of course you do, Mr. Palmer. You are, after all, my oldest baby."

"Mama!" he exclaimed in an embarrassed, boyishly endearing way.

Destinee giggled.

"That'll be enough out of you, young lady. Uh, Mama, I'd like you to meet Pandora Cooper and her daughter, Destinee. My mother, Lenora Palmer."

The woman wasn't what Pandora expected. She was tiny and seemed to be gentle and sweet. But what, exactly, had she expected? Julian wasn't very much like his mother physically, but they did have similar smiles. His rapport with his mother impressed her; they were obviously very close. It was the kind of rapport she'd had with her own mother.

Pandora had read in a financial magazine that his father had died of a heart attack the year Julian graduated college. According to the article, Palmer and Associates had been on the brink of bankruptcy, but he had taken over the company, working like blazes to transform it into the powerhouse it now was.

Julian relished the look on his mother's face. He could almost hear her humming the wedding march and mentally making wedding plans. For once, he didn't mind if she and his grandmother assumed whatever they liked. Pandora Cooper would one day be his wife if he had his way. And Destinee would become his stepdaughter. He would have his own family at long last.

Pandora recognized the matchmaking gleam in Lenora Palmer's eye. It was similar to the one she had seen in Julian's grandmothers. She shifted her gaze to Julian, whose own eyes danced with amusement. He was apparently enjoying allowing his mother to think there was more between them than there actually was. Pandora herself wasn't even sure what was between them.

"Before you arrived I collected vegetables from my garden. Just in time, it seems, to fix a salad for our lunch," Lenora said.

"I'll help, Mrs. Palmer," Pandora offered.

"No, please, let me," Destinee volunteered. "I think Mama and Julian want to talk—alone."

"Destinee!" Pandora gasped.

"Well, it is true, Mama." She turned to Julian for support. "Isn't it, Julian?"

"You're right, sweetheart. Why don't you go ahead and help my mother, while your mother and I have our talk."

Lenora looked at them knowingly and gave Destinee a conspiratorial wink before heading for the kitchen.

Destinee wore a smug expression as she followed Lenora.

As soon as they were gone, and before Pandora could object to being manipulated, Julian pulled her into his arms and kissed her. The caress of his lips on hers canceled whatever she was going to say.

What was this power he had over her? No man had ever made her feel this alive and this vulnerable. She had avoided any kind of deep relationships because she never wanted to be at such a disadvantage. This time she sensed that she did not have complete control over her feelings or the situation, and that was scary.

She pulled away from Julian, taking deep breaths to restore her composure.

"Don't," he softly commanded, but there was steel in his rich, velvety voice.

"Don't what?" she asked breathlessly.

"You know what, Pan. You wanted me to kiss you. Deep inside you want me to make love to you, too." He put a finger across her lips to head off any forthcoming denials. "Don't bother denying it. I want you to get to know my family because you are one day going to become an important member of it."

"I-I think you had better take us home."

"Always running, Pan. What, my darling, are you afraid of?"

"I want you to know I don't intend to marry again. And since I don't have affairs or engage in one-night stands, where does that leave us? Friends? What?"

"There's more to it than your not wanting to marry again." Not waiting for her reply, he went on. "Why do you feel so threatened by what is happening between us? Have I done anything to make you think my intentions are less than honorable?"

"Your intentions don't matter because I'll never marry again. And I won't be any man's mistress."

"Pan."

"I don't want to talk about it anymore."

"You're just as ripe, just as hungry for a loving relationship as I am, darling," he whispered in her ear, enclosing her deeper in his embrace.

Pandora pushed against his chest. His body heat radiated through the material of his shirt, causing flames of desire to race up her arms and blaze through the rest of her body. He was right, she did want him, but she was afraid, confused, unsure how to deal with these renegade feelings. Julian's fingers explored her body, and everywhere he touched was on fire now.

"Your father and I used to have 'conversations' similar to the one you're having when we were courting," Lenora said with a wicked twinkle in her eyes as she stood looking at them in the doorway of the dining room. "Lunch is on the table," she cheerfully announced. "It's time you two took a breather from your, uh, 'conversation,' to eat."

Embarrassed by her ardor and at being caught in such a compromising position, Pandora quickly moved away from Julian. He laughed. "All three of us are adults, Pan. My mother understands what goes on between a man and a woman, I can assure you. Or else I wouldn't be here."

Pandora started to say something, but what was the use? Julian had an answer for everything. The look he gave her said she should give in gracefully. She would now, she decided, but she would have to call a halt to his—what? Courtship? Whether she wanted him to or not, he was courting her, and he wasn't giving her a chance, or a reason, to object.

Pandora watched Julian as they ate their lunch. He was as true to her first impression of him—a black-maned lion patiently studying a prospective mate, waiting until she was ready to surrender to the inevitable.

Pandora shifted her attention to her daughter. She and Julian's mother were getting along swimmingly. Julian knew what he was doing bringing them here. Every move he made was geared toward getting what he wanted, which appeared to be her, and yet…

"Would you like to take a walk around the grounds?" Julian asked.

"You go with Julian, Mama. I want to stay and talk to Mrs. Palmer. She wants to show me some of her family albums. I can't wait to see pictures of Julian when he was a little boy."

Pandora wanted to refuse as much as she wanted to accept his invitation. In the end, she decided to accept.

The property boosted a green lushly wooded area and a clear-water creek. Julian took a well-traveled path leading down to the water.

"Oh, Julian, it's beautiful here. Is this where you grew up?" Pandora asked.

"No, I bought it for my mother about ten years ago. We lived in a Brooklyn brownstone when I was growing up. My mother is originally from North Carolina. I knew she always dreamed of having a place in the country. I vowed when I took over the family business that I would buy her such a place and I did. I'm sure you've noticed that my mother and I are very close. And I'm just as close to the rest my family."

Pandora sighed as they crossed a wooden creek bridge.

"I always wished for that kind of closeness between me and my father when I was growing up. Being a freelance photojournalist, he was forever rushing off to one assignment or another. When he didn't come back that last time, it was more of the same, only this time it was permanent."

"Your mother didn't mind his being gone so much?"

"Oh, she did, but where she came from, a woman went along with whatever her husband wanted. As you probably already know from what you've read about me, she was from India."

"You take after her quite a lot in looks, am I right?"

She nodded. "My mother used to say I got my eyes, my height and my brains from my father. No matter how smart she believed he was, I think he was selfish and insensitive for taking her away from her people, her way of life, globetrotting all over the world, leaving her behind to cope alone."

Julian could see now where her wariness toward and lack of faith in men originated—first with her absentee father, compounded, he was beginning to suspect, by her husband.

They came to two rock formations overlooking the creek. A runoff of clear blue water spilled over the rocks, down the center of the creek and into the rock bed below.

Pandora's reaction to her surroundings could be seen in her eyes.

"You're a nature lover at heart, aren't you?" he asked.

"Oh, yes," she answered, wistfully. "Every summer Destinee and I go to our cabin in the Catskills."

"Will you be going there this year?"

"Yes, definitely. It's been a busy year for me and my daughter. We need to get away for some R & R."

"You want to walk a little farther?"

"I think we'd better head back, don't you?"

"Why? Because you think I might throw you down on the ground and have my wicked way with you?"

"No, I don't think that."

"You sure?"

He took her hand in his and turning it over brushed her palm with his lips. Then he lifted his head slightly and said, "I want you, sweetheart, but I prefer to make love to you in a soft bed with satin sheets. There are thistles and rocks and all kinds of uncomfortable things lying on the ground."

"The thistles have soft purple flowers this time of year."

"Are you trying to talk me into or out of something?"

Pandora laughed. "I see your point."

"I wanted you to enjoy coming here. It was not my intention to seduce you."

"I believe you. Your mother might be biased where you're concerned, but I don't think she would go for that. Why, exactly, did you bring me here?"

"Just so you could meet my mother."

"And?"

"And nothing else. When a man courts a woman he's serious about, he wants her to meet his family, especially his mother."

"But I told you I would never marry again."

"I know, baby, but I intend to make you change your mind."

She wondered if he knew how close he was to achieving his goal. He made it sound so tempting. He himself was pure temptation, but…

Julian pulled her to her feet. "We'd better head back. My mother and your daughter will get the wrong idea if we stay away for very much longer. Not that I mind if they do."

Pandora put a finger across his lips. "Enough."

He kissed her finger. "All right, Pan."

She knew he wasn't giving up. He had only begun his campaign to win her over. Why couldn't he just believe her about not ever wanting to marry? Julian Palmer was one stubborn, determined man.

CHAPTER FIFTEEN

"You made quite an impression on Julian's mother from what I've heard," Cassandra told Pandora when she came into the office Monday morning.

"The Palmer grapevine must be faster than the speed of sound."

Cassandra laughed. "I told Drac the same thing last night. Julian's mother didn't waste any time calling Gramma Edna, and she in turn relayed what was said to Drac's father, who lives only a few miles from her. Then he passed it on to Drac, and he told me and..."

Pandora put up her hand. "I get the picture. So what does Drac think?"

"He thinks Julian is really hung up on you."

"And that worries him. Right?"

"You shouldn't let what he thinks bother you. Julian is his own man. I'm sure that whatever Drac's opinion might be, Julian won't let it influence him one way or the other once he's set his mind on something—or someone."

Uncomfortable with the direction the conversation was taking, Pandora changed the subject. "Any important calls or urgent business this morning?"

"No," Cassandra answered. Not at all put off by her employers evasive move, she asked, "How do you feel about Julian?"

Pandora didn't answer.

"I guess you haven't made up your mind yet."

"Cassandra."

"All right, I'll shut my mouth, but Julian is not going to go away. You can be sure of it."

Pandora was sure. Julian wasn't exactly crowding her, but...Suddenly, Monroe's warning crashed into her consciousness. If she wasn't prepared to marry Julian or be his mistress, what did she want? Deep inside she knew she wanted him to make love to her. She didn't do back-street affairs. If she should succumb to his determined pursuit of her, once would surely not be enough. How long could she continue to resist his overtures?

She and Destinee would be leaving on their trip to the cabin in another week. Maybe there she could sort things out and come up with a way to continue seeing Julian without becoming his mistress, thus getting Monroe off her case. It all seemed so impossible.

Flowers began arriving daily for Pandora, always just before lunchtime, and all from Julian. It was a good thing he was rich or he would surely go broke, she thought.

Pandora had a meeting at Phillips Investments Friday morning. She wasn't looking forward to tangling with Roscoe Phillips or Monroe, but it couldn't be helped. As the new chairman of the board, she had called the meeting to discuss new policies and ideas for improving the company's profit margin. She was sure that Monroe and Roscoe would be primed to shoot down whatever she proposed. But she had some bullets of her own, and she wouldn't hesitate to use them if they forced her hand.

When Julian walked into the conference room, Pandora's jaw dropped. True, he had a small interest in the company and had finagled a seat on the board, but she hadn't expected him to become actively involved, certainly not to show up at this meeting. She could tell from their faces that Monroe and Roscoe were as surprised as she to see him there.

Vice chairman Nolan Anderson called the meeting to order, then turned the proceedings over to Pandora.

She outlined her plans for building up and restructuring company policy regarding international bond exchanges, securities and investments. Roscoe's hand shot up, as did Julian's. Pandora saw them both at the same time, but recognized Julian first. Rage twisted Roscoe's face into an ugly mask.

Julian took the floor. "The plan is a sound one," he said, "but I think the board needs to vote on who it believes is best equipped to refine the details and handle anticipated negotiations."

"I nominate Monroe Cooper," Roscoe quickly interjected, not waiting to be recognized.

Murmurs of both agreement and disagreement were heard around the table.

"I'd like to make a suggestion," Julian countered. "I propose that Pandora Cooper and I work together on the project since we've had more experience in negotiating mergers and successfully adding subsidiary businesses to the primary companies."

Pandora declined comment, suggesting instead that the board take a vote on it.

Monroe looked from Pandora to Julian, suspecting that the two had already secured votes ahead of time. The outcome of the vote confirmed his suspicion. He shot her an angry look that said in no uncertain terms that he was anything but pleased, and he wasn't about to let her forget it.

Pandora saw the amused look Julian's face and knew he didn't care how angry Monroe was. He correctly surmised that the board would choose the two of them because of their successful track records in the financial world. She and Julian would be working closely for weeks on the Androzini project, and she would be constantly at the mercy of his devastating charm and his talent for persuasion.

Getting away for the next three weeks would give her a reprieve of sorts. She needed time away from Julian to gain perspective and to examine whatever it was between them without interference—from him.

Don't fool yourself. You have perspective; you're just afraid to act on your feelings, an inner voice reminded her.

She had no argument to the contrary.

"I wish we had invited Talaya to come with us, Mama," Destinee complained as her mother slowed the Navigator down at the turnoff leading to their cabin in the Catskills.

Pandora heard something more in her daughter's complaint. Soon her mother would no longer be the focal point of her existence. Destinee had never suggested bringing anyone on their trips to the cabin. It had always been just the two of them, and it had been enough—until now.

"I'm sure Selena has plans for herself and Talaya, honey." Selena had told Pandora that she was considering taking her daughter to visit her father. She had been divorced for three years and it had been difficult for her daughter, an only child, to adjust. Julian had stepped in and had become much more than a doting uncle, doing things with Talaya her father couldn't, or wouldn't, do.

Over the next few days, they settled into a routine of walks and swimming at a nearby pond the way they used to. Pandora noticed her daughter's restlessness. She had to admit she was experiencing a measure of it, too. But Destinee's mood bothered her. Evidently her mother's company was no longer enough and Pandora experienced a sudden feeling of alienation and loss.

"Are you sure this is the way to go with Pandora, Julian?" Selena asked her brother as he pulled his Escalade into the garage in back of his cabin.

"Yes, I am, sister girl."

She smiled. "You haven't called me that in a long time."

He glanced at his niece the backseat. Talaya had fallen asleep during the drive to the Catskills. If things worked out the way he hoped, he would be spending more time at Pandora's cabin than his own.

Turning to Selena, he said, "You understand what I want you to do, don't you?"

"I'm not convinced we should be doing this, Julian. Pandora is my friend."

"And I'm your brother." He was sympathetic to Selena's pangs of guilt, but it wasn't as though he was going to ravish Pandora. Well, not much. "I want Pandora in my life. Only one other woman has ever come close to meaning what she does to me."

A relieved smile lit Selena's face. "I feel that Pandora is better suited to you than Vanessa Armstrong ever could have been. Gramma Edna agrees with me."

"Mama said pretty much the same thing. Now if only Drac would see reason and come around."

"You know Drac."

He did, but what his cousin thought or felt wasn't the issue or his primary concern. "I need some time alone with Pandora."

"To work your magic, no doubt."

"Whatever it takes." His expression turned serious.

"Let's get these groceries and my child inside before you start working your usual magic with women."

"Magic? *Moi*?"

Shaking her head, Selena climbed out of the Escalade.

Lying on a blanket beneath a tree a few yards from the waters edge, Pandora watched Destinee swim back and forth in the pond. She had been in the water earlier, but decided she'd had enough. She was feeling so…she didn't know…at odds with herself, as if something was slightly off kilter in her world, as if something was missing. She finally had to admit to herself that Julian was that missing something. She wondered how he was, where he was and with whom he was spending his time.

"A penny for your thoughts."

"Julian? What are you doing here?"

"Vacationing in a cabin several miles from here."

"And you want me to believe your turning up here was just coincidence?"

"I want you to know to what lengths I'm prepared to go to be near you," he said softly, his dark eyes roving the length of her body.

Pandora was self-conscious at first, but the look of genuine appreciation in his eyes made her relax. Her swimsuit was a simple teal one-piece and she knew the color complemented her skin and hair, and the suit itself outlined her every curve.

Julian signaled to Selena and Talaya, who had waited at his SUV. "To prove my motives are pure, you see I've brought my sister and niece with me as chaperones."

Pandora gave Julian a look that said she wasn't at all fooled by his claim to purity of thought and motive.

Destinee came out of the water and ran to them.

"I'm so glad to see, you guys," she said happily, smiling fondly at Julian. "Did you invite them here after all, Mama?"

"Actually, no."

"Uncle Julian has a cabin about five miles from here," Talaya explained. "How is the water?"

"It's something else," Destinee answered. "Want to come in and find out for yourself? You have your swimsuit on?"

Nodding, Talaya quickly took off her shorts and top and raced Destinee to the pond.

Julian glanced meaningfully at his sister.

"All right, Julian, I can take a hint." Selena stripped down to her swimsuit and followed the girls into the water.

"Julian." Pandora looked at him suspiciously.

"I'll admit I wasn't very subtle, but I wanted you all to myself for a few minutes. Is that so terrible?"

"I guess not. I won't ask how you found out where we would be. But I would like to know how you managed to rent a cabin at such short notice? I know for a fact you have to reserve a place in the Catskills weeks, or even months, in advance."

"I bought the company that owns the cabin."

"Why doesn't that surprise me? Now that you're here, how long are you planning on staying?"

"As long as you and Destinee. Let's go for a walk."

"All right." Pandora picked up her matching wrapper, and slipped on her sandals. Julian was wearing an ordinary tank top and shorts, but on him ordinary was not the word that came to mind.

The tank top exposed Julian's muscular arms and hugged his impressive pecs.

"I can tell that you like what you see," he said, a wicked smile hovering on sexy, full lips. "You can have it, you know."

"There's a trail I like to trek over there," she said, pointing to a path to their left and ambling in that direction.

Julian fell into step beside her, and when they were out of sight of the pond, stopped and drew her into his arms.

"I've missed you," he said huskily.

"It's only been a few days."

"Seems like months to me." His mouth hungrily covered hers.

The kiss sent wild excitement surging through Pandora's body.

Releasing her lips, Julian stepped back, renewed determination in his eyes. "You can't keep me at bay forever, baby."

Not waiting for a response he pressed her lips to his, caressing her mouth more than kissing its soft fullness. He glided his hands down her back and cupped her buttocks, making her whole body quiver. He led Pandora over to a nearby tree and, bracing against it, he pulled her between his legs.

"Oh, Pan, what you do to me," he said, his breathing ragged.

The intensity of his words made Pandora try to wiggle free, but her movements only aroused him further. When he slipped his fingers inside the top of her suit and stroked her bare breasts, she closed her eyes. The touch of his hand was suddenly almost unbearable in its tenderness.

"Julian, we can't..."

"We can and we will. Maybe not at this moment, but it's going to happen." He moved her away from him and straightened up, appearing unsteady for a few moments. "Tonight I want you to think about this afternoon. I want you to dream about what it can be like for us to make love. I want you to burn for me the way I burn for you and will continue burning for you until we bank this fire within."

He took Pandora's hand and led her back to the pond, then he stripped down to his swim trunks and joined Selena and the girls in the water.

Pandora was shaken by what had happened between her and Julian, and seeing him in his snug-fitting trunks was almost more than she could stand. When her legs refused to support her, she plopped down on the blanket.

Julian left the water first. Pandora found herself staring at the rivulets of water streaming down his magnificent body. To be that fine was almost a crime.

Julian took a towel from his sports bag and dried himself. Everywhere it touched his skin Pandora wished she was that extremely fortunate piece of cloth. Then he sat lotus position and looked at her, grinning slyly, as if he knew exactly what and how he was making her feel.

"You could have joined us in the water, Pan."

Us? For a moment she had forgotten that they weren't alone.

Soon the others returned. Destinee plunked down beside Julian and started chattering nonstop. Julian managed to respond to the teen when expected and still keep his eyes on Pandora.

The conversation slowed, and the tension between Julian and Pandora became apparent to everyone.

Destinee shifted her eyes from Julian to her mother and back again. Her concerned expression moved Pandora to action.

"Come back to the cabin, and I'll fix us all some lunch," she said, collecting their things.

"You really don't have to go to all that trouble," Selena replied. "We brought a picnic lunch, and heaven knows it's enough to feed a battalion. Why don't you get the basket out of the Escalade, Julian?"

"Okay. Will do."

"Is anything wrong between you and Julian, Mama?" Destinee asked, frowning.

"No, of course not. Why don't you take these blankets over there and shake them out."

"Talaya, why don't you help her do that," Selena added.

The girls left to do as they were told.

"Just what was going on between you and my brother before we intruded? And don't tell me nothing, because I won't believe you."

"I can't tell you anything, Selena. I'm not sure myself."

"You may not be, but I'd say from the looks Julian has been giving you, he is. Are you really being honest with yourself about your feelings for him, Pandora?"

Pandora wondered. Was the way she was feeling similar to how high-wire performers feel when their safety net is taken away? To reach the other side and not plummet to almost certain death, they had to keep their balance without the smallest slipup. Right now she was teetering on an emotional high-wire, her balance evermore precarious. Was her fall imminent? Or could she make it safely to the other side?

CHAPTER SIXTEEN

Pandora tossed and turned most of the night. When she finally dozed off, erotic dreams of her and Julian making love invaded her sleep, taking control of her body, and causing it to tingle and her femininity to moisten and throb. Julian wanted her to think about him and she had. He wanted her to burn for him, and, oh, how she had burned. This definitely wasn't how she wanted to feel.

You're lying to yourself, girl. You want to feel these things for him, all right. You want to feel the pleasure he promised to give you when he makes love to you.

She got up and threw back the covers, then walked over to the window and looked out as the sunlight began to spill over the mountains. What was Julian feeling this morning? Had he lain awake all night thinking about her?

Pandora noticed how uncharacteristically quiet Destinee was at breakfast.

"Are you feeling all right, honey?"

"Yes," she said sullenly.

Pandora didn't believe her and waited for her to elaborate.

"Mama, is it serious between you and Julian? You know what I'm trying to say."

"I don't know what to tell you. I don't know where this relationship, if you can call it one, is headed." She paused. "I know you like him, but…"

"If he asks you to marry him, will you?" Destinee asked.

"He probably won't. He knows my feelings on the subject of marriage, Destinee, and so do you."

"My father hurt you; I know that, but Julian's not anything like him. Can't you change your mind about marriage and…"

"Aren't you getting a little ahead of yourself, young lady? Julian hasn't asked me to marry him."

"I want him for my father, Mama."

"There's more to consider than just having Julian for your father, honey."

"You like him; I know you do."

"Yes, I like him."

"I don't understand. If you like him, then why can't you two get together?"

"Desi, honey, I…"

"May I go for a walk down by the pond? Please."

Pandora hugged her daughter. She saw the shimmer of tears in Destinee's eyes when she walked away.

Destinee was subdued during lunch. Pandora longed to tell her what she wanted to hear, but couldn't.

"Honey, I know that you want a father and think Julian is the perfect person to assume that role, but you have to understand that your feelings aren't the only ones to be considered."

"I know, and I'm sorry for acting like such a brat."

Pandora didn't know whether she wanted to kiss Julian Palmer or kick his butt for so thoroughly disrupting her life.

"Do you want to just sit and talk for a while?" Pandora asked her daughter.

"What I want to talk about, you don't, so what's the use?"

"We could go swimming or exploring the way we used to."

"Not right now, Mama. Okay?"

"Destinee, we…"

The sound of a car engine intruded.

When Destinee saw Julian pull his Escalade behind her mother's Navigator, her expression turned from sullen to happy instantly and she ran from the cabin to greet him, Selena and Talaya.

Julian saw the distress on Pandora's face and wished they were alone so he could work on soothing it away. He gave his sister a pleading look.

Selena obliged. "Hey, girls, want to do some exploring. Later we can go back to our cabin and have dinner. Sound good?"

"Selena, I don't think..."

Selena smiled. "Destinee will be all right, Pandora. We won't get lost. I have a fairly good sense of direction. I'm sure you and Julian want to spend some time alone."

"I want to go, Mama," Destinee implored. "Please."

Julian touched Pandora's arm. "Let her go, Pan."

She hesitated before finally agreeing.

"I'll promise to bring Destinee back safe and sound after dinner." Selena promised. "At, say, six-thirty?"

Pandora watched the Escalade until it disappeared around the curve in the road. Then Julian turned her around to face him and lowered his lips to hers. The power of his kiss passed through her like an electric current, exciting her and making her experience overwhelming passion she had never felt before. Julian made her feel like a virgin, exalting in her first real taste of passion. Her body pulsed with anticipated pleasure and promised joy.

"Darling, your days of wanting and needing love and never getting it are over. I'm here to fulfill your every need, indulge your every fantasy. Just you, me and nature."

Julian lifted her into his arms and headed for the cabin.

Inside moments later, he lowered her to the floor, and then stepped back to marvel at her beauty. She was not only beautiful in body, but in mind. Pandora Cooper was the quintessence of womanhood, the sum total of every fantasy he could conjure up. Julian moved forward and locked his hands behind her neck, never once breaking eye contact with her.

She made a soft muffled sound, followed by feeble efforts to ease away from him.

"Don't be afraid of me, baby."

He covered her lips with his once more, effectively preventing her from uttering a word. He silently cursed Lyman Cooper for making her afraid to respond to desire without inhibition. Julian was glad now that he had been so patient with Pandora. Although he was eager to introduce this exquisite woman to pleasure, he wanted her to experience more than that. He wanted her to know what it felt like to be truly and completely loved.

"Do you really believe I would ever hurt you, Pan?"

When she didn't answer, he said, "I want to make love to you, but I won't if you believe I could do that to you. I know it's not easy for you, sweetheart, but I have to know."

"I don't believe you would hurt me—at least not intentionally."

"You're talking about emotionally now, aren't you? Is it one of the ways your husband hurt you? He didn't sexually abuse you, did he?"

Pandora turned her face away.

Gently cupping her chin, Julian brought her face back around. "The bastard did, didn't he?"

"Julian, please, I don't want to talk about it."

He drew her firmly, yet gently, against his body. How could any man mistreat this lovely woman? She deserved to be treated like a queen—loved, pampered and cherished. "I intend to do more than please you, Pan. I want there to be more between us than just sex. I don't want this to be a one-night stand, or an affair. I want to share my life with you." He paused. "Shh, don't say anything. You have made your position on marriage clear, but I believe with my heart and soul that you'll change your mind with the right inducement."

"And you think you're it?" she asked.

He touched her face with his fingertips. "I could be," he answered, his voice low and sexy.

"You're not playing fair."

"I'm not playing at all. I'm serious. How many times must I say it?"

Julian pulled the pins from her hair, combing his fingers through its silky softness, causing it to fall to her shoulders and flow down her back in shiny, rippling waves. She looked even sexier now, he thought, as he started unbuttoning her bright yellow blouse. He suddenly realized that she no longer wore stark black. If he knew Destinee, and he was coming to know her very well, she had played a major role in this transformation.

When Pandora tensed up he backed off, perceiving that she wasn't ready to make love yet.

"You want to go for a swim?" he asked her.

"A swim?"

"Yes, a swim." Julian smiled because she seemed rattled by his abrupt shift in mood.

"But, I thought..."

"Not yet, Pan. You came here to unwind, and that's what I'm going to help you do."

Pandora frowned, feeling disappointed and yes, even a bit peeved that he had postponed their lovemaking.

"You didn't bring your swim trunks," Pandora reminded him.

"Haven't you heard of people swimming in the nude?"

Her face felt hot. "Of course I've heard of it."

"But you've never tried it, have you?"

"No, but..."

"No buts. Selena and the girls won't be back for hours and there's no one around for miles to see what we do. Come on, let's have some fun."

Julian grabbed a blanket off the chair by the fireplace. "Get a couple of towels and let's go."

Pandora hesitated briefly and then walked down the hall to the linen closet.

They were soon heading down to the pond. After they spread out the blanket, Julian removed her sandals and began stroking her instep. When he inched his fingers higher she gasped. His fingers moved even higher still, and her thighs trembled. He moved his hands up over her hips to the waistband of her shorts.

"Would you feel better if I let you take these off?"

She nodded, but started with her blouse buttons, her fingers shaking as she undid the last one.

Then she removed her blouse and unhooked her bra. She hesitated before easing the straps off her shoulders and letting the bra fall free.

Desire surged through Julian when he saw Pandora's full, firm breasts. The nipples were like ripe cherries, and he longed to taste and savor them. Unable to stop himself, he enclosed the two perfect globes in his hands, caressing the nipples with his thumbs. The supple weight of her breasts caused his manhood to rise and harden.

Pandora stood and eased her shorts down her legs. She was now down to her sheer lacy panties.

Julian glimpsed the dark shadow of black hair inside her sexy panties and groaned as he waited for her to remove them.

"Do you want to do the honors?" she asked.

He couldn't wait to whisk those slightly scandalous panties down her legs and off. Completely naked, she was a goddess.

Pandora sat back down on the blanket. "Now you," she said sultrily.

Crossing his arms, he tugged his T-shirt off. Pandora reached out and stroked his nipple, causing Julian to groan. He wondered if his sex could possibly get any harder. Julian pushed his shorts and briefs down his muscular thighs and legs and tossed them on top of his shirt. Then he took her hand and led her into the water. When they were in waist high, they started to slowly swim, gliding as one across the water. They stood up in the middle of the pond.

Julian's breath caught at the sight of Pandora's breasts bobbing just above the surface of the water.

"Oh, Pan." He laced his fingers through her hair and arched her head back, planting little kisses on her lips. Becoming more aroused, he coaxed her mouth open and kissed her long and hard, not stopping until she was breathless.

"Julian," she whispered.

He covered a soft breast with his hand, feeling it become firm and seeing the nipple stiffen into a hard peak.

"You're so wonderfully responsive."

"Only with you," she admitted, realizing she sounded surprised.

"I want to make love to you now, baby."

"And I want you to, right now."

"Shall we go back?"

"Yes."

When they returned to their blanket, Pandora stretched out and Julian gently dried her body, letting the friction of the towel brush against her skin, teasing the sensitive nipples to aching hardness. She took another towel and let it soak up the beads of water clinging to his marvelous torso. She relished the sense of power she felt when Julian let out a sound that was part sigh and part moan.

"Are you ready, darling?" he asked softly, his words sliding over her senses like liquid velvet over sensitive skin.

"Julian."

"Yes," she said, lying flat on her back. He lay on his side next to her and covered her body with tender kisses that grew in intensity.

He moved his body over hers, saying in a sexy whisper, "Passion is like forbidden fruit—once tasted, the appetite is never quenched."

Held captive by his overpowering masculinity, her heart pounded wildly. She was beyond rational thought, wanting his touch, wanting him. Period.

He moved from her hair to her throat and down to a nipple, teasing it until she moaned in ecstasy. He skimmed his fingers along the side of her breast, coasted down her midriff, gliding along the curve of her hip. Her body shook as his fingers slipped between her inner thighs. When he reached her feminine juncture, she tensed.

"I won't hurt you, Pan. I promise," he whispered softly in her ear. "Let me give you a taste of paradise."

He gently spread the petals of her blossom and inserted a finger just a little way in. Then he slipped a second finger more deeply inside her moist niche. Her body bucked against this sensual invasion. Hot desire throbbed richly inside her womanhood and spread throughout her body. She moaned, eagerly anticipating more.

He did not disappoint. He stroked her bud of passion until it throbbed and swelled, clamoring for release.

Pandora cried out. "I need you; I want you now, Julian. Please," she murmured urgently, wildly raking her fingers up and down his back.

"I fully intend to please you, Pan, darling."

He moved his fingers back and forth across her slick, heated flesh, building delicious sensations in her velvety interior. Then his movements grew more frenzied, sending wave after wave of pleasure crashing through her.

"Julian."

"This is for you, my love."

He continued to stroke her ultra sensitive nub with his thumb, his fingers probing her honeyed folds until the friction drove her inner flesh to shuddering ecstasy.

"Now, you and I can move on to the ultimate pleasure together."

Pandora watched as he eased a condom over his manhood. He was beautiful, he was hard, he was ready.

"Touch me, baby," he said thickly.

She complied and he released a low groan as she moved her fingers up and down his shaft. Finally he eased her hand away and kissed her with a deep hunger.

He lay her down once more, then parting her thighs, slipped between them. She could feel the tip of his shaft when it found the entrance to her femininity. When he moved his hips forward and embedded himself to the hilt, a keening sound of pleasure left her lips.

He engaged his hardened flesh in a smooth gliding rhythm, sliding deliciously in and out of her slippery passage. The pleasure was so achingly sweet, she quickly adopted his movements, arching against him in strong, accompanying motions. He plunged deeper, harder, faster, driving her closer and closer to the edge of oblivion.

Their bodies rose and fell in passionate harmony again and again. When the moment of ultimate bliss came for Pandora, she collapsed, quivering in an unbearably sweet spasm of joy. Julian continued to move frenziedly against her until his climax burst forth and he shouted his fulfillment.

CHAPTER SEVENTEEN

Droplets of water awakened Pandora and Julian, who had drifted off to sleep, spent and sated, after their afternoon of lovemaking.

Julian looked up at the sky. He and Pandora had been so absorbed in each other they hadn't noticed that the sun had gone behind the clouds and was no longer warming the surrounding air.

Pandora rolled away from him and gathered her clothes. "We'd better hurry up and get to the cabin before it really begins to pour."

Julian hurriedly picked up his clothes and rolled up the blanket. They made a mad dash for the cabin, reaching it just as the rain started coming down in earnest."Look at that, will you?" Julian exclaimed. "It's raining cats and dogs."

"It sure is. The air is turning chilly, too."

"I know of a perfect way to warm us," he said opening the door and waving her in.

"I'll fix us some dinner," she said, wrapping it around herself as she headed for the kitchen.

Julian put his arms around her waist and tugged at the towel. "It can wait."

Pandora stopped him. "Selena and the girls will be back any minute."

"I doubt if she'll brave the rain. You see, she had a bad accident during a rainstorm, and she's deathly afraid of driving in one. If the rain doesn't stop or slow to a drizzle, she won't be here until morning. And if it hasn't let up by then..."

Pandora glanced out the window, the towel still pulled tightly around her.

"Maybe I should dress and drive over there and pick up Destinee."

"You don't know where the cabin is."

"And you're not going to give me directions, right?"

He shook his head, guessing that she was probably thinking what he was: They were going to be completely alone all night if he didn't. The prospect elated him. There definitely had to be an angel in heaven who favored him. He turned Pandora around to face him. She tried to hide it, but he saw the desire in her eyes and undid the towel hiding her body.

She surprised him by saying, "Since there's nothing to take off you maybe we should..."

Lifting Pandora into his arms, Julian started up the stairs, asking, "Which bedroom, baby?"

Pandora indicated the room. He went inside, put her on the bed and lay next to her. He raised up on an elbow and gazed into her eyes, now like melting gold in her aroused passion.

"I've dreamed about being with you like this for weeks. I was beginning to think it would never happen." He kissed her forehead and her nose, then homing in on her mouth and sliding his tongue between her lips.

When he released her mouth, she said, "I never thought it could be like this between a man and a woman."

"Surely your husband kissed you."

"Oh, he did, but never the way you do. His kisses were sterile and chaste compared to yours."

"Are you implying that I'm not chaste?" He raised one eyebrow wickedly.

"No, but I'm glad you're not."

"Woman, I'm going to make you pay for slandering me."

"How?"

"There are ways."

"Let's get on with it, then."

"I've never seen anyone so eager to experience retribution."

"I don't mind being your first."

Suddenly the rumble of thunder shook the cabin windows. Streaks of lightning followed.

Shuddering, Pandora moved closer to Julian. Her nipples brushing against his chest and her thigh rubbing against his caused him to harden.

"Oh, Julian, I'm so glad you're here with me."

"So am I." He stroked her back, moving his fingers down to her hip and massaging her skin in arousing circular motions.

He rolled her onto her back and continued his sensual exploration of her body with his hands and mouth. As the rain slashed the windows, he rained kisses along the soft column of her throat, moving on to a taut nipple and sucking it into a hard knot. Her little pants of pleasure aroused him even more.

"Do you want me, Pan?"

"You know I do."

He wanted to take it slow, but knew it was now impossible. He got atop her body and thrust himself deep inside her. The tightening of her muscles around his thrusting sex nearly drove him over the edge. He struggled for control and, finding a tiny measure of it, rolled onto his back, pulling her on top of him.

"Ride me, Pan darling," he said hoarsely.

Without a word, she began moving her body against his. He lifted his hip upward, each time hers came down, he managed to delve deeper. With every frenzied movement of her body, pleasure surged through Julian.

"Pandora! Oh, God! Yes, yes," he growled as he felt her climax vibrate around him. A scream of rapture tore from her throat and she collapsed atop him.

After a few moments to catch his breath, Julian murmured, "It keeps getting better between us, baby. No woman has ever made me feel the way you do. Is it East Indian sorcery at work here?"

"No sorcery, Julian, unless you are performing some of your own special magic."

He kissed her tenderly. "No, baby. I'm no wizard."

"I think you are."

When she kissed him, working her body against his, Julian felt himself harden inside her. He quickly rolled her beneath him and this time he took it slow, and together they reached the summit, then plunged over the side into an endless abyss of ecstasy.

Pandora woke first the next morning, a feeling of contentment flowing through her. Julian was lying on his stomach, his arm flung across her waist. He was such a generous lover, gentle yet exciting. She had been fighting him as well as her own feelings ever since they met. What exactly were her feelings? Love? Or lust? She needed time to figure out which.

"No regrets?" Julian asked sleepily.

"Not a one," she said softly. "In fact, I want more of you, Mr. Palmer."

He responded immediately to her open invitation and they again made love.

Later completely satisfied, but famished, they went down to the kitchen.

"I'm hungry enough to eat everything you've got in here," he said, opening the refrigerator.

"Me, too. I never knew lovemaking could make you feel this way."

"Pan, you are going to enjoy being my lover. I intend to turn you into a voracious woman."

"For food or your lovemaking?"

"Both. After we eat, let's shower together."

The rain finally slowed, then stopped altogether. Julian and Pandora were dressed when Selena and the girls returned several hours later.

"Mama, you look different. Were you and Julian all right last night during the storm?" Destinee asked.

"We were fine, honey. Weren't we, Julian?"

"I would have to say more than fine."

Pandora shot him a warning, but he only laughed.

"It's still pretty wet outside," Selena explained. "I would have come sooner, but…"

"Julian explained your aversion to driving in the rain," Pandora answered. "It's all right."

"We found ways to amuse ourselves," Julian added.

Smiling slightly Selena said, "I'll just bet you did. Well, what are we going to do with the rest of the day?"

Julian sat at the kitchen counter watching Pandora prepare lunch. Seeing her do the simplest things turned him on. He had been waiting for a woman like her all his adult life. Other women, with the exception of one, never made him want to make a commitment. Looking out the window, he saw Destinee and his niece and sister down by the pond. He wanted Pandora's daughter to become his daughter.

"You could help me, you know," Pandora said, breaking into his reverie.

"The kind of help I have in mind isn't remotely domestic."

"Never mind, Romeo."

After lunch, Julian suggested driving to lower Haines Falls on the Scholaris River.

Pandora had never ventured that far afield since buying the cabin. She was fascinated by the beauty of the falls. The clear blue water tumbling over the wall of rocks was a wondrous sight.

"Mama!" Destinee exclaimed. "Why haven't we ever seen this before?"

"I didn't know it even existed."

Julian took Destinee's hand. "Want to take a walk with me?"

"Sure."

Watching them walk away, Pandora wondered why Julian wanted to talk to her daughter alone. Laughing, she guessed they probably wanted to compare campaign strategies.

Julian walked Destinee to a formation of rocks in a lightly wooded area, several hundred yards from the falls.

"How would you feel about becoming my daughter?"

"As in adoption?"

"Yes," he grinned. "As soon as I can convince your mother to marry me, of course."

"That would be the ultimate, Julian. But how are you going to get her to change her mind?"

"I haven't figured that one out yet, but I'm working on it. You're with me, then, right?"

"Oh, yes, definitely. I think you two are perfect for each other."

"So do I. Now, the problem is convincing your obstinate mother of that."

Destinee's excitement faded. "Julian, my father was really mean to my mother. I remember how he used to talk to her. I never said anything to her about it, but I knew he sometimes went beyond just talking. Mama was leaving him and taking me with her when he had the heart attack. He was trying to stop us."

Julian saw the pain in Destinee's eyes.

"It was my fault he died, because I hated him and wished him dead." Tears streamed down her face.

Julian pulled her close and patted her back while she cried. When she was finally calm, he said. "Your father's death was his own fault, Desi. You had nothing to do with it. You didn't really hate him. And wishing something would happen doesn't make it come true."

"But he died, Julian."

"Shh, don't blame yourself," he said soothingly. He wondered if Pandora also harbored guilty feelings about her husband's death. Little by little, he was getting a better understanding of mother and daughter. His job wasn't going to be easy. He needed to repair the damage Lyman Cooper had done to both Pandora and Destinee. He wanted to make them his family. And, one day, they would be, because he intended to do all he could to make it happen.

When Julian and Destinee returned, Pandora sensed something different between them. What had they talked about? Why did Julian look at her daughter with such fatherly affection?"There is a wonderful restaurant about ten miles from here," Julian said. "Do you want to go there?"

They all murmured agreement.

On the drive to the inn, Pandora sneaked glances at Julian. He was gorgeous, but did what she feel for him go beyond desire and physical attraction? Something about him made her want it to be more and yet...

The inn had an authentic rustic flavor. The period furniture was polished to a high sheen and smelled of beeswax and lemon. There were organdy curtains at the lattice-cut picture windows. The soft lighting accentuated an inviting aura of happiness.

Selena insisted she and the girls share a table overlooking a creek bridge. She didn't fool Pandora. Selena wanted Pandora and her brother to be alone.

Julian smiled. "My sister's not very subtle, is she?"

"No, she's not."

"Now that we're lovers, there will have to be some changes, lady."

"What kind of changes?"

"We'll want to spend more time with each other."

"That won't be a problem, considering the new project we'll be working on together at Phillips."

"That's business. I'm talking about something more personal, like spending nights and weekends together. Things like that."

"Have you heard the adage that close proximity breeds contempt?"

"That's familiarity breeds contempt, but whatever. The kind of proximity I have in mind will do the opposite. Now stop fighting it, Pan. I care about you. I care about you for yourself. Business doesn't enter into it."

"Oh, Julian. I want…"

"What do you want? Me, I hope."

"I do want you. You don't have to hope, and you know it."

"We'll take it one day at a time and see how things develop. Okay?"

He took her hand and kissed her fingertips. "We're going to be good together, Pan. You'll see. Want to order now?"

CHAPTER EIGHTEEN

Pandora learned at the first board meeting after she and Julian were teamed on the Androzini project at Phillips that her brother-in-law had been appointed projects coordinator. He was to report back to the board on their progress, which meant that she and Julian would have to work closely with the man. And to make matters even more worrisome, Monroe's office was right next to theirs.

Pandora and Julian were to work three afternoons a week for six to eight weeks. Her evolving relationship with Julian was going to make it hard to keep her focus on her work. But once the project was underway and they were in a set routine, she was confident that would change. Getting to that point was the problem.

As Pandora was leaving the boardroom after the meeting, Monroe confronted her.

"There's something different about you."

"I don't know what it could be. If you'll excuse me, I have to get back to PanCo."

"If you're hiding something, I'll find out what it is."

"You're paranoid, Monroe."

"We'll see. Does this change have anything to do with your three weeks away?"

"Monroe."

"Go, by all means. But you had better remember what I told you. Like Caesar's wife, you had better stay above reproach or you'll lose Destinee. I'll see to it, I promise you."

"Stop threatening me."

"Oh, am I doing that, Pandora? Just don't forget what I said."

He left her with a feeling of trepidation in her gut. If he would just leave them alone. But she knew he wouldn't, as he knew that Destinee was her Achilles heel. It worried her that he and Sasha were so set on bringing her down, and that they didn't care if Destinee was hurt in the process.

Julian entered the boardroom. "Sorry I was late. The meeting was over kind of fast, wasn't it?"

"The only point of this hastily called meeting was to inform you and me that we now have a coordinator overseeing our progress. Guess who?"

"I saw Monroe leaving as I came in. It was probably Roscoe's brainchild to have his cohort appointed to the position."

"No doubt, but I'm not going to let it get to me."

"Me, either. How about having lunch with me?"

"I can't, I have a lot of work to catch up on at PanCo."

"Dinner, then?"

"Julian."

"I'm not going to let you revert to your old workaholic ways, Ms. Cooper. We've come too far for that."

"All right. But I want to have dinner at my place at, say, six-thirty?"

"It's all right by me."

After dinner, Pandora listened to her daughter chatting up Julian. It hadn't mattered to him that they had dinner with her daughter, he seemed happy either way. She admired him for that. Other men she had dated complained if she included Destinee. They always insisted on dining with Pandora alone.

"I'll be starting school at East Shore High next week. I'm so excited; Talaya is too," Destinee informed Julian. "She keeps teasing me about being the youngest freshman in the class."

"You can't help it if you've inherited your mother's superior brain, now can you?"

"I'm proud of that."

"You should be," Julian replied.

"I know you and Mama want to be alone, so I'm going to my room to listen to some music." She kissed Pandora and hugged Julian and headed upstairs.

"Smart girl," Julian grinned.

"Too smart for her britches sometimes."

"You're tense," he said, kneading her shoulder muscles.

"Dealing with Monroe tends to have that effect on me."

"Why?"

"Because he happens to be an obnoxious bastard, for starters."

"What is it with you two?"

"He hates me because I chose his brother over him, not that my choice was particularly wise."

Julian heard the bitterness in her words. After what Destinee had revealed to him about her father and mother and what Pandora herself was careful not to reveal, he wasn't surprised.

"Your judgment improved when you decided to be mine."

"I decided? As I recall, you wouldn't allow me to refuse you, Mr. Palmer."

"Ah, the magic words." He drew her into his arms and kissed her.

"You're incorrigible."

"Only where you're concerned. I've missed making love to you."

"I have to admit I've missed that too."

"So when are you going to let me rectify the situation? We could go to my place."

Pandora recalled Monroe's threat. The thought of him dictating the terms of her life made her angry.

"If my schedule wasn't so tight and I didn't have such an early day tomorrow, I would take you up on your offer."

"How about Friday night?" He kissed her behind her ear.

"Julian, you don't play fair."

"I've told you, I don't play. When it comes to you, I'm serious as a heart attack."

Her husband had said something similar when he was trying to convince her to marry him. She stiffened and broke away from Julian.

"What did I say?"

"Nothing. It's getting late, and as I mentioned before, I have an early day tomorrow."

"All right. One of these days you're going to trust me with your feelings.

Her eyes said, 'I don't know if you should hold your breath waiting for that day.' Julian frowned. It frustrated and angered him to see her slip behind that defensive wall. He knew who was responsible. Too bad he couldn't get his hands on the bastard and beat the hell out of him—not that it would solve anything.

Pandora saw the anger in Julian's eyes, and a frisson of fear crept down her spine. Lyman would have that look just before he hit her. But this wasn't Lyman, it was Julian, she kept reminding herself. This was the man who had made such sweet love to her and who adored her child. And said he adored her, too. Did she risk alienating him with her hang-ups about love and marriage?

Julian realized how he must look to her and turned his frown into a smile. "I'm not angry with you, Pan, just frustrated that we can't be together the way I want us to."

She relaxed, secure in the knowledge that he was looking beyond the physical aspect of their relationships. If their relationship never went any further, she would always cherish the time they had spent together.

"Maybe what you want is impossible, Julian."

"Oh, it's possible, sweetheart, just not yet. When it is, you'll know it. Until that time, I'll wait." He stood up and pulled her to her feet. "Walk me to the door."

Once they got there he embraced and kissed her, moving his mouth over hers as if the taste of her was ambrosia for his senses.

"Just a little something to remind you of what you're missing and don't have to miss if only you'll agree to marry me." With that, he opened the door and left.

Pandora's legs felt like jelly. Why did he have the power to make her feel this way every time he touched her? Surely, she wasn't falling in love with him! She didn't want to consider that possibility.

Consider it, girlfriend?

She walked over to the window and watched Julian drive away.

He was gorgeous. He was intelligent. He was all man. Then what was wrong with her? Why couldn't she do as he asked?

Because you have to learn to trust. True, your late husband damaged your ability to do so, but he's dead and you're very much alive.

So what do I do?

Just let things happen. Take one step at a time. Live one day at a time.

"Was the time you spent in the Catskills worth the price you paid that realty company just so you could be near the black widow, Julian?"

"Drac, I've asked you not to call her that," he said, turning away from his computer screen to look sharply at his cousin. "What I do or don't do with Pandora Cooper is none of your business."

"What is it about her that makes lovesick idiots of men?"

"Drac."

"All right. I just don't want to see you make a fool of yourself over this woman, okay?"

"If I do, it's my choice, not yours. Now can we drop the subject and get some work done? What have you found out about Lyman and Monroe Cooper?"

"A pretty intense rivalry went on between the brothers, especially regarding Pandora Benning. If my sources are to be believed, Monroe still wants her."

"What sources are those?"

"Julian."

"Look, Drac, I need to know."

"His secretary was very informative."

"You sure it isn't just office gossip?"

"Don't you know me better than that, Julian? At his health club he was overheard saying he wanted her and intended to have her."

"I wonder how far he's willing to go to achieve this. I already know what you think, so don't go there."

Looking disgusted, Drac left his cousin's office.

Julian turned away from the computer screen and gazed out the window. He wanted to know what was between Monroe and Pandora in the worst way. If she would just open up to him, he was sure he could help her. Once he gained her confidence and she began to trust him, their relationship would grow. Patience and persistence would win out in the end.

CHAPTER NINETEEN

"We have to fly to Rome to confer with the head of the Androzini Investment Corporation," Pandora informed Julian, sitting at her desk at Phillips.

Grinning, he sprang from his chair, crossed the room and parked a lean hip on the edge of her desk. "As they say, when in Rome, do as the Romans do. It is the city of love."

"Julian, this trip is about business."

"I know, and I never allow one to infringe on the other. In fact, I aspire to get the first one done with so I can enjoy the second."

"You're impossible."

"I'll expect a full report," Monroe rudely interrupted, striding arrogantly into their office.

"And you'll get it, Monroe," Pandora answered sharply. "Why are you in our office? We don't have a meeting scheduled with you today."

"It's my job to keep a watchful eye on you two and make sure all your actions are for the good of the company. You were chosen to represent Phillips, and what you do and how you act reflects on the company."

"What are you trying to say, Cooper?" Julian demanded.

"Only that you should curb your amorous urgings and indulge your lust for each other at the appropriate time and place, preferably after hours in the privacy of the bedroom or motel."

"Just a minute." Reacting to Monroe's vulgar insult, Julian bounded off the desk.

"Don't bother, Julian," Pandora said, glaring at Monroe. "He was just leaving. If we have anything to report, you'll have it in writing."

"I'd better," he threatened, glowering at Julian and then at Pandora before exiting the room.

"What I would like to do is break his neck."

"Forget him, Julian. It's not worth the energy it would take. Now, getting back to our trip to Rome."

"So, when do we leave?"

"I wish I could come with you," Destinee said, watching her mother pack.

"You have school. I'll only be gone for two weeks, honey. Maybe not even that long. I'll be back before you know it."

"I'm glad Julian is going with you. Will you get to see the Colosseum and the Pantheon and those beautiful fountains I've seen in magazines and travel books?"

"This is a business trip, Destinee."

"Aren't you gonna take time to do some sightseeing and have fun?" she asked incredulously. "Why go there at all if you can't do any of those things?"

"Destinee, Destinee. You'll find there is more to life than having fun."

"But you never have any. I bet Julian will see that you do. Don't forget to bring me back some souvenirs."

"*Some* souvenirs?" Pandora had to admit she was looking forward to this trip, and business wasn't all she intended to enjoy.

She stopped daydreaming, realizing she was being infected by her daughter's enthusiasm. At best, they would have a day or two before they had to come back.

"Julian, I can come with you and..."

"No, Drac," Julian said, cutting him off, "you're needed here."

"You're just using this as an excuse to be with her, aren't you?"

"I want to be with her, yes, but this is also a business trip."

"Julian, listen to me, I..."

"How's your relationship with Cassandra coming along?"

"Changing the subject won't stop me from trying to convince you not to get any more involved with that woman than you already are."

"The subject is closed, Drac. I advise you not to mess around in my personal life. I should be back in two weeks. I expect you to hold down the fort until then."

"You know I will, but..."

Julian glared at his cousin.

"All right," he said, reluctantly conceding defeat. "You know you really shouldn't let your guard down so totally with this woman. Mark my words, if you do you're going to live to regret it. Don't say I never warned you."

"Warning taken."

"And totally disregarded."

"I never thought we would dispatch the Androzini account so easily or so quickly," Pandora said to Julian over lunch at the Cafe Grecco near the Spanish Steps in Rome ten days later.

"Evidently, Giancarlo Androzini was more eager for American business than we thought. I'm glad the negotiations went so swiftly. It gives us more time to enjoy Rome. Where do you want to go first?"

"I'll leave it up to you, Mr. Romantic."

After leaving the restaurant, Julian took Pandora to the Seven Hills of Rome, to which all roads lead. They passed by fountains that sparkled, danced and sounded as if they were playing a special kind of music to entertain passersby. They walked up to Quirinal Hill, then on to the Forum. Julian had brought a camera along and asked a passing tourist to take pictures of them in front of the Flavian Amphitheater, better known as the Colosseum.

"Destinee will love these pictures. Come on and get closer," he said, pulling her into his arms and kissing her as the man took the picture.

"Julian, stop," she chided him playfully when she caught her breath.

"We're in Rome. Can I help it if you bring out the lover in me, sweetheart. I'll signal for a *carrozze*."

"What's that?"

"An open horse-drawn carriage."

"You've really got a thing for carriage rides, don't you?" she remarked, remembering a horse-drawn carriage ride they'd taken around Central Park.

"You did call me Mr. Romantic."

They had dinner on the terrace of Rosati's, and then went to the Piazza Barberini to see the Triton Fountain. The base of the fountain was held up by dolphins, and the Triton above them blew into a conch shell through which jets of water sprang. She was fascinated by Bernini's magnificent marble statuary.

"You've got to visit Trevi Fountain before we go back to the hotel," Julian said, relating a bit of its history and the legends it had spawned.

Pandora threw coins into the fountain and made a wish, even though she had little confidence it would ever come true. She wished he could belong to her, but didn't see how that could happen short of marriage, and she didn't want any part of that institution.

"Why the look of doom and gloom? Don't tell me; I think I already know. Pan, I want you, but I'm not going to push you into something you're obviously not ready for, sweetheart."

"I know you wouldn't mean to, but…"

"Let's drop the subject and concentrate on having fun and really enjoying ourselves, all right?"

She smiled. Away from business, Julian was a free spirit and his enthusiasm was contagious.

"There is much more to see, but we won't be able to see even a third because I have plans for the rest of our stay."

"Do I get a hint?"

"You don't need one."

After seeing more of the fountains lit up by moonlight, Julian and Pandora returned to the hotel. The beautiful displays put them in an even more romantic frame of mind.

Julian arranged to have cocktails set up on the balcony of his hotel suite. Pandora's suite was across the hall, and he good-naturedly complained to her about that.

"It would have been better if you had just agreed to share a suite with me. Less expensive, too."

"Since when did expense ever concern you?"

"It never has; I was just messin' with you. You packed away your black widow image after this morning's meeting, and I just want to make sure you leave it out of sight."

"You're determined to change my image, aren't you?"

"No, it's a part of you, Pan. What I want to do is see that you keep it separate from the passionate, giving woman you become when we're together or making love."

"And are we going to make love?"

"Honey, yes. Most definitely."

Pandora raised her glass to take a sip of wine, but Julian took it from her and set it down on the table, saying,

"I want you, Pan."

"Almost as much as I want you." She unzipped her dress and let it fall around her feet. Her slip, bra and panties quickly followed.

"Oh, girl, you put the goddess Venus to shame."

"I'm no statue. I'm a flesh and blood woman, and I want you to make love to me."

"What have I unleashed by setting you free?"

"A passionately hungry woman. Come on, Professor Higgins. I'm your Eliza Doolittle. You have my permission to instruct your protégée further."

"I don't believe you need any more instruction." He drew her into his arms and kissed her mouth, then, moving down her body, rained more kisses on her heated skin. "Just more practice."

Pandora pushed him a little away from her. "I want you to be as naked as I am. I want to see that splendid body of yours aroused and ready to do my bidding."

"Yes, Your Highness. Your wish is my command." By the time he was naked, his manhood was rigid and angled straight out from his body.

"Oh, Julian," Pandora sighed.

He positioned her legs around his waist, and guided his hardened flesh slowly, deeply, inside her. Her shrieks of pleasure when he moved her body against his excited him.

"Anyone ever die from making love?" she asked.

"There is, of course, the little death when all control is abandoned for the most indescribable pleasure ever."

With his hardened flesh still intimately sheathed in Pandora, Julian headed for the bedroom. With each step, the friction was building, increasing the sensations aching for release. Inside the bedroom, he rolled them onto the bed. He kissed her neck, her collarbone, and rained kisses on her breasts. When the roughness of his tongue caused her nipples to peak, he licked his way back up to her waiting lips.

"Oh, Julian."

"You're fantastic, baby." He slid his hands beneath her hips and raised her buttocks, moving her body against his and embedding himself deeper. "You feel so good, Pan."

He felt good, too, she thought as he thrust against her, moving his body in circular motions, his sex filling her more deeply than it ever had.

"Julian! Julian!" she cried out.

"Yes, baby, yes!"

The continued hot rub of his body against hers drove her closer and closer to the edge. She returned his thrusts, arching wildly into him. Moments later they came in rapturous release.

"Is it being here in Rome, the city of romance, the reason you gave yourself to me so completely this time, Pan?"

"I guess so."

"And I thought it was my technique."

"You nut."

"What a thing to say to a man at a time like this."

"You're crazy, Julian Palmer."

"Yes, crazy about you, Pandora Cooper."

Their remaining days in Rome were spent in Julian's suite making love. As he had predicted, many of the sights went unseen.

CHAPTER TWENTY

"Who is the woman in your office?" Pandora asked Cassandra on the way to her private office her first day back at PanCo.

"Kiah Williams," Cassandra said, following Pandora. "I hired her to help me because you've been so busy with the Adrozini project. She's only a temp."

"If you need her on a more permanent basis, ask her to stay on. It's all right with me. I trust your judgment."

"I think I will. She's very efficient. How was Rome? And don't tell me you didn't take time to enjoy yourself, because I won't buy it. You had Julian Palmer with you."

Pandora smiled. "As a matter of fact, I did enjoy myself."

"He made love to you nonstop, didn't he? Don't answer; it's written all over your face. You've changed since knowing him."

"Monroe intimated as much."

"I think you had better keep Julian. It would be a shame to let that gorgeous hunk of man get away."

"You want to go to your office and get some work done now?"

"The black widow is back," Cassandra smiled.

"Julian, I need to talk to you about something I learned while you were in Rome," Drac said, walking into his cousin's office.

"Not now, Drac. I'm knee-deep in follow-up paperwork on the Adrozini project," he said, motioning to the stack of papers on his desk.

"It's been over a month since you began work on this project. When will it be finished?"

"I don't know. Probably another six weeks."

"What I have to tell you can't wait that long."

"What is it, Drac?"

"There's a problem at Gaines Financial, the company we took over three years ago."

"What's the problem?"

"Well, its financial advisor resigned without giving proper notice or an explanation. That's not at all like Chris Gaines. He is methodical, responsible and usually considerate."

"I agree," Julian said thoughtfully. "Maybe he got an offer he didn't want to risk losing if he waited," Julian laughed.

"This is not funny, Julian."

"Replace him, Drac."

"I will, but he left several important projects floundering. And he's not the only one to bail. Cedrick Temple, CFO for New York Network Securities, the company we acquired four years ago, has also resigned."

That got Julian's attention. "You think it's more than a coincidence?"

"I don't know. Well, not really, but it does seem odd."

"What have you been able to find out?"

"That's just it, I haven't been able to find out anything. No one knows why Chris resigned, not even his brother. All he knows is that Chris suddenly pulled up stakes and moved to Los Angeles."

"What about Cedrick Temple?"

"He took a position at Mid-Northern Investments in Chicago. And, get this, at a salary comparable to that of Network Securities, not more. Why make the switch, if not for a higher salary or better fringe benefits? He was very closed-mouth when I talked to him about it."

"So what do you suggest we do?"

"I can't suggest anything at the moment. I just wanted to make you aware of what's been going on."

"I'm aware. If anything out of the ordinary happens I want to be informed about it right away."

"Will do."

Pandora and Julian lounged before the fireplace in his living room, listening to music.

"Being here with you is wonderful."

"It's wonderful to see you so relaxed."

"I am that, all right. I'm enjoying life for the first time in a long while, and I have you to thank."

"I love the way you reward me." He stroked her face with his fingertips.

"You want to be rewarded now?"

She gave him a sexy smile, and waited for him to get started. He brought her closer, and she responded freely to his passionate kiss.

"You want more?" he asked huskily.

"Oh, yes, that was just an appetizer." It was divine to feel his hands move over her body.

"Pandora Cooper, I'm in love with you. I know you aren't in love with me yet, but I know you're more than attracted to me. For now it's enough."

"But for how long? I meant it when I told you that I will never marry again."

"I know you think you mean it, but I'm not going to give up on changing your mind."

"You want…"

He silenced her with a kiss. "What I want to do right now is make love to you. We can talk about the other thing another time."

Pandora was slightly disoriented when she woke. Seeing that it was three in the morning, she started scrambling off the bed.

"Where are you going?" Julian asked, his voice thick with interrupted sleep.

"I should have left hours ago."

"It's the middle of the night. Stay with me, baby."

"I really shouldn't."

"Why not? You don't really want to leave, do you?"

"No, I don't."

"Then don't." He pulled her into his arms and began stroking her hip.

"Julian…" Her breath caught in her throat when he began rubbing her most sensitive spot. Soon, she had forgotten all about leaving.

Destinee was having lunch when Pandora came down the next day.

"Miranda wants me to go with her to check out the new ice skating rink on Forty-fifth."

"I thought you didn't like being with your cousin."

"Oh, she can be fun sometimes. Besides, Talaya is going."

"How are things at your new school?"

"Just great. How are things between you and Julian?"

"Destinee."

"He's crazy about you, Mama. And you're serious about him, right? I can hardly wait for you two to get married."

"We are not at that point, and I don't know if we ever will be."

"Oh, you will," she said with a confidence only kids her age have. "Talaya should be here any minute. We're going to meet Miranda at the skating rink."

"You want me to give you guys a ride?"

"God, no! We're taking the subway."

A sure sign, Pandora thought, that her little girl was growing up fast, maybe too fast. This would be the first Saturday she and Destinee didn't have plans to do something together.

Those special times she had always shared with her daughter were numbered. Soon Destinee would be old enough to drive, then…Pandora knew the day was coming when she would be alone. But she need not be alone—if she could just get past her hang-ups about marriage.

Thoughts of what it was like to be married to Lyman darkened her mood. She must forget about that time and keep reminding herself that Julian was nothing like her brutish husband.

"My family and I are getting to you, aren't we, Pan?"

They were on their way back to New York City after a Sunday visit with Julian's grandmother and Drac's father, Howland.

"With a lot of help from my daughter."

"And all this time I thought it was the irresistible Palmer charm."

Pandora glanced back at her sleeping daughter.

"I—we really enjoyed today, Julian."

"There will be many more times like today. I won't push, but I can see you're weakening."

"Julian, don't get your hopes up."

"I understand your feelings about marriage. I'm not rushing you—well, not much anyway."

"You're impossible."

"I want you in my life permanently, Pandora. It's that simple."

"Nothing in life is ever that simple, Julian."

"I'll try to make it so just for you, sweetheart. You're worth waiting for."

After Destinee had gone up to bed, Julian lingered, clearly itching to talk.

"Monroe has been unbelievably cooperative lately, don't you think?" Julian asked Pandora.

"I agree. I thought he would be a pain, but surprise, surprise. And you're right, it is unbelievable," she said, not sure what to make of her brother-in-laws unexpectedly civil behavior.

"Maybe he's mellowing."

"I doubt it. I'll bet he thought he would be able to discredit us in some way. It was probably the reason he accepted the position in the first place."

"We've handled everything professionally and aboveboard. He can have no complaints about our methods or the results. I've felt that it has more to do with a personal axe to grind. What do you think?" he asked, watching Pandora closely.

"He resents my success, that's all."

"It's more than that, and I think you know it. I want you to tell me what's going on between you two."

"Nothing is going on. Why do you keep harping on that?"

Julian sighed heavily. "All right, I won't ask you again to trust me. You obviously feel you can't."

"You're wrong; I do trust you."

"But not about that, right? You don't have to answer. I'd better go. I'll see you at Phillips tomorrow."

"But, Julian…"

"Walk me to the door, Pandora."

He kissed her good night and left.

Pandora knew her transparent denials annoyed Julian. She wanted to confide in him, but old habits died hard. Why couldn't she heal and go on with her life?

You can do it, girlfriend. Just give Julian a chance. He'll help you.

CHAPTER TWENTY-ONE

"We need to replace James as CFO," Cassandra informed Pandora as soon as she walked into the office.

"I thought he was recovering from his heart attack."

"He is, but the doctors don't think he'll be able to handle the pressures of the position."

"All right, then go ahead and start interviewing for his replacement. I want you to make sure that a twenty percent increase is added to James's retirement package to show our appreciation. He's a good man, and we're going to sorely miss his expertise."

"There aren't many around who are as good or as experienced and who aren't already taken, but we'll find one."

"I know I can count on you, Cassandra. How is Kiah working out?"

"She's a godsend. She doesn't mind working overtime or Saturdays."

"That's good, because I have to go to Los Angeles next week. You'll be in charge."

"Why do you have to go out there?"

"It's the first company I took over, and they need my help. It seems the new director is having problems jelling with the staff. They need a mediator, and it looks like I'm it."

"There's someone who's going to miss you. And I don't mean Destinee."

"I know, and I'm going to miss him, too."

"You're finally admitting to having more than lustful feelings for the man!"

Pandora smiled. "Yes, I am, Ms. Know-It-All. When I get back, Julian and I are going to have a serious talk."

"I'm glad to hear it. I know one person who won't be happy."

"Drac. I figured as much. I met his father at Gramma Edna's a couple of weeks ago. He's an original. He really likes you, Cassandra. He said that after you and Drac were married and you had a daughter, he wanted to name her."

"Let me guess. He wants to name her Elvira, right? Or Buffy."

"I see he's been talking to you."

"Not to me, to Drac." Her smile faded. "He's been acting funny lately."

"Funny how?"

"Oh, I don't know, distracted, or maybe worried."

"Do you think it's about business?"

"Could be. With Drac you never know. He can be so closed-mouthed sometimes that I feel like choking him."

"Haven't you heard that men are from Mars and women are from Venus?"

"I can believe it. I'd better get back to work. It's all I can do to stay on top of things since you've been so involved with Phillips Investments. Now with this trip to Los Angeles, work is threatening to bury me."

"I am confident you can handle it, Cassandra."

"I could arrange to fly to Los Angeles with you, Pan," Julian said over dinner that evening at Robaire's.

"You would be bored stiff. I'll be too busy to be good company for you. Besides, one of us has to be here to deal with Monroe."

"You're right. It's just that I'm going to miss you."

"I'm going to miss you, too. I can hardly wait to get back from this trip and be with you, Julian."

"You have no idea how happy I am to hear you say that. I was beginning to think I needed a refresher course in the art of loving a woman."

"You know you don't. You're a wonderful lover and a pretty special man."

"Ooh, hurry up and come back from Los Angeles."

"Julian." She almost told him she loved him, but decided to wait.

"Heavy thinking?"

"Let's go to your place."

"An eager woman. I love it. And I love you."

While in Los Angeles, Pandora made a point to call Destinee every evening. "How's it going, daughter mine? You haven't been giving Rachel a rough time, have you?"

"I'm okay and, no, I haven't been sweatin' Rachel. I miss you, Mama. When are you coming home?"

"I'll be here a few more days. You haven't been too lonely without me, have you?"

"No, Julian and Talaya and her mother have been keeping me company. We went to visit Gramma Edna yesterday. She's so cool, Mama. I helped her collect leaves and twigs to make an autumn wreath. I've never done anything like that before."

"I'm glad you're having a good time, honey. I'll call you tomorrow. I love you. Bye now." Julian knew the way to her heart was through her daughter.

The phone rang seconds after she had hung up.

"Pan?"

"Julian."

"You sound happy. It must be hearing your master's voice that did the trick."

"You're cruisin' for a bruisin', Mr. Palmer."

"Too bad I'm not there to kiss you for your insolence, Ms. Cooper."

"I know."

"When you get back and we wrap up the Phillips project, which I think we will in another week, let's go away to the Catskills for a long weekend."

"Your cabin or mine?" she asked, laughing.

"Mine."

"Isn't it supposed to snow?"

"The Weather Channel predicts that there's a sixty percent chance of that happening over the next two weeks. There's nothing I'd like better than to be snowed in with you."

"We could be snowed in for longer than the weekend."

"Doesn't that sound like heaven?" he asked, his voice husky and heavy with meaning.

"You shouldn't be saying things like that when I'm three thousand miles away."

"I want you to ache to be with me."

"I already do."

"Then hurry back, sweetheart."

"I'll be there as soon as I can. You can believe that."

"Have I at last cornered the market on your affection?"

"The astronomical rate of return dividends would blow your mind."

"What's wrong, Cassandra? Any catastrophes while I was away?" Pandora asked her assistant when she entered the office a few days later.

"No."

"Man problems, then?"

"Big time."

"What's Drac done now?"

"You remember me telling you that he'd been asking a lot of questions about PanCo?"

"Yes."

"I mentioned we had hired a new man to take over from James. When I told Drac who he was, he got a funny look on his face and stalked out of the office as if I'd told him we had hired the mad bomber or something."

"That is strange. Why would hiring Colin Whitley bother him? From looking over the man's credentials, he's good at what he does."

"Drac's antagonism toward you is getting on my nerves. He's so moody sometimes."

"But you care for him, don't you?"

"Yes."

"He'll tell you what's bothering him sooner or later."

"He'd better make it sooner. Did you get things straightened out in Los Angeles?"

"Yes. I think Christopher Gaines will work out just fine."

Just as Pandora was about to leave for the day, Destinee called.

"Since you're going to the mountains with Julian this weekend, may I spend the weekend at Talaya's? Please."

"I don't know, honey. We don't want to take advantage of Selena and wear out your welcome. You're over there so much as it is."

"She won't mind. She told me that she's glad to have me over so Talaya won't be so lonely. Her dad got remarried, and his wife is expecting a baby. Talaya told me she feels left out of his life."

"I'll bet she does. I'm glad you two are friends."

"Besides, Rachel is spending the weekend with her daughter. I absolutely refuse to stay at Aunt Sasha's for a whole weekend."

"I don't mind if you spend the weekend with Talaya as long as it's all right with Selena. I'll call her later. How about going shopping with me tomorrow? You have such good taste in clothes, my future dress designer of America."

"Oh, Mom."

"This mint-green sweater will go well with the gray wool slacks," Destinee suggested to Pandora from the waiting area of the fitting room at Juliet's Exclusive Salon.

A tall, elegantly dressed woman sauntered into the fitting room.

"You certainly have good clothes sense for someone so young. It's about time Juliet got someone to help who really knows something about fashion."

"Thank you, but I don't work here, although I do hope to one day be a fashion designer."

"You're so tall I thought you—now that I look at your face, I can see you couldn't possibly be old enough to work here."

"She may be young, but she's serious about being a designer. Someday she's going to turn that dream into a reality," Pandora said proudly, poking her head through the curtain opening.

"You must be her mother; I see the resemblance." Then she said to Destinee, "You have to help me pick something out." Her tone contained a hint of presumption. "You see, I'm flying to Aspen for a ski weekend."

She looked at Pandora. "By the way, my name is Vanessa Armstrong. And yours?"

"Pandora Cooper, and my daughter's name is Destinee."

"Pleased to meet you," Destinee answered politely.

Pandora closed the curtain, but continued to listen to the conversation between her daughter and Vanessa Armstrong.

"With your hair coloring, I think this jacket would look great on you, Ms. Armstrong."

Armstrong. Pandora had heard that name before. Then she remembered. Could she be the same Vanessa Armstrong who had hurt Julian so badly? She pulled the curtain back a bit to get a better look at the woman. She was tall and very elegant, not beautiful, but attractive in a coolly superior sort of way. Her hair was dyed a becoming shade of golden brown that complimented her whiskey brown eyes and lightly bronzed skin. She wore heavy plain-gold jewelry that had to be worth a mint.

Pandora couldn't—or didn't want to—imagine Julian going for a woman like her. She seemed so superficial, not at all the kind of woman she would expect him to be attracted to.

So this was Vanessa. It took another woman to instantly recognize tendencies men often failed to see in women like that. Even so, Pandora couldn't help the feeling of jealousy squeezing her heart.

"You've helped me so much, Destinee," Vanessa said, smiling sweetly.

Pandora stepped outside the curtain. "It was nice meeting you, Ms. Armstrong."

"The pleasure has been mine, I assure you, Ms. Cooper. I really must be going," she said, giving Pandora the once-over before walking away.

Pandora had a feeling the woman knew exactly who she was and about her involvement with Julian. Pictures of them leaving restaurants had appeared in the tabloids. She was sure to have seen them.

"So what do you think of her?" Pandora asked Destinee.

"She's okay, I guess," she offered, "but only If you like the haughty witch type."

"Destinee, shame on you."

"It's only the truth, Mama."

Pandora realized that her daughter was perceptive for a girl her age. And she wasn't shy about voicing her opinion. Then again, kids her age hadn't yet learned the niceties of social interaction—how to use subterfuge to mask their true feelings. This could be both refreshing and potentially disastrous.

CHAPTER TWENTY-TWO

"Maybe we should postpone this trip and go another weekend, Julian," Pandora suggested when she saw grey clouds gathering.

"I thought you liked the idea of being stranded alone with me for an entire weekend."

"What I don't like is the look of those clouds. Maybe we should turn back."

"This is a four-wheel drive, Pan. I also have snow chains, so stop worrying."

A little later, Pandora glanced at Julian's profile. He was so confident about everything all the time. She wondered if he had been like that with Vanessa. He seemed so confident that he could get Pandora to change her mind about marriage. She guessed that he had some reason for thinking that way. Her resolve was most certainly weakening, but it was more that her feelings for Julian were deepening and growing stronger. And she did want to please him. It started snowing as they neared the cabin.

"It looks like we made it just in time," Julian asserted. "I'm glad I had the cabin fully stocked with wood as well as food. I have all we need for the roaring fire I plan to build," he said, flashing a sly, wicked smile. "In the fireplace, of course."

"Right."

"I did say in the fireplace. That's all I meant."

"Sure it is."

"What other place did you think I meant?"

Pandora laughed. "Life with you on a daily basis definitely would not be boring."

"Are you seriously considering sharing it with me, Pan?"

"I think we had better get inside and start that fire. I'm getting cold."

"Yes, ma'am. I absolutely don't want you to be cold."

Pandora kept her coat on and wandered around the living room while Julian built the fire. His cabin was certainly more well-appointed than hers. Whereas hers was built of oak, his was of pine. The high, hand-finished cross-beamed ceiling gave it an airy, uncluttered look. The custom-designed Pella windows seemed to bring the sky inside.

"You like it?" Julian asked.

"Oh, yes. It has all the extras mine doesn't."

"I had it redone since I was here last. I wanted it to reflect my taste and personality. So what do you think?"

"You've succeeded. I thought you just bought the cabin to impress me."

"Originally I did, but once I moved in here I knew that I wanted more."

Pandora took off her coat and put it across the back of the couch. "I should make some coffee to warm us."

"Let's do it together." He took her hand and led her into the kitchen.

There was a cozy dining area to one side of the huge kitchen, with curtain-free windows revealing a tree-lined vista just beginning to fill with snow. The open and relaxed atmosphere began to mellow Pandora. She walked over to one of the hand-varnished, knotty-pine counters where a coffee maker stood ready. Julian took a can of coffee from one of the matching cabinets.

Pandora started the coffee while Julian rummaged in the freezer for something to fix for their dinner. She then explored the contents of the cabinets, finally settling herself on a wooden stool at the counter.

Julian held up several freezer-wrapped packages. "I'll put these in the microwave to defrost. In the meantime, we can take our coffee into the living room and warm up."

The spicy aroma of burning Jack pine wood filled the living room. Julian set the tray with the coffeepot and mugs on the coffee table.

Then he began arranging huge thick cushions on the enormous fur rug in front of the fireplace. He turned the lights down low so that the glow from the fire produced an intimate, romantic aura in the room.

"What kind of music are you in the mood for, Pan?" he asked, walking over to the entertainment center.

Pandora smiled. "I'm sure you have everything. You decide."

"Oh, I have what you need, everything you could ever possibly want." He chose a CD by the Isley Brothers called "Mission to Please". Then he sat down on the fur rug and held out his arms for her to join him. She snuggled into his embrace, letting the heat from his body warm her.

"Are you really on a mission to please, Julian?" she asked.

"Sweetheart, I think you know the answer to that question. Let's get you out of this pink sweater. It's new, isn't it?"

"Destinee helped pick it out. She said you'd like it."

"I do, but I want to see you out of it."

"Your wish is mine to grant."

She raised her arms, and he pulled the sweater over her head. Her body heat caused the thin silk blouse to cling to her lacy bra, molding her full breasts. He quickly unbuttoned her blouse and tossed it to the floor, then unhooked her bra, allowing her breasts to spring free.

"Oh, girl," he groaned, slipping the straps off her shoulders and lowering his lips to a nipple.

She moaned with pleasure as she held his head in place, inviting his tongue to worship her aroused flesh more fully. Her boots, wool slacks and silky panties were off in short order.

"Pan," he finally managed to whisper, "no words can describe how you look to me at this moment." He slowly slid his fingers down the curves of her body to her hips. "Your skin is soft and warm, and heaven to the touch."

"Now I want to see and feel all of you, Julian. I want you naked."

In no time he was down to his briefs. When he peeled them off, she touched his erect shaft and her excitement spilled over. She continued to move her fingers over him, unable to get her fill of touching him. The look in his eyes and his growing tumescence said he was eager to strike a chord of desire within her.

"Oh, Pan," he uttered hoarsely as he eased his body over hers.

The contact was so electric. He groaned as he rubbed his chest against her breasts, his hips against her hips, his hair-roughened legs against her smooth ones.

"Julian, oh, Julian," she cried out, circling her arms around his waist.

He covered her lips and throat with kisses, then returned to her mouth. "Your taste is sweet, so sweet."

Pandora raised her head, bringing her lips to his and darting her tongue inside his mouth. She felt him shudder and heard a sound somewhere between a groan and a growl come from his throat. She felt the throb of his sex against her stomach and wriggled her body beneath his, inviting him inside.

"Open for me, Pan."

When she did and he slipped inside her, slowly filling every inch of her moist passage until he was surrounded, pure male power contained by her, wanting her, completely consumed by his need for her. Her body convulsed, and intense vibrating sensations emanated from her center, where he lay within, thick and hard and deep.

He thrust once, and heat infused her, spiraling through her body. He thrust again and the sensation sent her senses spinning and she screamed. He delved even deeper between her damp velvety folds. She wanted the sensual slide in and out of her flesh to go on and on forever.

"Oh, yes," she cried out. "Once more, once more again and again and again—yes, yes now."

He dove relentlessly into her over and over, and over again, heightening the feeling, pulling it from her, compelling her to come, demanding her pleasure as the culmination of his own. Suddenly it was there. The wonder of him surrounding her passion, and his tumultuous thrusts echoing reverberantly through her. In that glorious moment her entire being was centered around him. Her body quivered with undulating pleasure that would not stop. She didn't want them to stop. A torrent of sensations burst from deep inside her, a feeling like nothing she had ever felt before.

With one last powerful thrust, Julian gave himself up to his own explosive climax.

Long moments later, they lay entwined, basking in the aftermath of glorious fulfillment.

"Next time, I want to lead you into rapturous bliss," Pandora told him.

"A take-charge woman. I don't know if I should give you that kind of power."

"Why not? You afraid I might abuse it?"

"On the contrary, I want you to." He kissed the top of her head. "You think if I did give you the power, I'd still be able to set your world tilting on its axis?"

"I know you would."

He gazed at the dying fire. "I know I need to put more wood on the fire, but right now I don't want to be away from you for even that short a time." But he reluctantly eased out of their embrace. "Promise you won't run away."

"Where would I go in all this snow. The only other place I might run to is your bedroom."

They ate a meal of grilled chicken, baked potatoes and vegetables in their robes. He was even sexy in his robe. He was all the man any woman could ever want. She couldn't understand why Vanessa Armstrong had thrown it all away. But who was she to talk? She herself had hesitated before making the ultimate commitment to this man. Before, she could have blamed it on her past relationship with her husband, but she had come to know Julian and knew he was as different from Lyman as heaven was from hell.

Julian reached for the wine bottle. "Would you like another glass?" he asked.

"Are you trying to get me drunk?"

"Do you want me to get you drunk?" He took her hand and turned it palm side up and flicked the center with his tongue.

She sucked in her breath. "I demand that you make love to me."

"You still on that power trip?"

"No more delaying tactics, Julian."

He rose from his chair and held out his hand to her. She took it and led him out of the room and up the stairs to the master bedroom. There were three other bedrooms upstairs. She thought the cabin was the perfect place for a large family to spend time together. Julian had said he wanted her and her daughter to be his family.

It was time to face the fact that she loved him enough to make a life with him, even if it meant marriage—especially if it meant marriage. She had mulled this over long enough, and it was time for her to slay her dragons once and for all.

"Stand right there," Pandora commanded when they entered the bedroom.

Obeying, he stopped. His dark eyes were hot with desire. She opened his robe and kissed his neck, then eased it off his shoulders, letting it slide down his body.

Pandora flicked her tongue over his nipple and felt his breathing quicken. His eyes were closed, lost in the exquisite pleasure he was receiving at her hands. She kissed her way down his flat stomach. When she reached his hardened member and felt him shudder, she moved her lips away.

Julian opened his eyes. "Why did you stop?"

She removed her robe. "You want me to continue?"

"Yes, oh God, yes!"

"You are mine, Julian Palmer."

"As you are mine, Pandora Cooper," he said thickly, sucking his breath in sharply when her fingers began to dance up and down his throbbing flesh.

Her hands retraced the contours of his body on the journey back up, skimming over his narrow hips, lean waist and rib cage. She flicked her tongue over his nipple, and then licked her way up his throat and devoured his mouth.

His breath turned ragged when she reached for his sex and holding it her hand, then began working his hot flesh.

"You're going to kill me," he rasped.

"But what a delicious way to die." When Pandora moved away from him, she saw he was unsteady on his feet. She took his hand and guided him over to the bed, ordering him to lie down across it. She spread his legs and knelt between them and ran her long hair back and forth over his groin. He made a low savage sound.

"Oh, baby," he muttered mindlessly.

She moved her mouth over him, letting the friction of her tongue pleasure him.

"Yes, yes—more. More, please!"

And she did, pushing him close to the edge before withdrawing. She instructed him to move lengthwise on the bed. She then lay on top of him, straddling his hips and moving against him.

"Enough!" he growled. Grasping her hips, he thrust himself to the hilt within her. Then he lay still, reveling in the feel of her vibrating hotly around him. She cried out, urging him to move so that he could give her more exquisite pleasure. He exerted every ounce of control to stay still.

Unable to stand him not moving, she begin a sliding friction against him. When he felt her shudder followed by spasms of pleasure, his endurance ended and he came in a mind-shattering climax.

Throughout the night they made love—from slow to wild then back to slow. At dawn, they fell into an exhausted sleep.

CHAPTER TWENTY-THREE

Pandora was the first to awaken Saturday morning to discover the cabin was unusually silent. She eased out of Julian's arms and padded over to the window to look out. A deep, heavy snow covered the ground; they were snowed in. There must have been a blizzard during the night. She and Julian had been totally oblivious to anything but each other.

"Come back to bed," Julian murmured sleepily.

"We're really snowed in, Julian. I hope it melts enough so we'll be able to leave tomorrow."

"If it doesn't, we can stay in bed and snuggle."

"Julian."

"Don't worry, Pan. I'll call for help on the cell phone if we can't."

"You left it in the Escalade. Come look outside."

Julian left the bed and came up behind her and looped his arm around her neck, drawing her into his body with the other arm. He frowned when he saw that the path to the Escalade stored in the garage was covered by a ton of snow, and it was still coming down hard.

"When it stops snowing, I'll dig a path to the Escalade and retrieve the phone. Now let's go back to..."

"If you say bed, I swear I'm going to kill you."

"Oh, kill me, baby. Please, kill me."

"You idiot." Pandora kissed him and then let him carry her back to bed.

Later that morning Julian revived the banked embers in the fireplace and soon had a cozy fire blazing. He and Pandora went into the kitchen and had breakfast.

"There is an important question I want to ask you when we get back to New York," Julian said, to her smiling.

"I bet I know what it is."

"I wonder if you'll give me the answer I want."

"You'll have to wait and see, won't you?"

"Maybe I should ask it now."

"I think you should wait. Although I'm sure I know what my daughter is going to say, I want to talk it over with her, anyway. It'll make a big change in her life. I'm not sure she's considered how much of a change."

"You're right. I'll pop the question with both my girls present. I don't want any hitches." He paused. "You sure you don't have any lingering doubts about marrying me?"

"You asked me to trust you, so I am. I love you with all my heart and soul, Julian."

"And I love you, Pandora, very much. I can hardly wait to get papers on you."

"Are we going to form a merger after we get married?"

"Palmer and Cooper. Palm Co, I like the sound of that."

"Why not PanCo and Palmer?"

"We'll worry about the order when the time comes."

"I can just see Drac's face when that happens."

"Once he really comes to know you, his attitude will change. If he doesn't, it'll be his loss."

"Want to help me clean up the kitchen?"

"No, but I will if you'll promise to reward me afterward."

"A negotiator to the end."

"We're going to have a fantastic life together, baby."

"I know we will."

By Sunday morning it still hadn't stopped snowing, but it had slowed enough for Julian to shovel his way to the garage and retrieve his cell phone. But when he tried to make a call, all he got was static. They whiled the day away playing chess, eating and making love. They couldn't get enough of each other.

Pandora was worried about not being able to get back on Monday. It was Tuesday morning before they were able to leave the cabin.

"I'm grateful to Selena for getting Destinee off to school yesterday and today," Pandora said after finally getting Selena on the cell phone.

"Me, too. You don't regret going away with me, do you?"

"No, never. I thoroughly enjoyed you and our time together."

The drive back to New York City was slow and treacherous, testing Julian's driving skills every mile of the way. It was late afternoon when they reached Selena's house.

"I know it's useless to ask that you didn't worry about Destinee," Selena said to Pandora, taking their coats and leading them into her warm, comfortable living room.

"What can I say, Selena. I'm a mother." Pandora said, taking a seat on the caramel colored, L-shaped couch. Julian sat beside her and draped his arm along the back.

"The girls should be home from school any minute." Selena looked at her brother. "Drac has been calling nonstop since yesterday."

"He has? I wonder what he wants. Didn't he try to get me on the cell phone?"

"He said he did, but could never get through. It must be important. You had better call him." She studied her brother and Pandora. "You two must be tired."

"Actually, I'm feeling revitalized," Pandora answered, gazing lovingly at Julian.

"Does that look mean what I hope it means?" Selena asked.

"Maybe," Julian grinned.

Destinee burst into the living room, Talaya close behind.

"I saw Julian's Escalade parked outside. I'm really glad you're back. We were so worried."

Pandora rose from the couch and hugged her daughter. "I'm glad to be back."

Destinee went over to Julian and hugged him. "I knew you would take good care of my mother."

"I'm glad you have that kind of confidence in me, Desi," he said softly.

"What did you do for school clothes?" Pandora asked her.

"When you didn't make it home Sunday morning, we went to the house to get a change of clothes. This morning I wore one of Talaya's outfits. We're more like sisters than friends, and we wear the same size."

Julian drove Pandora and Destinee home, glancing every now and then at the woman he loved. When Destinee had mentioned that his niece seemed more like a sister to her than a friend, he saw the look on Pandora's face and wondered if she was thinking the same thing he was. What would it be like to have a baby of their own? They'd never discussed it, but then the possibility of their marrying had just begun to seem real.

"How would dinner out Friday night appeal to my girls?" Julian asked.

"Is it a special occasion?" Destinee wanted to know, her eyes sparkling in eager anticipation.

"I have a very important question to ask you both."

"Can't you ask it now?" Destinee pleaded. "Waiting until then is going to kill me."

Julian could tell by the excitement in her voice that Destinee knew the question. But her mother was quiet. He wondered if she was having second thoughts. She smiled reassuringly, and he relaxed.

He felt as anxious as a teenager on the way to a first date. He finally acknowledged that he had been trying to convince himself that he wasn't worried that she would turn him down. He had never wanted anything as badly as he wanted Pandora to be his wife.

Pandora had phoned Rachel at her daughter's and asked her to go to the house and prepare a simple dinner. When they entered the condo, they could smell of Rachel's famous chili, and they were soon digging in with gusto.

After dinner, a happy Destinee said goodnight and went up to her room. "That's the happiest I've ever seen my child, Julian, and it's all because of you," Pandora said with a kiss.

"It's because of you that I'm a happy man, my love."

"I want you to always feel that way. I want us to always be as happy as we are right now."

"So do I. And we will, if I have anything to say about it."

"It's getting late, I'd better go."

"One day soon you won't ever have to leave."

"I look forward to that day." He rose from the couch and pulled Pandora to her feet. His arm around her shoulders, they walked to the door.

"I'll call you in the morning. You know, now that the Phillips project is finished, I'm going to miss working with you."

"We'll have to find another project to collaborate on."

"The one I have in mind has nothing to do with business."

"Oh?"

"What are your feelings about making a baby?"

"I hadn't given it any thought until a certain dynamic man swept into my life."

Julian grinned. "I take it you like the idea?"

"Love it." It might, in fact, already be a distinct possibility. Julian had used up all his condoms, so the last time they had made love had been without protection. Since she had already made up her mind to marry him, having a baby wouldn't be a problem.

"I'm glad. Julian Darius Palmer Jr. doesn't sound bad."

Pandora smiled mischievously. "It might be a girl."

"Juliana, then. I don't care as long as she's as beautiful as her mother and sister."

"She may look like you."

"Poor girl."

"No, lucky girl."

He pulled her into his arms, fitting her soft curves into his lean frame, and then he reluctantly backed away declaring, "I'd better get my coat or I'll never leave." He kissed her one last time and left.

CHAPTER TWENTY-FOUR

"It's about time you got back," Drac said irritably, waving the file folder and following Julian into his office.

"If you must know, Pandora and I were snowed in at the cabin." Julian hung his coat up and walked over to his desk.

"You don't sound like it was any hardship," Drac said sarcastically. "I hope it was worth it."

"What is with you, Drac?"

"Your precious black widow has me ticked off, that's what."

Julian glared at his cousin. "If you have something to say, spit it out."

"I have more than just my words to back me up."

"Drac!" he warned, nearing the end of his patience.

Drac threw the folder on Julian's desk. "Take a look at this."

Julian frowned. "What is this all about?"

"Read it, then you'll begin to understand."

Julian opened the folder. The first few pages were inquiries made by PanCo concerning Palmer and Associates. Two were dated before the takeover of Phillips Investments; the latest, a few days ago. His eyes widened in shock when he came to the changes in personnel within his companies over the past few months. There were two that stood out. Chris Gaines going to Star Pacific and Cedrick Temple to Mid-Northern Investments.

"This is only the preliminary report."

Julian looked up. "I was aware of Gaines and Temple resigning."

"But neither of us knew that they had taken jobs at companies either owned by PanCo or Cooper Corp."

"What are you trying to say? That Pandora lured our top people away from us?"

"Read the rest of the report, Julian," Drac urged.

Julian did just that. Colin Whitley took a job as chief financial officer at PanCo after resigning from one of Palmer and Associates' subsidiary companies a few weeks ago. Julian shuffled through the papers until he came to the sheet on Chris Gaines. Star Pacific was in Los Angeles. He closed his eyes.

Pandora had flown there two weeks ago to—what? She had said to act as mediator between the new head of finances and the staff of one of her companies. She had discouraged him from going along when he had suggested it.

Julian looked at Drac. "It could just be a coincidence."

"Julian, wake up and smell the coffee. Is Cedrick Temple's resignation and sudden move to Chicago to work at Mid-Northern, which happens to be a subsidiary of PanCo, a coincidence, too?"

"There has to be an explanation."

"Oh, there is. Pandora Cooper is holding true to her name and reputation. What explanation can she possibly give for keeping this from you? Unless she's guilty of corporate espionage."

Julian flipped to the next sheet. Jonathan Fremont had gone to work for Peterson Investment Group. "Is Peterson one of PanCo's subsidiaries or holding companies?"

"No, but it's affiliated with a company she co-owns with Monroe Cooper."

"Are you saying Pandora and Monroe are…"

"Conspiring to ruin us," Drac finished.

"I don't believe it," Julian said vehemently. "I won't. Pandora happens to hate the man."

"It's probably what she wants you to believe. And get this, one of Monroe Cooper's former secretaries is now working with Cassandra at PanCo. In the head office, no less. What more proof do you need that the woman has been double-crossing you big-time, Julian?"

Julian stood and stepped over to the window, thrusting his hands deep inside his pockets. This had to be some kind of horrendous mistake. The Pandora he knew would never…She had integrity, superior intelligence and was savvy concerning Wall Street and the Exchange and many other financial organizations. She had no need to do something this underhanded. He reminded himself that she had pulled off takeovers many had found impossible to engineer. He also remembered her deep-seated mistrust of men. But she no longer had reason to feel that way, not after all they had shared, did she?

She was his woman, and that had to count for something. He wouldn't condemn her on just circumstantial evidence. He had to be sure in his own mind that any of it was true.

Was it possible she had sought to distract him with her display of vulnerability? It was shades of Vanessa all over again. He shuddered at the thought. Could it have been an elaborate act to eventually gain control of his company? No woman was that good an actress. The way she had responded to him couldn't have been faked. No way.

Because she responded to his lovemaking didn't necessarily mean she wouldn't...but he recalled her casually mentioning something about merging and renaming their businesses once they were married. But hadn't she only been kidding? Or had it been part of her plan all along? Was it why she had gone out with him in the first place, letting him get close to her and her daughter, hoping he would become so besotted that whatever she did wouldn't matter or be noticed? Just like Vanessa.

"Drac, I think you should go. I need time to absorb all of this."

"Jules, man, I..."

"Just go, all right?" he said in a barely controlled voice.

"I was afraid this would happen, that she might..."

"Drac!"

His cousin finally got the message and left. Julian dropped heavily into his chair. He buzzed his secretary and asked for a pot of coffee. He thought about all the time he had spent with Pandora and Destinee. He loved that girl like a daughter; they had connected almost immediately. His family, excepting Drac, had liked and accepted them. Was getting to know them all a part of some kind of game plan? But the Pandora he knew and loved was not a game player—maybe in business. But that was different, wasn't it?

Julian picked up the folder again and looked at its contents more closely. Drac had contacted stockholders in several of Palmer and Associates' subsidiary companies. They'd all been approached either by PanCo or Monroe's company, Cooper Corps, about selling their shares. Julian checked the dates and realized how recently most of these contacts had been made. Most had been handled by Monroe, but the latest were initiated by Colin Whitley. These actions were taken during his and Pandora's recent trip to Rome.

Had making Monroe coordinator of the Androzini project really been the board's doing? Or had Pandora personally suggested he work with them? No, no, he wouldn't believe that. No one could be that devious, especially not the woman he loved. But did he really know her? Did he actually know what she was capable of? Did anyone ever completely know the workings of another's mind?

He had made the mistake once of thinking he did, and he had barely survived the experience. Julian closed his eyes. *Oh, God, I can't—I won't go through that kind of agony again.*

He opened his eyes and checked his watch. He had an appointment in less than fifteen minutes. He wasn't in any mood to deal with business right now. He would get Drac to take over for him. He had to get a grip on his emotions. The anger he felt at this moment was threatening to devour him.

Julian had his chauffeur drive around for hours before asking him to stop at the Club Paradise. He walked back to the bar and ordered a double scotch and listened to a guest performer sing "As We Lay", an old classic originally recorded by Shirley Murdoch.

"Julian, I'm surprised to see you here—alone," Vanessa said, sliding onto the seat next to his. "I expected to see you with the new love of your life, Pandora Cooper, the infamous Black Widow of Wall Street."

Julian's insides contracted at the sound of Vanessa's voice. He couldn't believe he had once thought he loved this woman.

"I didn't think anything could ever surprise you. Where is your latest conquest, or should I say fool?" Julian responded, taking a deep swallow of his drink.

"There's no need to get nasty, darling."

"Isn't there." He finished the scotch and ordered another.

"I understand now. The light of your life has dumped you." She reached out and touched his cheek. "And since we are both between lovers, I thought..."

"Don't say it! Don't even think about it, Vanessa. After what you did, where do you get the unmitigated gall to suggest something like that to me?"

"People make mistakes, Jules."

"Now you're going to tell me you've changed, right? Well, frankly, my dear, I don't give a damn." He laughed.

"That's not funny, Julian. You used to..."

"*Used* being the operative word. Go find yourself another fool, Vanessa. I've been there, done that. And I have no intention of ever going there with you again."

"If you change your mind I'm still..."

"Available? I don't care what you are."

"The offer still stands. *If* you change your mind you can call me anytime."

The bartender walked over to Julian after Vanessa had left.

"I couldn't help overhearing. She's one hell of a classy broad, if you get my drift."

"I seem to be drawn to that type. You can have them all." He saluted the bartender with his empty glass. "Another drink."

"You're not driving, are you?"

"No," Julian answered, laughing at the relieved look on the man's face.

Pandora virtually floated into her office. She couldn't remember ever being this happy. Not even graduating at the top of her class came close to topping this wonderful feeling. Only the birth of her daughter rivaled how she was feeling. At last she would have the husband of her dreams.

Julian was nothing like Lyman. He wasn't trying to control and mold her, and he really cared for her and her daughter. For the first time since her mother died, she trusted someone, a very special someone. Julian had been so patient with her and so understanding of her hang-ups. She sat in her chair, but didn't immediately turn to work. Her thoughts were too centered on the man she loved.

"I would definitely have to say you have it," Cassandra said, walking into Pandora's office.

Pandora smiled. "And just what is it that I have?"

"That love-struck look, what else?"

"Oh, you mean the look similar to the one you've been wearing for the last few months?"

"The very same. But Drac has been so preoccupied lately. I thought it might be another woman, but the only serious competition I have is his fierce loyalty to the family business and to his cousin."

"He's overly protective when it comes to Julian. I think he sees me as some kind of threat. He takes my reputation way too seriously. I was hoping he would change his attitude, but that hasn't happened and may never happen. If anything he's more hostile than ever."

"He mentioned that all the women Julian has known in the past have always wanted something other than his loving attention. According to him, Julian almost married a woman who had designs on his fortune. Drac says he'd been hurt pretty badly."

"Julian has never said anything to me about it. At first, I had just assumed that he had always been a carefree bachelor, but I had heard it from his grandmother that he had been dumped by a woman named Vanessa Armstrong. Evidently he had cared very deeply for her. I've met the woman, and I'd say she's definitely not his type." Pandora tried to recall something Drac had once said, but it evaded her memory.

Cassandra grinned. "But the Black Widow of Wall Street is his type? I know you aren't the ruthless witch you've led people to believe. I know it's all a protective mechanism."

"All right, Dr. Brothers, I'm busted."

"If I could just convince Drac not to take your reputation so seriously."

"Maybe he'll come around in time, once he realizes how much I love his cousin and believes that I would never, could never, do anything to hurt him."

Pandora started sorting through the papers on her desk. "How is Colin Whitley working out?"

"He certainly knows his business. He has already organized a committee to oversee the more mundane things, freeing us both to work on more important projects. I would say he is a godsend."

"You said that about Kiah. I guess we're lucky, then."

"When I asked Colin why he left Richards Investments, he said he just wanted a change."

"I can certainly understand that. I'm glad he chose us. We need him, what with the heavy work load lately. I'm up to my eyeballs in it, and will be the rest of the week. I want to be all caught up by Friday."

"So what's happening on Friday, may I ask?"

"Julian is taking me and Destinee out to dinner."

"Not just any dinner, though, right? Come on, give," she nagged.

"He's going to ask me to be his wife," she said dreamily. "He wants Destinee to be with us when he does."

"Oh, Pandora. I'm so happy for you, girl. Maybe Drac will get the hint."

"I don't know how I'm going to get through the next few days."

"You're a different person since getting involved with Julian Palmer. Being in love has worked miracles."

"I whole-heartedly recommend it."

"I don't need to ask how Destinee feels about this, do I? She's probably in seventh heaven."

"You're right. She's crazy about Julian. They have a special rapport. He's going to be the kind of father my baby has always wanted and deserved."

Destinee couldn't contain her excitement at dinner that evening. "Just one more day and it'll be Friday, Mama. You and Julian will be officially engaged to be married. Oh, I can't stand it. How can you?"

"It's hard, but I'm managing—just barely."

"Miranda is even happy for us, Mama."

"Miranda? You two have grown closer lately, haven't you?"

"She's not like Aunt Sasha. I told her you and Julian were really in love and we were going to be a real family."

"I'm glad you two are friends, and that she is one member of your father's family you can relate to."

"When you and Julian get married, Talaya will become a member of my family, too." Destinee smiled, obviously delighted by the prospect. "I think we should go shopping tomorrow afternoon. This is a special occasion, and we need something special to wear to celebrate it."

"Any excuse to buy new clothes. Why don't you come to the office after you get out of school and we'll go shopping."

"Julian, I'm so glad you called," Pandora exclaimed happily the next morning. "I've missed hearing the sound of your voice the last couple of days."

"I've been kind of busy. Listen, I have some disappointing news. Something has come up and I won't be able to keep our date this evening. Tell Destinee I'm sorry."

"I will. She'll understand." Pandora disguised her own disappointment. "I know it must be important or you wouldn't be cancelling at the last minute."

"No, I wouldn't. I have to go out of town."

"When will you be back?"

"I don't know. I'll call you. I have to finish packing, so let me get off this phone."

"Julian, if there is anything I can do, you know I'd be more than happy to do it."

"There is nothing. Look, I'll get back to you, okay?"

Pandora slowly cradled the phone. It must be pretty important. The last thing Julian would ever do is disappoint her or Destinee. He knew how her daughter felt about their getting married. She buzzed Cassandra; maybe she could tell her more.

"Yes, boss lady?"

"Julian has to go out of town and won't be able to keep our date this evening. Do you know anything about this urgent business trip?"

"Drac didn't mention anything to me about it last night when we went out. It must have come up since then."

"I have a bad feeling about this, Cassandra. Julian didn't sound like himself."

"Maybe he was just distracted by the suddenness of the emergency."

"You're probably right. I'm just being paranoid. It's just that I'm so happy. I don't want anything to spoil it."

"I can understand that. Nothing is going to spoil it. If I hear anything at all, I'll be sure to give you a call."

"I'd appreciate it." The feeling that something wasn't quite right continued to plague Pandora for the rest of the morning. She would just have to wait until Julian got back. She trusted him implicitly, and her love for him knew no bounds. This was only a temporary postponement. Very soon she and Julian would be married. She felt secure in that knowledge.

CHAPTER TWENTY-FIVE

"I hope Julian gets back tomorrow," Destinee said hopefully when she arrived at PanCo that afternoon.

"I wouldn't count on anything this weekend, honey. He probably won't be back until the middle of next week."

"We can still go shopping, though, can't we?"

"Yes, we sure can."

Later, at Collette's Boutique, Pandora and Destinee were trying on dresses when they heard familiar voices.

"Hurry up, Miranda. I haven't got all day." It was her sister-in-law, Sasha.

"Aw, Mother," Miranda grumbled.

Pandora and Destinee came out of their dressing rooms at almost the same time.

"Destinee!" exclaimed Miranda. "Girl, what are you doing here? You didn't tell me you were going shopping today. We could have come together, and I wouldn't have had to come with my mother."

"Miranda!" Sasha gasped.

"Sorry." Miranda turned back to Destinee. "That dress has got it going on!"

"Pandora," Sasha said, staring agape at the teal evening dress she was wearing. "I thought black was your color."

"I saw an outfit I know you'll like, Miranda," Destinee said, ignoring her aunt's dig at her mother. "Come on, I'll show you."

"All right."

The two cousins headed for the clothes racks in the front of the boutique.

"So the black widow has finally shed her widow's weeds. Is it for any particular reason?" Sasha asked, her claws on full display.

"I know it taxes your limited intelligence, Sasha, but can you manage to be civil, for once?"

"I am being civil, Pandora. Whether you deserve it remains to be seen."

Pandora rolled her eyes. "Sasha, please."

"I've been reading about your, ah, escapades with Julian Palmer in the local tabloids. It's obviously not in you to be discreet."

"Sasha!"

"Monroe has been keeping me informed about you and your tacky little affair."

Pandora made a move towards her. Sasha backed up. "Since you believe I'm undeserving of your high opinion, I wouldn't push it, if I were you."

"If you lay a finger on me, I'll have you arrested for assault so fast it'll make your head spin."

"Always the threats. Don't you and Monroe know anything else?"

"You'll find out soon enough what else we know."

"What is that supposed to mean?"

Sasha laughed. "You think you want to know, but you really don't. When the time comes, Pandora, you'll be sorry for the way you've treated me." She eyed her up and down. "That is a stunning dress, even on you." Then she turned on her heel and headed in the direction their daughters had gone.

Pandora wondered what that was all about. With Sasha there was no telling. She was a habitually vicious woman. Pandora went back into the dressing room and changed into her own clothes. She decided to buy the teal dress.

Pandora saw Destinee talking animatedly with her cousin while Sasha glared at them, impatiently tapping her foot. Finally, Miranda chose a pants outfit. Sasha went to the register to pay for it. Destinee and Miranda said their good-byes. On their way out the door, Sasha looked at Pandora with a curious mix of contempt and triumph. She couldn't understand what the woman had to feel triumphant about. Knowing Sasha, it wouldn't be long before she found out.

Pandora didn't care about Sasha's little intrigues, but she was beginning to be concerned about Julian's. Her mind kept replaying her last phone conversation with him. There was a coolness in his voice that was definitely new. It was strange, but she wasn't going to worry about it. Julian loved her. She was confident that when he got back, she would get a full explanation.

Julian returned from his trip late the following Wednesday and went to his office Thursday morning. He found his cousin waiting for him when he walked in.

"Well, did you reach any conclusions?" Drac asked Julian.

He sighed heavily and headed for his desk and tossing his briefcase on top of it.

"Your preliminary report was right on target, Drac. I followed up everything in it." Julian opened his briefcase and handed Drac the in-depth compilation of facts. "This should make you happy."

"Jules, man, I…"

"I can't believe you're at a loss for words. It's got to be a first for you, Drac. From the beginning you tried to discourage my involvement with Pandora—the infamous Black Widow of Wall Street. Go ahead and say I told you so."

"I never wanted to see you hurt, Jules. You've been like a brother to me."

"You're the younger brother I wished for when I was growing up. Look, I know you only had my best interest at heart. You have no concept of how much it hurts to find out the woman you love has betrayed you. You'd think I'd have been more alert to the possibility after that fiasco with Vanessa."

"Vanessa Armstrong is nothing compared to Pandora Cooper."

"I agree. I don't see how I could have been fooled so easily, so completely, a second time."

"You let your heart rule your head is all I can think."

Julian rose from his chair and paced back and forth in front of the wall of windows, his hands deep in his pockets, his thoughts in obvious turmoil.

"You know the one who's going to be hurt the most by this, Drac?"

"Her daughter."

"Yes." He let out a soul-weary sigh. "I love that girl as if she were my own child. Dammit, I don't want to hurt her, but there's no way I can avoid it."

Drac put his hand on his cousin's shoulder. "I'm sure it must feel that way. Curse the black widow for putting you through this."

"I can take it, but it's going to destroy Destinee."

"I don't envy you the job of telling her, Jules."

After Drac left, Julian sat down in his chair and propped his elbows on the desk, then covered his face with his hands.

Facing Destinee wasn't the only thing he dreaded. He dreaded seeing Pandora, knowing what she had tried to do to him. He still couldn't—didn't want to—believe she could betray him like this.

When he was checking a questionable instance that pointed to her treachery, he was hoping against hope that he would be proven wrong. She had personally hired Chris Gaines and, according to him, when he felt guilty about leaving his brother in the lurch on several ground-breaking projects and wanted to return to his old job, she bribed him with a substantial inducement to forget about it. As her face floated before his mind's eye, he started remembering little things about her—

like how she laughed when he whispered explicit suggestions in her ear. How delighted she was to visit his mother and grandmother. It couldn't have all been an act. The longing he'd seen in her eyes couldn't be faked. Tears stung his eyelids.

He had to stop this and get on with what he had to do. He stared at the phone for a few minutes before picking it up and dialing a number.

"PanCo. Kiah Williams speaking, how may I help you?"

"May I speak with Ms. Pandora Cooper?"

"I'm sorry sir, she's in a meeting."

"Is Cassandra Jones, her personal assistant, available?"

"Yes, sir. May I ask your name?"

"Julian Palmer."

"If you can hold, I'll connect you to her extension."

"Julian, are you back from your trip?"

"Yes. When will Pandora be finished with her meeting?"

"Another twenty minutes. If it's urgent I can…"

"No, don't interrupt her. Does she have a lunch date or any appointments later this afternoon?"

"No. You have plans for the rest of her day, huh? I'm sure she won't mind being interrupted if it's from you."

"No, I don't want you to do that. Tell her I'll be there at noon to take her to lunch."

"Julian—you sound strange. Is everything all right?"

"Yes. If you could just…"

"All right, I'll give her the message."

"Thanks, Cassandra."

Pandora walked in just as Cassandra hung up. "Any calls?"

"Yes, Julian called."

"You should have buzzed me in the conference room."

"He said not to, and then asked if you were free for lunch and was the rest of your afternoon free."

"I hope you told him it was. Nothing is more important to me than being with him." Pandora's smile faded when she saw her assistant's preoccupied demeanor. "What's wrong?"

"Oh, it's nothing, just—I don't know how to explain it. Something about Julian's voice...It's probably my imagination working overtime."

A feeling of unease washed over Pandora. After she saw Julian she was sure it would go away. She'd spoken to him only once since he had gone on his mysterious trip, and that had been just a few quick words. He had sounded cool and remote. What could be bothering him so much? What could be wrong?

"When you said lunch, I didn't think you meant at your place," Pandora said to Julian as the driver swung the limo into the underground garage of his penthouse. "Not that I mind, you understand."

"I thought we could be more private here."

The uneasiness Pandora had felt earlier returned. Julian's voice sounded cold, detached, and almost ominous. When they stepped into the elevator and she got a good look at his face, she saw that it was stripped of any telling emotion. His trip must not have gone well.

"Julian, is anything wrong? Did things not turn out the way you expected them to?" she asked as he stuck the card into the door lock of the penthouse.

"No, they didn't."

"I'm sorry," she said, her voice filled with sympathy.

"Are you?" he said, pushing the door open and waving for her to precede him inside.

"Julian." She reached out to him. He moved away.

"Let's go into the living room," he said.

Pandora grimaced. He sounded so cold. She walked over to him and slipped her arms around his neck. She heard him groan. He needed to be loved, that had to be what was wrong. She kissed his neck, then his lips. She felt his body shudder with need and started unbuttoning his shirt. When her fingers moved over his bare skin, she heard his sharp intake of breath.

"Julian, baby, you're so tense. Let me love your disappointment away."

"Yes, I want that so bad," he said in a voice spiked with desire.

As if he were on a mission, Julian hurriedly undressed himself and then Pandora. When she stood naked before him, he murmured her name again and again, then pulled her into his arms.

"Let me love you, Julian," she whispered in his ear and then kissed it.

"God, Pandora!" he groaned, backing her against the wall. He raised her legs around his hips and slid inside her. Again and again he stroked, withdrew, stroked, withdrew, each time building the pleasure a little higher. When he felt her body shudder, he buried his throbbing flesh deep, bringing them both to a quick climax. But it wasn't nearly enough. He had to have more.

"Pan, Pan," he murmured over and over, then picked her up and carried her into his bedroom.

"Julian, baby, what is it?" she rasped when she could catch her breath.

"Don't talk," he growled, silencing her with his lips.

"You are so beautiful, Pan." This time he aroused her slowly, starting with mind altering kisses on her throat; moving down to her breasts, he took a nipple into his mouth and sucked strongly, urging Pandora on to a fever pitch. He loved seeing her respond to his touch. He forced back the thought of her treachery and gave himself up to the passion of the moment.

"Julian," she said when her breathing had slowed to normal. "Baby, what is it?" she asked, trailing her fingers down the side of his sweat-dampened face. He stiffened and moved away from her.

"I didn't intend for this to happen," he groaned. "When I'm near you, every logical thought flies out of my head."

Pandora smiled. "That's the way it's supposed to be between two people who love each other as much as we do, my love."

"Don't say another word. Don't make this any harder than it already is."

"What? I don't understand."

He glared angrily at her. "You understand me, all right."

"I won't *understand* anything until you tell me what you're talking about." She sat up on the bed and reached out to touch him. He jerked his body away from her. "Julian, please. Tell me what's wrong?"

He sprang off the bed and strode over to the closet. He yanked a robe off its hanger and put it on.

Fear wedged the words she wanted to say in Pandora's throat. She drew the sheet up over her breasts and waited.

Julian stood at the foot of the bed, his jaws flexing, his eyes intense. "I don't know where or how to begin. I'm so angry with you...I thought you were the one woman in the world besides the women in my family that I could love and trust, but obviously I was wrong. Not since Vanessa have I ever come so close to falling in love."

"Vanessa is the woman you almost married, isn't she?"

"Yes, she's the woman who betrayed me in a way no woman should ever betray a man. She used her beauty, her body and her intelligence to destroy me. And she almost succeeded. Does the scenario sound familiar?"

"Why are you putting me in the same category with her?" Pandora demanded.

"You can drop your little pretense, Pandora. I know all about it," he roared.

Pandora flinched. "About what? I don't know what you're talking about."

"You're an even better actress than Vanessa. Maybe you should take your act to the Broadway stage."

"Act? Will you stop with the sarcasm and tell me what it is you think I've done, for God's sake!"

"I don't think it; I know it." He spat the words out like a bitter pit. "You betrayed me in a way I'll never be able to forgive. Is being the black widow more important to you than being an honest, loving and compassionate woman?"

"What are you talking about?" she shouted, nearing her wits' end.

"The game is over, baby."

"Game? What game? Julian!"

"It was Palmer and Associates you wanted all along, wasn't it? I'm just another man to grind into the dirt for whatever sick, twisted revenge that drives you. You couldn't buy us out or take us over, so you resorted to other means, playing the innocent put-upon widow, the vulnerable abused woman, the brave, courageous mother. You and your daughter against the world. Oh, I fell for it hook, line and sinker, didn't I? But you miscalculated, didn't you, baby? You didn't manage to get me to the altar before I found out what you were up to."

Pandora shot off the bed, dragging the sheet with her.

"You think I've done something dishonest? That I've betrayed you? Our love? How could you make love to me if this is the way you feel?"

"Because God help me, I still love you in spite of your treachery," he cried. "And you're after all a very beautiful woman and you do have an extremely sexy body."

"What you're saying is you love my body, but despise my mind?"

"No more than you've despised me and wanted my body and my company. I thought you were kidding about merging our two companies and renaming it, but you were dead serious about that, weren't you?"

"I don't believe you're saying these things to me." Her voice cracked. "Julian, I love you."

"You only loved the sense of triumph deceiving me gave you and for whatever sexual gratification you craved. You didn't have to carry your campaign quite this far. Is the reason you did because you were curious to know what it would feel like for me to be your besotted lover?" He laughed bitterly. "I was a fool. I ignored all the warning signs not to trust you, not to become involved with the formidable Black Widow of Wall Street. It seems I had to learn my lesson the hard way."

"I'm still in the dark about what it is I'm supposed to have done." A sick feeling spread through Pandora's insides as she waited for him to answer. Her body still tingled from his lovemaking. None of this was making any sense to her.

"I know everything, Pandora. I know that you and Monroe Cooper are in league to ruin me."

"Monroe! What does he have to do with this?"

"Everything, apparently." He slashed his hand in the air. "Oh, come off it, Pandora. Are you and he lovers? Did the two of you plan this from the beginning? Was all that animosity you directed at him all a pretense for my benefit? You don't need to answer, I think I already know."

"If you think that, then you don't know me at all, Julian."

"Is it a coincidence that you hired Chris Gaines away from Gaines Financial to head up Star Pacific? It's the reason you didn't want me to come with you to Los Angeles, isn't it? Is it a coincidence that Cedrick Temple resigned his position to move to Chicago to work at Mid-Northern, a company that you own in partnership with Monroe Cooper? And is it also a coincidence that you lured Colin Whitley away from Richards Investments, which I happen to own, to come work for PanCo?"

"Colin? We knew Richards was a subsidiary of Palmers, but Julian, he told us that he just wanted to make a change. It really was a coincidence that he came to us."

"So you're saying it's a coincidence that you hired him? You can drop the innocent act, Pandora. I'm not buying it. There's more. When I went out of town on business, it was to find out the truth. God, I wanted it to be some kind of horrific mistake. But there's no mistake, huh, sweetheart? You're nothing but a deceitful, conniving bitch. But I'm the fool. I believed you loved me." His voice became harsher. "Isn't that the joke of the century? The only person you love is yourself."

"How can you believe that about me?"

"You haven't denied any of what I've said because you can't. It's all true. There are probably a lot more things you've done that I just haven't found out about, yet."

Pandora slapped his face with all her strength. "You despicable bastard, you want me to deny it, but would it do any good if I did? You obviously think I'm capable of plotting to destroy someone I love." Tears coursed down her face. She quickly wiped them away and started to walk past him out of the bedroom. He advanced toward her. She backed away.

"Don't touch me! I don't ever want you near me again. Do you understand, Julian? Let me by so I can dress and then get the hell out of here."

He opened his mouth to say something, but hesitated, then said. "You're acting like the wounded party when you did all the wounding," he said, rubbing his cheek.

"Good-bye, Julian."

"Is that all you're going to say?"

"What do you want me to say? Whatever I say won't change anything. What we had is gone—no, we never had anything to begin with. It was all a figment of my deluded, love-starved imagination." She let out a weary sigh. "You know what hurts the most? How my daughter is going to take this. She loves you so much. She wanted us to be a family, the kind of family she's always dreamed about. Now I have to tell her it's not going to happen. God, how I hate you for that."

Pandora glared at him one last time before dropping the sheet and marching out of the room. She gathered up her clothes and purse from the living room floor and stalked into the guest bathroom. When she opened the door minutes later, Julian was standing there, waiting.

"I'll talk to Destinee and explain."

"Explain what? That the man she thinks of as a father is not the man she thought him to be?"

"Pandora."

"You can come to the house this evening. I'm only agreeing because…"

"I know the reason. I'll be there around six-thirty."

"After that you stay the hell away from us. We don't need you. Oh, God, when I think..." She gritted her teeth.

"I...never mind. It's over."

"Let me call my chauffeur to take you back to your office."

"Don't bother. I'll call a taxi on my cell phone when I get in the elevator."

When Julian saw her head for the door, he had an insane urge to stop her from leaving, to tell her that what just happened between them wasn't because of any misplaced revenge. But his pride and the deep hurt he felt at her betrayal stayed his feet and silenced his tongue. Instead, he watched her go and, despite what he had learned about her, he found that he still desired her, still wanted to hold her, make love to her. Did that make him some kind of masochist? His pain wasn't physical, but it was no less painful because it was emotional.

Pandora was right, it was over between them. Now the only thing left was to break the news to Destinee. He would rather die than hurt her like that, but her mother had left him no choice. There was no way he and Pandora could ever...

"Why did you betray me, dammit? Why?" he growled. He snatched his clothes up from the floor, stalked into his bedroom and slammed the door.

CHAPTER TWENTY-SIX

Pandora was in a state of shock by the time she arrived back at PanCo. She felt numb, disoriented, bruised, destroyed. She had been so sure that Julian really loved her. His betrayal was incomprehensible; her pain indescribable.

Pandora walked numbly past Cassandra's desk into her own office and shut the door without uttering a single word. Seconds later she heard a knock at the door.

Cassandra eased the door open. "Can I come in?"

"Yes, why not?"

"I would have thought that you and Julian—what's wrong? You look like hell."

"Believe me, I feel a lot worse than I look."

Concerned, Cassandra asked, "Are you sick or something?"

"Oh, Cassandra." Pandora burst into tears.

Cassandra pulled her into her arms and let her cry. "What is it?"

"It's over between Julian and me," she sobbed.

"It can't be. You guys were all set to get married. I've never seen anyone so much in love as you are with that man. I don't understand."

"Neither do I. For some insane reason, Julian believes I've betrayed him. That it was my intention all along to use his feelings for me to destroy him. The things he said..."

Cassandra reached for a tissue and blotted Pandora's face.

"Tell me about it."

Pandora had regained control by the time she finished filling Cassandra in on the details.

"On the surface, there are things that point to your being guilty of what he's accused you of. But I know, and you know, it's not true." A horrible look came into Cassandra's eyes. "Oh, God. Drac is somehow involved in this. I just know it."

"What are you saying?"

"When we first met, he asked me so many questions about you and about PanCo. I thought it was just out of simple curiosity, but it was more than that, much more. I see it all now. He was using me to get the lowdown on you and this company. How could I have been so stupid? A man like him going for a girl like me."

"That might not be the way it was. Drac Palmer isn't one of my favorite people, but I'm sure he genuinely cares for you and he would never..."

"Turn on me the way Julian did on you? Given his penchant for overanalyzing everything and everybody, not to mention his overprotective tendencies, I'm sure Drac is involved in this in some way, and I'm never going to forgive him for it." Cassandra returned her attention to her friend and employer. "You shouldn't have come back to the office, Pandora. Why don't you go on home? I'll take care of things here."

"You're right. I should go home. I do need time to prepare myself," she said, sniffling. "Julian is coming over this evening to break the news to Destinee. And I know I'm going to need every ounce of strength I can muster to get through that."

Inside she was dying a little bit at a time. She wanted to rail against the injustice of it all. She still had her daughter. Julian was right about one thing: It was she and her child against the world. She didn't need, or want, anyone else in it. If she had Destinee she had everything she needed to survive this crushing pain that was tearing her apart.

A feeling of dread squeezed Pandora's heart like a vise when she heard the doorbell. It was Julian. Watching her daughter's face light up when she opened the door made Pandora want to cry. In a few minutes her child's happiness would be destroyed the same way hers had been earlier that day.

She saw a deep sadness in Julian's eyes when he looked at Destinee. Pandora felt a flicker of satisfaction. Julian was beginning to know the pain she felt at his betrayal of her trust. He was the only man she had ever unconditionally given it to, and he would be the last.

"You came to ask Mama a very important question, right, Julian?"

"Destinee, I..."

"If you want to be alone with her, I can go upstairs."

"No, stay. You know how much you've come to mean to me, don't you, sweetheart?"

Destinee smiled. "Of course I do. You mean just as much to me. I've been looking forward to the special dinner you promised us. We bought new dresses for the occasion. I can hardly wait for you to become my father, Julian. I've dreamed about it for a long time. Talaya's mom will be my aunt, and Talaya my cousin. But most important of all, you and me and Mama will be a family."

Julian's jaw clenched. "Let's sit down so we can talk."

"You look funny. Are you sick or something?" She sat down next to him on the couch.

"No, I'm not sick, it's just that..."

"Just what?"

"I hate to have to tell you this, but your mother and I won't be getting married after all."

Destinee's face looked as if a glass of ice water had been thrown into it. Her shocked expression was heartbreaking to see. "Not getting married! Why? Did I do or say something to make you change your mind?"

"No, honey, you didn't do anything," Pandora quickly reassured her. "The relationship between Julian and me just isn't going to work out."

"But why? I know you love him, Mama." Tears drizzled down Destinee's cheeks, and she gave Julian a desperate look. "Can't you do something, Julian? I want you for my father. I need you to be my father."

"Destinee, I wanted that, too. More than anything."

"But not enough to change your mind about marrying my mother?" Her shoulders shook with the force of her sobs.

Seeing the heartbreak in her daughter's eyes finished tearing Pandora's heart to shreds. She glared at the object of their misery.

He tried to take Destinee in his arms and comfort her. She sprang off the couch, tears gushing down her face.

"I don't understand any of this. Just last week we were all so happy." She turned to Pandora. "Was the reason Julian went away your fault? He was all set to ask you to marry him before he left, and now he's changed his mind."

Pandora reached for her daughter. "Honey, I…"

"Stay away from me, both of you. I can't deal with this." She fled up the stairs.

"I think you'd better go, Julian."

"Maybe I should go up and try to…"

"Do what? You've already hurt my baby more than her natural father ever had, more than anyone else has or ever could. You can blame me, but it won't change what you've done to Destinee."

"I know that, Pandora, and I'm sorry."

"You're sorry! Please, leave my house, Julian. Just get out."

He glanced up the stairs, a pained expression on his face. Then he turned and quietly left.

Pandora slowly ascended the stairs and headed for her daughter's room. She found Destinee sprawled across the bed, crying her eyes out.

"Destinee."

"Go away," she sobbed. "I don't want to talk to you."

"Honey, I'm sorry that we had to hurt you like this."

"What happened? We were so happy, Mama."

"I know we were. Julian thinks I betrayed him, but it's not true. Things have been happening—and he blames me for them. But Destinee, I would never do anything to hurt him."

"Then why does he think you did?"

"I don't know, but I intend to get to the bottom of this."

Pandora drew her daughter into her arms. "You know how much I love you, don't you, honey? You're all I've got. You are my life, my darling girl." She brushed the hair back from Destinee's tear-ravaged face. "I don't know what I would do if I didn't have you."

"Do you think Julian will change his mind once he knows the truth?"

"It won't matter if he does. It would never work. I can't trust him."

Destinee cried all the harder. Pandora sat rocking her child until she calmed down.

"We'll survive this, honey. You'll see."

Julian drove back to his penthouse and went straight to the living room and plopped into the easy chair in front of the fireplace. All his hopes and dreams had turned to ashes. The woman he loved obviously never felt the way he thought she did about him. The evidence was indisputable. He got up and began pacing before the fireplace. At the moment, he felt like committing murder. There was one other person he had to deal with—no, make that two. Monroe and Roscoe were as thick as thieves and were probably in on it together.

Monroe Cooper had played him like a fine instrument, starting with his insistence that Julian accept the invitation to the summer party he and his sister had given. The pretense of animosity between Monroe and Pandora was what really ripped his guts to ribbons.

It all couldn't have been staged. The lovemaking had been real. Her response to him had been very real, not at all faked. Destinee's concern for her mother and what she revealed about the relationship between her parents had been the truth. Pandora's not wanting to talk about her life with her husband was understandable.

He was driving himself crazy thinking about this. He closed his eyes and he could see the look on Destinee's face when he had told her he wasn't going to be her father. It broke his heart. He had never felt so devastated in his life. Somebody was going to pay for making him hurt her. Monroe and Pandora were about to find out there was a price for smashing another person's hopes and dreams.

The fires of rage burned hotly within Julian. He had stoked the fires of passion within Pandora into scorching flames of ecstasy. But by the time he was through with her, Pandora would experience the heat from a different kind of fire. She would feel the fires of hell. This was a vow he intended to keep.

The next morning Julian strode past Monroe's secretary's desk.

"Do you have an appointment, sir?" She asked, springing to her feet. "You just can't barge in here and..."

Julian opened the door to Monroe's office, then closed it in the secretary's face, effectively cutting off the rest of her words and thwarting her indignation at being so blatantly bypassed.

Monroe looked up from the papers he was poring over.

"Palmer. What do you want? Have you ever heard of making an appointment?"

"I don't need an appointment to see scum like you."

"Now wait a minute."

"I just want to warn you that you made a huge mistake when you messed with me, Cooper. A mistake I intend to make you pay for in spades. I want you to worry about when and how I will exact my revenge. By the time I'm through with you, you'll wish you had never heard the name Julian Palmer." With that, he strode out the door.

"You'd better hurry or you'll be late for school, Destinee," Rachel said Monday morning.

Destinee cast a pleading look at her mother. "Do I have to go?"

"Yes, you do, young lady. I know it's hard, but you have to get on with your life. I didn't insist Friday because you were too upset."

Destinee's shoulders slumped as she left the table.

"I hate seeing her like that," Rachel said, nodding her head sadly.

"So do I, Rachel. But it can't be helped. In time she'll get over it."

"And will you get over it?"

"Rachel."

"I could kill Julian Palmer for hurting you both like this."

"I don't want to talk about it, okay? I need to be getting to the office."

"You haven't eaten your breakfast."

"I'm not hungry."

"You're leaving kind of early, aren't you?"

"Work is the best healer. And believe me, I have plenty of that waiting for me at the office."

"I don't want you to go back to being a workaholic. You've come so far."

"Don't worry about me, Rachel. I'll survive." She took a sip of her tea.

"But I do worry, Pandora. I've come to think of you more as a daughter than an employer."

Pandora smiled. "I'll be fine, really."

When Pandora entered the office, Cassandra was sitting at her desk crying.

"Cassandra, what's the matter? Are you sick?"

"No. Drac confirmed what I've halfway suspected all along."

Pandora put a hand on her arm. "What did he tell you?"

"That when we first started talking, he only did it because he wanted to gather all the information he could about you and PanCo to help his cousin figure out a way to gain control of your company."

"That shouldn't have shocked you. We knew Palmer and Associates' reputation for takeovers. Remember how we laughed about it because PanCo's track record came close to rivaling Palmer and Associates and we hadn't been in business as long."

"Drac said I came to mean more to him than just a source of information. But how can I believe him? He's admitted compiling a report concerning you and PanCo, then handing it over to Julian. He hates you more than ever for hurting his cousin. I tried to convince him that he was all wrong about you."

"But he didn't believe you. I don't understand any of this. It's as though somebody has deliberately set me up. And that someone has got to be Monroe. It has to be him and Roscoe Phillips who are behind this."

"Probably, but how are you going to prove it?"

"I don't know, but there has to be a way. They must have made mistakes somewhere along the line."

"Monroe is a master of deception. You can bet he's covered his butt."

"Getting back to you and Drac."

"He's mangled my trust and faith in him, Pandora. I don't know if I want to be bothered with him and his attitude."

"But you love him, Cassandra."

"You love Julian."

Yes, she did. "We'd better try to get some work done."

CHAPTER TWENTY-SEVEN

"Julian, you've been working night and day. We hardly ever see you anymore," Selena said from the doorway of her brother's office.

"What are you doing here, Selena?"

"I'm here because I'm worried about my big brother."

"He's doing just fine."

"No, he isn't. You still haven't told me what happened between you and Pandora."

"I really don't want to get into it with you, all right?"

"I've tried to contact Pandora, but she won't take any of my calls. What did you do to her? Destinee hasn't been to our house in weeks. Talaya says she won't even talk to her at school anymore."

"I'm sorry to hear that. I was hoping..."

"What?"

"I can't talk about it, Selena."

"No, you're just working yourself into the ground for the hell of it, right? Come on, Julian."

He glanced at his watch. "I have a meeting scheduled to begin in fifteen minutes."

"So you're giving me the boot. You need to talk to somebody, Julian. When you're ready..."

He gave her a half smile. "I know."

Julian was about to leave his office and go into the conference room when the phone rang. He picked it up.

"What is it, Paula?" He clenched his jaw. "Send her in."

Destinee entered his office.

"What are you doing here? You should be in school."

"I had to see you, Julian, and convince you that Mama didn't do what you accused her of. She loves you. Don't you understand?"

"Destinee, I…I understand, but do you? I don't want to say anything against your mother because she is your mother and I know you love her. Sometimes the people we love do things—how do I say this?"

"Julian, she didn't betray you. Was it Uncle Monroe who told you that? He hates my mother and would say or do anything to hurt her. Or was it Aunt Sasha?"

"I'm not taking your uncle's or your aunt's word for anything. Listen, why don't I have my chauffeur drive you home?"

"What kind of proof do you have?" Destinee persisted.

"You know the business trip I went on. It had to do with what your mother did on her trip to Los Angeles. I don't want to get into this with you."

"Well, I want to get into it with you. It's important. We were going to be a family, Julian," she sobbed.

He pulled Destinee into his arms. "I know, sweetheart." God, this was hard. He didn't know how he was going to get through it without hurting this beautiful girl any more than she already had been.

"Your mother doesn't want me to see you or come visit and I have to respect that."

"You won't even…"

"No, Destinee, I can't. I'm sorry."

"When I begged her to let me come see you, she said no, it wouldn't do any good because you wouldn't change your mind. She was right. I should have listened." Destinee backed out of his arms.

"Don't leave like this, Desi."

"Don't call me that. Don't ever call me that again. I hate you, Julian, for hurting me and my mother."

"Destinee…"

Her chin went up. "We'll be all right." When she got to the door, she turned and said. "Good-bye."

When the door closed, Julian dropped his head. *Oh, God, Pandora. Why did you destroy our future together?*

Selena marched through the doors of Pandora's office suite.

"Is she in, Cassandra?" Selena asked.

"She is, but..."

"She doesn't want to talk to anyone related to Julian, right?"

"I'm sorry, Selena."

"You know why they broke up, don't you?"

"I—yes, but I can't discuss it with you. If you want to find out anything, you have to ask either Pandora or Julian."

"What about you and Drac? Why has he been moping around lately? Don't tell me you're on the outs, too? Oh, Cassandra."

"Cassandra, I need the report on—Selena!" Pandora exclaimed from her office doorway.

Selena walked toward her. "Girl, we need to talk."

"It won't do any good. My relationship with your brother is over."

"Does that also include our friendship?"

"All right, come into my office. Cassandra, don't forget to get me the file on Security International so Colin and I can discuss what to do about them."

Pandora closed the door. "Before you start, Selena, I'm sorry for not taking your calls. It's just that I didn't want to talk about what happened between Julian and me."

"Exactly what did happen between you?"

Pandora gave her an edited version.

"He was hurt pretty badly by Vanessa. I can see how he would go off like that if he thought you had betrayed him."

"He doesn't just think it. There is proof. Trumped up proof, true enough, but proof nonetheless."

"In time he'll recognize it for the lie it really is and apologize."

"Don't bank on it, Selena. Even if he does come to his senses, I could never trust him again."

"You love him, Pandora. Can't you guys make up?"

"I do love him despite how he's hurt me. Love isn't something you can turn off and on like a light switch. Or because you want to."

"But can you forgive him?"

"I don't think so, Selena."

"The other reason I wanted to talk to you is Destinee."

"She's taking it pretty hard. It breaks my heart to see her so unhappy, but there is nothing I can do."

"You could let her come visit us."

"I haven't forbidden her to do that."

"Talaya said she won't even talk to her at school anymore. And after school she avoids her."

"I'll talk to her, but I won't make any promises. She's very hurt, Selena."

"I wish there was something I could do."

"So do I, but there isn't."

"Pandora, Rachel is on the phone. She says it's urgent," Cassandra told her employer.

"Rachel, what's wrong? Is it Destinee?"

"The school called. Evidently she cut her afternoon classes. Since she didn't come home, I don't know where she could be. She has her cell phone, but she hasn't called."

Pandora's heart lurched. "Stay by the phone in case she does call. I'll see if I can find her."

She put the receiver down. "Oh, God, don't let anything happen to my baby." *Maybe she went to see Julian; that has to be where she had gone.*

She started to call Julian—no, she decided to go there.

Fifteen minutes later, Pandora entered Palmer and Associates. The secretary was away from her desk, so she went to Julian's private office door and knocked.

"Come in, Paula. I have...Pandora! Why are you here?"

"Not to beg you to forgive me my alleged sins and take me back. Destinee's school called. She evidently cut her afternoon classes. I thought she might come here."

"She was here at noon. You say she didn't return to school and she isn't at home?"

"No. Rachel called. How did she seem to you?" Pandora asked, growing more agitated by the minute.

"She was very upset about our breakup, naturally."

"What did you say to her?"

"I told her I was sorry, but that we weren't going to get back together."

"Oh, my God." Tears trickled down Pandora's cheeks.

Julian's heart turned over at the sight of her tears, and he pulled her into his arms.

Oh, how she hungered for his touch, reassurance of his love, but knew it wasn't going to happen. She moved out of his embrace.

"Where could she be?" she cried.

"I have an idea."

Pandora and Julian reached Central Park in minutes. They found Destinee feeding the ducks at the pond.

"Destinee," Pandora called to her. "Honey, are you all right?"

She looked dully at her mother. When she saw Julian, her eyes lit up, then they dimmed and she returned her attention to the ducks.

Julian stepped forward. "Destinee."

"Are you and Mama..."

"No we aren't, but that doesn't matter. You are important to both of us. Just because we aren't going to be married doesn't mean that I'll stop caring about you. You'll always be special to me."

"My mother never will be, though, right?"

"Destinee, what Julian is trying to say is..."

"Oh, I understand what he is saying, all right. He really never loved us."

"That's not true, Desi."

Destinee glared at Julian. "Don't ever call me that again." She shifted her attention to her mother. "I know you came to get me, Mama. Can we go now?"

"I wish to God I had never hurt you, Destinee. Please believe that." Julian reached out to her, but she darted past him.

"We'll get a taxi home, Julian. You don't have to worry about us anymore. Neither one of us will ever bother you again. I promise."

"Pandora."

"Good-bye, Julian. And thanks for helping me find my daughter," she said, slipping her arm around her daughter's shoulder as they walked away.

With a heavy heart, Julian watched them go. His pain had multiplied ten-fold with this encounter. His jaw tensed. Someone was going to pay for what he was feeling right now. He intended to see that they paid big-time.

A few days later a messenger delivered an envelope to Pandora at home. After signing for the envelope, she closed the door and tore it open. She was being summoned to attend an urgent meeting of the board at Security International at twelve o'clock today. She frowned. She'd been having problems with that company lately. It was one of the ones that her husband had left jointly to her, Destinee and Monroe. She had tried to convince Monroe to let her buy out his shares, but he had refused. According to Colin's report, the company was in deep financial trouble.

Because Lyman had intended it to eventually go to Destinee, Pandora felt she should give it her full attention.

Pandora was shocked to see Drac at the meeting. He soon made it clear as to why he was there.

"As of two days ago, Palmer and Associates owns fifty-one percent of Security International. We demand an accounting from Monroe Cooper, the former controlling shareholder and still presiding CEO of the company. If he can't provide one, we are demanding that he tender his resignation."

"I refuse. Tell Palmer he can't—you can't do that," Monroe sputtered, scowling indignantly at Drac.

"We can, and we are. Effective as of today your refusal gives us no other option but to remove you from the position of CEO of this company. If you'd like to take the matter to a higher authority, feel free to do so."

"You're referring to Julian Palmer, aren't you? I didn't know the Palmers were associated with TelCorp or I would never have sold them the shares or signed a contract with them. The terms were provisional."

"If dissatisfied with your work performance per the agreement. As TelCorp is now a subsidiary of Palmer and Associates, we reserve the right to appoint a CEO of our choice. We are hereby exercising that right, Mr. Cooper," Drac matter-of-factly asserted.

Without uttering another word, Monroe stalked angrily from the room.

Drac cleared his throat. "The twenty-nine percent in trust for Destinee Cooper has been increased to controlling-shareholder status. Until her twenty-fifth birthday, Julian plans to personally supervise the handling of the trusteeship—if it is agreeable to her mother."

Pandora was floored.

"Do you have any objection, Ms. Cooper?" Drac asked.

"I—no, I'm sure Julian will handle it to the best of his ability. Answer me one question. Why did he send you to do his dirty work?"

"He felt he couldn't trust himself around you and your associate, Monroe Cooper. He doesn't want to go to jail for murder."

"So he's left us to your tender mercies. You are every bit as bloodthirsty as your name implies, aren't you, Dracula Palmer? Julian knows I'd never do anything to hurt my child or jeopardize her future." On that note, Pandora walked out of the conference room.

As the taxi drove her back to the office, Pandora knew this was just the tip of the proverbial iceberg in Julian's vendetta against her and Monroe.

"I knew Julian Palmer could be ruthless, but not like this!" Cassandra exclaimed when the third summons in just a few weeks arrived at PanCo.

Pandora was weary of it all. "I wish there was something I could do to convince him that I never betrayed him. Each of the companies he's acquired the proxies for and gained control of are connected in one way or another to Monroe because of Destinee's inheritance. Doesn't he realize that they are the only connections between Monroe and me?"

"Oh, I think he does."

"He is like a tenacious terrier after a bone, and I'm his dinner."

"He'll get tired of this game and move on to something more challenging."

"I don't think so. He's out for blood. Mine."

"It's really getting to you, isn't it?" Cassandra asked worriedly. "You've lost weight, Pandora. Can't you see that working sixty-hour weeks is killing you?"

"It's the only way I can forget about my personal problems."

"You can't forget that you love Julian Palmer, no matter how many hours you work."

"I know you're right."

"Why don't you take a few days off, and you and Destinee go away somewhere?"

Pandora brightened. "I know why I hired you. How about your relationship with Drac?"

"There is no relationship. I gave him back his ring."

"Cassandra. It's just another thing for him to hate me for."

"I don't think he really hates you. He's just overprotective of his cousin."

"If you know that, then why did you give him back the ring?"

"Drac knows what he has to do to change my mind."

Pandora wished her own situation was as easy to fix. A simple ultimatum wasn't going to do it for her and Julian. Not even a million of them would be enough.

An hour later, just as Pandora came out of her office to speak to Cassandra, a uniformed man knocked on the door.

"Are you Pandora Cooper?" he asked.

"Yes." *Oh, no, not another one of Julian's summonses,* she groaned.

"This is for you," he said, handing her a legal document.

"What is this?"

"You are hereby ordered to appear in family court on the date indicated."

"Family court?" Pandora felt faint when she read the document. Custody! Monroe was suing her for custody of Destinee! Her head started spinning, then everything went black.

"Pandora! Are you all right?" Cassandra asked anxiously.

Pandora opened her eyes. Why was she on the floor with her head cradled in Cassandra's lap?

"What happened?" she asked groggily.

"You fainted."

Suddenly, it all came back to Pandora in a rush. The subpoena! "Monroe and Sasha are trying to take Destinee away from me."

"They can't do that. You're an exemplary mother."

Pandora rose slowly to her feet. Walking on unsteady legs, she made it to a chair and collapsed into it.

"Give me the subpoena, Cassandra."

Pandora re-read the document. "Monroe is suing for custody on the grounds that I'm a bad influence on my teenage daughter. He and Sasha must be on drugs or something. There is no way in hell he can prove something like, that because I am a good mother."

"He knows that."

"He must not if he's going through with this."

"You don't have a thing to worry about. No judge in his right mind is going to favor awarding custody of Destinee to a man like him and his harpy sister-in-law over you."

Pandora appreciated her friend's fierce loyalty. "You're right, Cassandra. He's bitter, and I'm the scapegoat for his having been ousted from his position at Security International. He has a nerve trying to blame me after what he's done."

"Let me call your attorney. Surely, she can sort this out for you."

"I don't know what I would do without you."

"You would put Kiah in my place."

"Not a chance."

Judith Sanders examined the subpoena Pandora handed her the next afternoon.

"I received a letter from the court this morning. Monroe and Sasha have hired Colton Foster to represent them."

"But they can't possibly have a case."

"Monroe must think he does to have hired someone like Colton Foster. I've already talked to the man. He assures me that the evidence he has is solid. We'll just have to see about that. In the meantime, don't worry. I'll let you know in a few days what kind of case they have."

Pandora couldn't concentrate on anything, and left the running of PanCo to Cassandra and Colin Whitley for the next week. She hadn't been feeling well. She knew it was because of the stress she had been under. The last thing she needed was Monroe trying to take her daughter away from her now.

"Mama, what's wrong?" Destinee asked at dinner. "You've lost so much weight it scares me. You're not going to die like Daddy did, are you?"

"Of course not, honey. I'm just going through something heavy at the office."

"It's really because of Julian you've lost your appetite, isn't it? Maybe I should have a talk with him."

"No! Don't do that."

"But, Mama, he said he still cared about us."

"I said no. We don't need Julian. I'll get over him in time."

Destinee didn't look convinced, but didn't, to Pandora's relief, relief, say anything more. If what she was beginning to suspect was true, she would never get over Julian Palmer. He had wanted a baby so badly and now...They were going to be so happy once. There was no hope of that ever happening, thanks to Monroe and Roscoe.

Monroe hated her for choosing his brother over him. She didn't really understand why Sasha hated her so much. Roscoe Phillips, she knew, would do anything he could to bring her to her knees.

"I'll answer it, honey," Pandora said to Destinee when the phone rang.

"Just the person I wanted to talk to."

"What do you want, Monroe?" she asked, her voice dripping with contempt.

"My niece, of course. Since you're an unfit mother, it shouldn't be a problem."

"You wish. You haven't got a prayer of winning."

"Oh, but I do."

"What do mean?"

"Several articles written about you and Julian Palmer's sordid little affair have appeared in the tabloids."

"If that's all the evidence you have, you don't have a leg to stand on."

"Oh, it's not all, I can assure you. Remember the night you spent at Palmers penthouse and didn't get home until after nine the next morning? Oh, and all the time you spent in Palmer's hotel suite when you were supposed to be attending to business in Rome."

"You son of..."

"Tsk, tsk, such language. I've had you followed, and there are some pretty explicit pictures I think a judge would be very interested in seeing. According to my niece, Miranda, you and Julian Palmer spent a long intimate weekend at his hideaway in the Catskills. The man I had following you lost you or I would have some, shall we say, rather erotic pictures to show the judge. And on top of that, you left Destinee in the care of strangers."

"Selena Andrews is hardly a stranger, Monroe."

"You really should have left her with Sasha instead of your lover's sister. It can be construed as a form of neglect. According to what my attorney tells me, courts take a very dim view of that kind of behavior by a mother."

"You can't do this."

"We'll see. You have a good night's sleep now. In a couple of weeks I'll have custody of your daughter. Good night, Pandora."

"Monroe!" She heard the hum of the dial tone in her ear.

"Mama, what was that about?"

"Business, honey. Your uncle was just being his usual obnoxious self, that's all."

"You sure? I heard you mention Talaya's mother's name. It sounded like more than just business to me."

"It's not. Believe me and stop worrying, okay?" She reassured her daughter. But could she reassure herself that what Monroe was prepared to do would fail? It had to fail. She couldn't survive losing Destinee. She had already lost Julian, but she had a part of Julian growing inside her.

CHAPTER TWENTY-EIGHT

"Julian, I've been trying to get your attention for the past five minutes."

"What did you say, Drac?"

"The black widow and Colin Whitley. Will you stop staring at her like that? You've got to forget about her, man."

"Easier said than done. I invested my heart and soul into loving that woman."

"I can relate to that."

"How do things stand between you and Cassandra?"

"She barely speaks to me and..."

Julian's mind drifted away from the rest of what his cousin was saying. He watched Pandora conduct business over lunch. She looked too thin. He wondered if she was all right. It was the first time he had seen her since that scene in the park when he had hurt Destinee again. He noticed that she had gone back to wearing stark black. A twinge of guilt jabbed his heart sharply.

"You can't still feel anything for the woman after what she's done!"

"Do you feel anything for Cassandra?"

"Of course I do, but that's different."

"Is it?" Julian returned his attention to Pandora. She was getting up to leave. He wondered if she had seen him when he and Drac walked in.

Just then Vanessa Armstrong entered the restaurant. Drac saw her first.

"Oh, no!"

"What is it?" Julian asked.

"You don't want to know who just walked in and is headed for our table."

Julian grimaced when he saw Vanessa.

"What does she want?"

"It's certainly not me she has her sights set on."

"She can't have them on me, either. I told her as much when I saw her weeks ago at the Club Paradise. If she didn't get the message then, her ego must be made of granite."

"Julian," Vanessa called to him in a low, sexy voice. "May I join you and Drac?" Not waiting for an answer or an invitation, she slid into a chair directly in front of Julian. Vanessa smiled at Drac. "How have you been?"

Drac squirmed uncomfortably. "Look, Vanessa, I don't think you should..."

"Relax, Drac. Can you go to the men's room or something? I would like to speak to Julian alone for a few minutes."

"We have nothing to talk about that Drac can't hear, Vanessa. Now, if you would please just go."

"I'm delighted to know that you and Pandora haven't made up." She flashed Julian an inviting smile. "What you need is a little TLC."

"But never from you."

"Now, don't be like that, Jules." She lowered her eyelids and widened her smile, then wrapped her arm around his. "I've admitted that I made a mistake."

"A mistake? Is that what you're calling it now?"

"Can't you find it in your heart to forgive me?"

"You were the one who kicked me to the curb in search of greener pastures. I guess you found they weren't as green as you thought. Elton Powell didn't marry you after all. That's too bad. I don't want to embarrass you in front of all these people, but I will if you don't get up and leave right now."

The message must have finally sunk in because Vanessa rose from her seat, but before Julian could stop her, she bent and kissed him on the mouth. With a seductive smile playing on her lips, she brushed his cheek with her fingers before leaving the table and heading in the direction of the ladies room.

Julian could have strangled her. Vanessa had no doubt seen Pandora and had decided to stage that little scene.

Pandora had stood up to leave when she saw Vanessa join Julian and Drac. Nausea bubbled in her stomach and she closed her eyes and sat back down. Beads of perspiration appeared over her upper lip.

"Excuse me, Colin," she said, rising unsteadily to her feet. "I have to go to the ladies' room."

Lines of concern creased his forehead. "Are you sure you're all right, Pandora?"

"I'm fine. I'll be back in a few minutes." She made it to the ladies room just in time. Her stomach gave up the little bit of lunch she had been able to keep down. After rinsing her mouth and washing her face, Pandora sank down weakly onto one of the lounges. Why did she have to see Julian, of all people, with that woman? He evidently couldn't wait to go back to Vanessa. How could he after what she had done to him? Pandora realized that once and for all time she would have to forget him.

Who was she trying to convince? Cassandra was right, nothing short of a permanent case of amnesia could ever make her forget Julian Palmer. Work and more work certainly hadn't done the trick. All it took was seeing him one time to dispel that particular fantasy.

Right now she had more than her feelings for him on her mind. The hearing to discuss her fitness as a guardian for her daughter was a week away. Her nerves were on edge and her emotions raw. Monroe's threat hung suspended over her head like an anvil, ready to crush the life out of her. Could he possibly have what he said and really use it against her? She shuddered at the thought. She knew to take his threats seriously. She had known that he cared for her and had tried to tell him at the time they were involved that her feelings for him hadn't deepened into love, but Monroe had refused to accept it. As for Sasha, her attitude went beyond simple jealousy, bordering on obsession and close to incest where her older brother had been concerned.

Having re-applied her makeup and regained her composure, Pandora was about to leave the ladies' room when Vanessa opened one of the stall doors and entered the lounge.

"Knowing Julian prefers me to you has made you feel sick, hasn't it? I heard you vomiting."

"If you want to believe that, you're quite welcome to do so. But for your information, the lunch was a little too rich and my stomach wouldn't tolerate it. Now if you'll excuse me."

"You're a cool one, I'll give you that. I don't know if I could be so calm if I were in your place."

"What is there not to be calm about? Tell me, Vanessa, were you calm when you walked out on Julian five years ago?"

"I'll be the first to admit that I made the wrong decision, but now that Julian has given me another chance..."

That she intended to correct her mistake was what she didn't have to say. The sickness Pandora had experienced a few minutes earlier overcame her again, making her feel even more miserable, if that were possible. Had Julian forgotten everything they'd shared? Obviously he had. He had decided to believe all those lies about her and pretend she no longer existed. Well, he could have Vanessa if that was what he wanted. When all was said and done, she would have their baby.

"I wish you all the luck in the world, Vanessa, because if he's taken you back after what you did to him just to get even with me, you're both going to need it." With that parting shot, Pandora exited the room with her head held high.

Colin stood up when he saw Pandora coming toward him.

She smiled at him. "We had better be getting back to the office."

"Maybe you should let me drive you home."

"Thanks, Colin, but I'm fine. Really."

His expression said she hadn't convinced him of that. She took a cleansing breath and prepared herself to walk past Julian and Drac's table, hating that it was the only way out of the restaurant.

"Pandora," Julian called to her politely.

"Julian, Drac. You know Colin Whitley. If you'll excuse us, we have to get back to the office." Walking past, she stumbled. Julian reached out to steady her.

"Thank you." She looked at Colin. He cupped her elbow and escorted her out of the restaurant.

"The look you gave Whitley...Surely you're not jealous of him, Jules?" Drac asked.

"Why don't you mind your own business, cousin."

When Vanessa walked out of the ladies' room—a smug, triumphant smile on her lips—and headed for the door, Julian vaulted to his feet and reached the exit before she did.

"If you've said anything to hurt Pandora, Vanessa, I'll make you the sorriest woman to ever walk the face of this planet. From now on, you stay away from her as well as from me. Do I make myself clear?" he said, his tone relatively civil in spite of his anger.

"Very," she answered weakly, her eyes huge, the savage intensity she heard in Julian's voice and saw on his face obviously having made an impression on her.

Julian shot Vanessa one last look of pure, unadulterated contempt before leaving the restaurant.

On the day of the hearing, Pandora and her attorney stood waiting in the corridor outside the courtroom. Monroe appeared with his attorney, Colton Foster, and smiled arrogantly at her.

"Your coming here today was a waste of time, Pandora. You might as well start packing Destinee's things."

"Mr. Cooper, I must warn you against harassing my client," Judith Sanders admonished.

"The ever lovely Judith Sanders," Colton Foster drawled in his heavy Texas accent. "See ya'll in the courtroom, darlins." He smiled and he and his client moved down the hall a bit.

"That man is as thoroughly obnoxious as his client." Judith said, wrinkling her nose in disgust. "I'm sure the judge won't grant custody of an impressionable teenage girl to a man like Monroe Cooper."

"I hope you're right, Judith. But there is Sasha waiting in the wings to back him up."

Twenty-five minutes later, Pandora walked out of the courtroom, numb with shock. She couldn't believe what had just happened.

"It's only the first round, Pandora," Judith reassured her.

"The first round! There shouldn't be any round at all. I can't believe the judge could possibly think that Monroe might actually have a case."

"Judge Gardner is a hard nose, a traditionalist down to her black leather pumps. She's rigid when it comes to custody cases."

"Monroe intends to blacken my name and reputation."

"His character is not all that sterling, Pandora. We'll have to convince the judge that money and revenge are motivating him, not concern for the welfare of his niece."

Looking as though he had already won, Monroe swept past Pandora on his way out of the courthouse.

Pandora ground her teeth. "Oh, how I despise that man."

"Since it's so close to Christmas," Judith said, "the judge will probably put off scheduling the case until after the first of the year."

"I hope so. I want this over and done with, but I'm scared, Judith. Everything inside me says to expect the worst and I won't be disappointed."

"You've got to think positively, Pandora."

"I'm trying, Judith, but it's hard."

Two weeks before Christmas, Pandora and Destinee were in the living room listening to music, when Rachel showed Monroe and a stone-faced woman in.

"Why are you here, Monroe?" Pandora demanded. "And who is this person?"

"Show her the order, Ms. Sloane."

"What order? Who are you?" Pandora asked the woman.

"My name is Evelyn Sloane. I am an officer of family court," she said retrieving her badge and a legal document from her briefcase and handed them to Pandora.

After Pandora started reading the paper, it slipped from her fingers and floated to the floor.

"Mama? What is it? What's wrong?" Destinee asked, glaring daggers at her uncle.

"It's a court order…" Monroe began.

"I'll handle this, Mr. Cooper." Ms. Sloane interjected. "Destinee, I have a court order that says you have to come with me."

"Come with you? Where? Why? And what for?" she asked, glaring at her uncle and then back at Ms. Sloane.

Panic and fury consumed Pandora. She picked up the court order and finished reading the rest of it. "I'm going to call Judith."

"It won't do you any good," Monroe snapped.

"Mr. Cooper, I'll have to ask you to stand aside. Or leave the premises. As an officer of the court it is my job to see that procedure is strictly adhered to."

"Yes, of course." He cleared his throat and backed away.

Ms. Sloan walked over to Destinee. "I think you should go and pack your things, dear. You'll be staying with your Aunt Sasha until the judge rules on your case."

"My case? What case? Mama, what is this all about?"

Holding back tears, Pandora walked over to her daughter. "Honey, ah, your uncle has petitioned the court to grant him custody of you."

"But why? He and Aunt Sasha don't even like me. You're my mother and I belong here with you. I don't care what some dumb old court papers say. Mama, tell them I'm not going," Destinee pleaded desperately.

"It's only temporary, Desi."

"I won't go."

"I'm sorry, Destinee, but you have no choice," Ms. Sloane told her.

"You mean I really have to go with them!" Destinee exclaimed, her voice high-pitched and disbelieving. "I won't go," she yelled defiantly.

"I think you'd better pack your things," Ms. Sloane said gently to the now nearly hysterical teen.

Pandora squared her shoulders and said, "Rachel and I will help you, honey."

Rachel nodded agreement, but looked at Monroe with searing contempt. If looks could kill, he would have collapsed then and there.

"I don't want to go with them, Mama," Destinee cried inconsolably, her eyes filling with tears.

"And I don't want you to go, honey." Pandora glared at Monroe. "You're going to pay for this, Monroe. I'll get my baby back."

"I wouldn't count on it if I were you."

In Destinee's room Pandora held her daughter close. She couldn't believe this was happening. Judith had been so confident that the judge wouldn't rule on the case until after the first of the year. What could

Monroe have possibly said to the woman? She couldn't bear it, but she knew she had to be strong for Destinee's sake.

"Mama, why is Uncle Monroe doing this to us? He's never cared about me. He knows that I don't want to live with Aunt Sasha."

"He's only doing it to hurt me."

"But why? You've never done anything to hurt him."

"In his mind I have."

"Just like Julian blames you for things you never did. Are all men such jerks?"

"I know it looks that way, but no, they all aren't."

"From what I've seen so far, they are. Daddy was awful, too. I believed that Julian was different. I wanted him to be my new father. I thought we would be a family. Now I'm losing my only real family—you, Mama," she cried pitifully, burying her face in Pandora's shoulder.

"You're not losing me, Desi. You'll be back here where you belong before you know it. You'll see."

Twenty minutes later, patting her daughter's back, Pandora said, "Don't cry, honey."

"I can't help it, Mama."

"It's time to leave, Destinee," Ms. Sloane said gently.

Pandora felt her daughter's body tremble. It was agony to have her precious child ripped from her care. She bit her lips to keep from crying. "You had better go with them, Desi. Never forget how much I love you. We'll be back together real soon."

"Please, Mama, hurry up and make it happen."

"I will, honey, don't worry," she said with a confidence she did not feel.

"You really shouldn't make promises to the girl that you won't be able to keep," Monroe callously advised.

Clenching her fists, Pandora watched as Ms. Sloane led her daughter out the door, Monroe following close behind.

"I thought that husband of yours was the worst human being to ever draw a breath," Rachel grumbled after the door closed. "I stand corrected. His brother is ten times worse. You better sit down, Pandora, before you fall down."

Pandora let Rachel lead her over to the couch.

"I don't understand how any judge could do something so totally insane," Rachel said.

"Me either," Pandora answered, reaching for the phone to call her attorney. "Judith, Monroe and an officer from family court just took Destinee. What can we do to get her back?" Her voice cracked, her mind teetering on total collapse.

"Calm down. What does the order say?"

Pandora picked up the document and read it to her.

"It's only a temporary order. I wouldn't worry too much. I'll call the judge in the morning. and find out why she issued it and see if I can get her to rescind it. Where will you be tomorrow afternoon?"

"At the office. I can't stay here without my girl, Judith, I have to get her back."

"You will. I'll help you."

"You shouldn't be going to work, Pandora," Rachel scolded her the next morning.

"Don't fuss, Rachel. I have to occupy my mind or I'll go stone crazy."

"What about the baby? Yes, I know you're pregnant with Julian Palmer's child. When are you going to tell the man he's going to be a father?"

"I haven't decided."

"I know how much he has hurt you by believing all those lies. But, Pandora, he has a right to know something as important as this."

"Maybe later after I get my daughter back."

"I think…"

"I know what you think. He's gone back to his ex-fiancée. There can be no future for us." Pandora rose to leave the kitchen when a pain sliced through her lower abdomen, causing her to double over.

"Are you all right, Pandora?" Rachel asked anxiously.

"It was just a twinge. It's gone now."

"Maybe you should call your doctor."

"There is no need. I'll come home early and rest, I promise."

In her office Pandora paced, waiting for her attorney to call. She realized that she shouldn't have come in to work. There was no way she could concentrate on work or anything else until she knew…

The phone buzzed.

"Yes, what is it, Cassandra?"

"Judith Sanders is on line two."

"Good." Pandora punched the intercom button. "Judith, what did you find out?"

"Monroe told the judge that you had left Destinee with your lover's relatives to have a carnal affair with Julian Palmer. She wouldn't change her mind. I'm sorry. Destinee will have to stay in Monroe's custody until the case comes up on the schedule. The judge promised to make it as soon as possible, though."

"Oh, God!"

"I'm sorry, Pandora."

"It's not your fault. Thank you for trying to help."

"It's not over yet. Don't give up."

"I won't."

"We'll get your daughter back where she belongs—with her mother."

Pandora hung up the phone and sat staring into space, her mind a blank one minute, filled with anxious thoughts the next.

Her one clear thought was that she had to get her daughter away from Monroe and Sasha. Talk about bad influences; they were the worst. Pandora got up from her chair and walked over to the windows.

Suddenly a sharp pain shot through her lower abdomen.

She had just made it into her chair when Cassandra walked in. Taking in the situation, she rushed to Pandora's side.

"What is it? What's wrong?"

Perspiration beaded Pandora's forehead and she was groaning in pain. "I'm pregnant and I'm bleeding."

Cassandra reached for the phone. "I'm calling 911."

CHAPTER TWENTY-NINE

Pacing before the windows in his office, Julian kept revisiting how Pandora had looked that day in the restaurant. Up close he had seen the dark circles her makeup had failed to cover. Was it from lack of sleep? Or was something else the cause? He wondered and worried.

The satisfaction he thought he would derive from exacting his revenge remained elusive. And from what Drac had told him, Pandora hadn't joined forces with Monroe as Julian had expected her to after finding out her plan to betray him had been cut short—if in fact it had been her plan. There had to be more to it. Driven by anger, he now conceded that he might have overlooked some extenuating detail. He had not given Pandora a chance to defend herself; he had just gone on the attack.

Betrayal or not, he ached to have Pandora in his arms again. He missed not spending time with Destinee. He wanted the family life that had been within his grasp. He reached impulsively for the phone to call Pandora, but the intercom buzzed before he could dial her number.

"Julian, it's Cassandra. You've got to come to Mercy Hospital right away. It's Pandora; she's in emergency. She didn't want me to call you, but she needs you."

"I'm on my way." Pandora was in the hospital in the emergency room! Had she been in an accident? How badly was she hurt? Oh, God no! Cassandra had sounded pretty upset. Panic slammed through him with hurricane force. He could lose her. Julian had his secretary call a taxi; he was too upset to risk driving, and he didn't want to wait for his chauffeur. If anything happened to Pandora...

When Julian arrived, Cassandra was pacing the hall outside the emergency room. When she saw him, she rushed to him.

"I'm so glad you're here, Julian."

"What happened? Was she hurt in an accident?"

"No, she collapsed at the office." Before Cassandra could elaborate, the doctor came through the emergency room doors.

"I'm Dr. Margaret Sturgis, Pandora's doctor," she said, extending her hand to Julian, then to Cassandra. "Are you Pandora's family?"

"How is she, doctor?" Julian demanded.

"She's stable at the moment, but I'm concerned for the baby."

Shock rendered Julian speechless.

Mistaking the look on his face for just worry, Dr. Sturgis went on. "I've been concerned about her for several weeks now. This is a warning sign. Stress this early in the pregnancy isn't good for her or the baby."

Julian was numb. Why hadn't Pandora told him she was carrying his child? That was a stupid question. Why should she have told him anything after the way he had treated her?

"Can I go in?"

"Only for a few minutes. I've arranged to have her moved to the prenatal ICU on the fourth floor in a little while."

Cassandra put a hand on Julian's arm after the doctor walked away. "I didn't know for sure that she was pregnant until today, but I had suspected it."

"I'm surprised you can even stand to talk to me after what I've put her through…I've been a real first-class bastard. She wasn't a part of the plot to ruin me, was she? You don't have to answer. I should have had more faith in her. I let what happened to me in the past influence our relationship. The funny thing is that I was always the one saying trust me—then what do I do? Oh, God, if she loses our baby, I'll never forgive myself."

"Julian, don't. You know, I think…"

"Don't make excuses for me. I'm guilty as hell."

"That wasn't what I was going to say. I think Monroe and Roscoe really weren't trying to ruin you. I believe their aim was to destroy Pandora, and they just used you as their instrument to accomplish it."

"You could be right about that, but right now I have to see her." He started to open the emergency room door, then stopped. "Does Destinee know her mother is in the hospital?"

"No. I called the house. Rachel told me that Monroe came by with an officer of the court and they took Destinee to live with her aunt and cousins."

The news stunned Julian. "I don't understand. Why would he…would they want her? Pandora is Destinee's mother."

"She and Monroe share joint guardianship as specified in her late husband's will. I don't know all the details; you'll have to ask Pandora about it."

"But doing that might upset her further. You heard what the doctor said."

"I know, but she'll be more stressed out if you try to avoid the subject. She'll think you're trying to hide something and worry even more, and that's not good."

"You're right, it isn't." He slammed his fist into his palm. "I'm roasting in a fire of my own making; damned if I do anything, and damned if I don't." Regaining control of himself, he entered the emergency room. He found the cubicle Pandora was in. She lay on a gurney, her eyes closed. He wondered if she was in pain.

"Pan."

Her eyes opened. "Julian!"

"How do you feel, sweetheart?"

She looked confused for a moment, and then her expression changed. "You know about the baby, don't you?"

"Yes." He pulled up a chair and took her hand. "Why didn't you tell me?"

"I was going to, eventually, but Monroe took me to court, and now has temporary custody of Destinee."

"I know. Cassandra told me what happened."

"Monroe showed the judge pictures of me leaving the penthouse, and also told her what we did on our trip to Rome. Destinee mentioned to her cousin Miranda about the weekend we spent in the Catskills."

Because of him, Pandora was going through this. She was in danger of losing their baby.

"Julian, I didn't betray you. I know it looked that way, but I didn't."

"Shh, don't worry about that now. Concentrate on keeping our baby safe." He kissed her forehead and held her close. She was his life. He hoped that he hadn't ruined any chance they had of being happy.

Later, Julian was outside the door of the prenatal ICU after they had transferred Pandora upstairs. He signaled the doctor when she came out.

"I've given her some medication to relax the uterus," Dr. Sturgis informed him. "It's imperative in the next forty-eight hours that she remain calm and lie completely still."

"You mean she could lose the baby?"

"I'm sorry, but yes, it's a very real possibility. There was some bleeding. We've managed to stop it, and we'll be monitoring her closely. You can go in now, but don't stay too long. And please—I can't stress this enough—please don't say or do anything that will upset her."

Julian followed the doctor inside. After he found Pandora's room, he stood for a moment watching her. She looked so fragile, his eyes stung and tears threatened to fall. God, he loved this woman, his woman. She was carrying his child. He had let her down when she needed him most, and he was ashamed of himself for the way he had treated her. Could he ever make it up to her? Would she even want him to?

Julian found it hard to believe a judge would actually hand custody of Destinee over to someone like Monroe Cooper and his sister. The pain and grief Pandora was enduring was partly Monroe's and Roscoe Phillips' doing. To be honest, it was his, too.

"Julian," Pandora called.

"Yes, Pan. I'm here, darling."

"I'm not going to lose the baby, am I?"

"No, you're not."

"But Dr. Sturgis said…"

He caressed her cheek. "Don't worry, all right?"

Her eyes misted. "But I can't help it. I want our baby, Julian."

"And you'll have him. You'll see."

"About Destinee. I have to know how she is."

Julian touched her forehead. "Shh, don't get so worked up. I'll see that she comes to see you. I promise."

"How can you keep a promise like that when Monroe…"

"Just leave it to me. I'll arrange it." He bent to kiss her lips. "You rest, okay? I'd better go. The doctor said not to stay too long."

"Julian, we have to talk."

"I know we do, but not now. After you and the baby are out of danger and you have Destinee back with you, then we'll talk, all right?"

"All right."

Julian stayed with Pandora until she fell asleep, then quietly left the room.

"Julian, where have you been? We had an important meeting this afternoon. Did you forget?" Drac asked when Julian walked into his office.

"Forget about the meeting. I've been at the hospital."

"The hospital?"

"Yes, the hospital. Pandora was rushed to emergency. We were dead wrong, Drac."

"About what? Is she all right?"

"No. She's in danger of losing our baby, and it's all my fault."

"How can—how is it your fault? She's the one who…"

"Don't say another word against her, Drac. Monroe Cooper and Roscoe Phillips are the only ones responsible. Why hadn't I seen that? Somehow they made it look as if Pandora had betrayed me when all the time they were aiming their guns at Pandora. Because of their sick obsession, and my own obsession with exacting revenge, I could lose everything that holds any meaning for me."

"How do you know she isn't involved?"

"My gut feeling is that they alone planned what happened, and they used me to do it. Monroe, that dirty son of a gun, has gained temporary custody of Destinee just to torture Pandora further."

"It means that Cassandra was right all along. I'm sorry for my part in all this, Jules."

"Tell that to Pandora. She's terrified she'll lose the baby. If she does I'll never forgive myself. And I know she'll never want to see my face again."

"What about Cooper?"

"Oh, I'm going to take care of him and Roscoe Phillips. Neither one of them is going to escape my wrath. What I want to know is how they pulled it off. But right now I have to pay a call on Monroe Cooper and convince him to let Destinee visit her mother in the hospital. It's paramount that Pandora see her daughter. Monroe will curse the day he was born if he refuses to do as I say."

Drac swallowed hard. He had never seen his cousin this angry. He wouldn't trade places with Monroe Cooper or Roscoe Phillips for all the money in the world.

"Mr. Palmer, I have strict orders not to let you in to see Mr. Cooper," Monroe's secretary warned Julian. "He's in conference with his sister."

Ignoring her warning, Julian stormed into Monroe's office. "I think you had better leave," he said to Sasha.

"Now just wait a minute. Who do you think you are?"

"Palmer, I'm calling security if you don't leave."

"I'll do it," Sasha said, reaching for the phone.

"I wouldn't touch that if I were you. Tell her, Cooper."

Reluctantly Monroe said, "Don't bother. Listen, Sasha, you go on home. I'll call you later."

"You want me to leave you alone with this maniac? There is no telling what he might do."

"He won't harm me."

"If it's all the same to you, I'll wait outside. If you or he doesn't come out in the next ten minutes, I'm calling the police," she said. closing the door behind her.

"If you put a hand on me," Monroe began, "I'll…"

"Do what? I strongly suggest that you don't say another word, Cooper. You're going to listen to what I have to say. I'm already an inch away from killing your lying ass as it is, so don't push me."

"What do you want?"

"I want you to take Destinee to see her mother in the hospital."

"Hospital! Pandora's in the hospital?"

"Yes, thanks to you." Julian said derisively.

"I don't know what you're talking about."

"I haven't got time to explain it to you. And even if I did, believe me, you wouldn't like the method I would use to enlighten you."

"And if I refuse to do what you want?"

Julian smiled menacingly. "I would advise you not to piss me off. It could prove very injurious to your health."

They heard a loud pounding on the door.

"It's security, Mr. Cooper. Is everything all right in there?"

"Everything is fine."

"You sure, sir? Mrs. Haynes said..."

"My sister overreacted. You can go back downstairs." Monroe cleared his throat. "What hospital is Pandora in?"

"Mercy. I knew you would see the wisdom in doing as I've suggested. If you're not there with Destinee within the hour, I'll come after you. And believe me, there's nowhere on the face on this earth you can hide that I can't find you."

Julian strode to the door. "You can tell Roscoe Phillips his time is coming."

"I'm so glad to see you, honey," Pandora said through happy tears when her daughter walked in. Destinee rushed to her mother's side and hugged her.

"When Uncle Monroe told me you were in the hospital, I was so worried. Why are you here?" When Pandora hesitated, Destinee's eyes widened in fear. "You're not going to die, are you?"

"No, it's nothing like that. I'm pregnant, and almost lost the baby."

"Does Julian know?"

"Yes, he does."

"And?"

"And nothing. We haven't had a chance to talk about it yet. He only found out today."

Julian appeared. "Don't worry, Destinee. I'm going to take better care of your mother in the future."

"I hope you mean that. She's been so sad. And now this."

"I know, and I'm going to make it up to her, and you, too. We had better go. We don't want to tire your mother out."

"Destinee just got here," Pandora complained.

"I'll be back tomorrow, Mama. Uncle Monroe said as long as you're in here, he'll see that I visit you everyday. I can't believe how nice he's being about letting me come see you."

Pandora looked at Julian's face and comprehension dawned. She smiled and mouthed her thanks.

"Will she and the baby really be all right, Julian?" Destinee asked him once they were outside the unit.

"God, I hope so, sweetheart."

"You still love her, don't you?"

"I never really stopped."

"But you thought she had betrayed you."

"I was wrong."

"Are you and Mama going to get back together?"

"I hope we will."

"Me, too."

CHAPTER THIRTY

"I'm doing so well, the doctor is moving me to a private room in the morning," Pandora told Cassandra the next evening.

"Seeing Destinee and knowing Julian was there for you worked wonders, didn't it?"

"I wouldn't go that far, Cassandra."

"I know you're still upset with him for believing the worst. I can't really blame you, but he's trying to redeem himself."

"He convinced Monroe to let Destinee come see me. I'm grateful to him for that."

"I think gratitude isn't the only thing you feel for him."

"Not now, Cassandra. How are things going at the office?"

"Colin has everything under control. I believed him when he said it was a coincidence that he decided to leave Richards Investments to come work at PanCo. It was just something that he wanted to do. That the company happened to be a subsidiary of Palmer and Associates is the real kicker. Monroe capitalized on his timing. When I interviewed Kiah, she admitted to having worked for Monroe in the past. She says she'll understand if you don't want her to stay on."

"She's good at her job, isn't she?"

"Yes, very good."

"Then you decide if you want her to continue."

"I think she should stay." Cassandra laughed. "You have to admit that she moved up a rung when she left Cooper Corps to come work for us."

"You're right, she did." Pandora yawned.

"I'm tiring you out. I'll come back to see you tomorrow."

The next time Pandora opened her eyes, Julian was sitting beside the bed watching her.

"How long have you been here?" she asked.

"Not long. I've been content just watching you and listening to the beep of the monitor. It reassures me that our child still lives. Dr. Sturgis said they were moving you to a private room in the morning if you continue to improve."

"For a while there I was so scared, Julian."

He took her hand and kissed it. "I know you were, and so was I." His voice brightened. "Destinee should be here in a few minutes."

"How did you manage to convince Monroe to let Destinee visit me? You never did tell me how you pulled off that particular miracle."

"And I'm not going to now. I don't want you worrying about Monroe or anything else. Everything is going to be all right, Pan. You'll see."

"I wish I had your confidence."

"You can always borrow some of mine. You always said I had more than my share."

"Monroe doesn't care about Destinee, so why is he really seeking permanent guardianship?"

"I'm sure we'll find out the answer very soon, if my suspicions are correct."

"Your suspicions? What do you think his motives are?"

"To bring you down."

"But he went after your company. If his real aim was to hurt me, then why..."

"I don't know the answer to that. Is there anything he wants that you have?"

"Only PanCo, but surely..."

"Why do you think he wants it so badly? And why use Destinee as part of his scheme to get it?"

"I started a stock portfolio for Destinee. She owns thirty-five percent of PanCo. As for why he wants the company, he's angry because of the way I outmaneuvered him where Phillips Investments is concerned and, of course, Cooper Corps. My husband left forty-five percent of that company to me and Destinee. I converted thirty-five percent of the stock to cash and took my ten percent and started PanCo. He's always resented me for it, but I never thought he would stoop this low to hurt me."

"Monroe Cooper is a very vindictive man. I figured it had something to do with money, lust, revenge or a combination of the three. I think he'll reveal his true intentions soon. Your stay in the hospital has only postponed it."

"Since we share joint guardianship of Destinee, that means he'll have access to her portfolio if he gets full custody. Oh, Julian, what can we do?"

"Nothing, until he makes his move. When he and Phillips make their move we'll be ready."

"We?"

He smiled. "Yes, we, my darling. I'm going to help you nuke the bastards."

A few days later Pandora had a visit from Gramma Edna, Julian's mother, and Selena.

"When are they going to spring you out of this place?" Selena asked.

"Dr. Sturgis says tomorrow. She's assured me that the danger is past."

"Us Palmers are a pretty sturdy bunch," Gramma Edna said.

"I almost miscarried in my fifth month when I was carrying Julian," Lenora recalled. "The doctor said he was a fighter. This baby you're carrying is a Palmer, so he's got to be a fighter like his father."

"Drac told us about what that low-life Monroe Cooper did. Somebody needs to take a two-by-four and go upside his head. It would probably break in two," Gramma Edna grumbled.

Pandora smiled. She loved Julian's family.

"Uncle Howland said to tell you that if it's a boy he has the perfect name for him," Selena said with a laugh. "You want to know what name he picked?"

"I don't think so. Not after he named his sons Dracula and Frankenstein."

"I told him Julian reserves the right to name his first-born."

"What did he say to that?"

"He wants dibs on the next child. What else?"

"Stop fussing, Rachel," Pandora groused. She had been home two days, and the woman was driving her crazy. Every time she moved, Rachel was there.

"I just want you to take care of yourself and that baby."

"I know, but you're smothering me. I'm going into the office tomorrow."

"You really think you should?"

"I feel fine. I don't intend to overdo. Cassandra and Julian have already told me they won't stand for it. I won't endanger the baby. I want it too much."

"When are you two going to get married?"

"Rachel."

"It's a logical assumption, considering that you still love each other."

"I don't want to discuss it."

"You'd be a fool to let him get away a second time. That's all I'm going to say on the subject," she said, marching from the living room.

The doorbell rang. Pandora went to answer it.

"Monroe!"

"May I come in?"

"Why? What do you want?"

"Let me in and I'll tell you."

She didn't want to, but why not? Maybe this is the break she and Julian had been waiting for. Was Monroe ready to deal? she wondered.

"All right, Monroe," Pandora asked impatiently after he was seated on the couch.

"I take it you're all well now?"

"I'm fine."

"By the way, what exactly was wrong with you that Palmer felt he had to insist, no, demand that I let Destinee come see you?"

"It's none of your business. You don't really care, so just get to the reason for your visit. You know the judge has scheduled the case for after the first of the year."

"I know. I also know that she's allowing Destinee to spend Christmas with you."

"You object to that?"

"No, I have more important things to discuss with you."

"Such as?"

"Such as you signing PanCo over to me."

"You must be out of your mind or, as Destinee is fond of saying, on drugs."

"I'm not crazy or on drugs. I'm serious."

"And why would I do that?"

"You want your daughter back with you, don't you?"

"Are you blackmailing me, Monroe?"

"No, of course not, just bargaining. I have something you want, and you have something I want."

"You're a nasty piece of work. You know that?"

He got up from the couch. "You made me this way. I really loved you once, but you chose my brother over me." He cleared his throat. "Think about it and get back to me by the end of the week."

Pandora barely noticed when Monroe left. She absently picked up the phone and punched in Julian's number.

"Can you come over right now?"

"What's wrong? It's not the baby, is it?"

"Nothing is wrong there. I just had a visit from Monroe. You were right. He is using Destinee as a bargaining chip to gain control of my company and, in effect, end the black widow's reign." She relayed what Monroe had said.

"You're going to have to outmaneuver him again."

"How do you propose that I do that?"

"I'll explain when I get there. I'm leaving right now."

"I knew it wouldn't take you long to make up your mind," Monroe said confidently when Pandora walked into his office several days later. "You brought the necessary papers, I take it?"

"Yes, she did," Julian said, following her inside.

"I see you brought your watchdog. It doesn't matter; the outcome will be the same."

Julian set his briefcase on the desk and handed a sheaf of papers to Pandora.

She cleared her throat. "I have an agreement I want you to sign. It says you willingly relinquish custody and guardianship of Destinee to me and you will never seek to sue for custody again. In exchange, I'll agree to sell PanCo to you for twenty million dollars." Pandora laughed when he opened his mouth to protest.

"Considering all my holdings, anything less would seem strange. It's all legal. I had my attorney draw up the agreement if you want your attorney to look it over."

"I don't need an attorney for this."

"You know what they say about a man representing himself," Julian warned. "He has a fool for a client."

"Not in this instance, Palmer. I know exactly what I'm doing."

"What I'd like to know is how you managed to convince my people to leave their jobs. I already know from talking to Colin Whitley that his approaching PanCo for the CFO position was a coincidence."

"Gaines resented you making his brother head of Gaine's Financial instead of him. It was Roscoe's suggestion that he seek the CEO position with Star Pacific. You see, we've been keeping a close eye on the black widow's empire."

"For future reference, or takeover, no doubt."

Ignoring Julian's sarcasm, Monroe went on to explain. "I made Christopher Gaines promise not to say anything about my part in his defection if he was hired. And by the way, the bribe not to return to Gaines came from me; I led him to believe that it came from Pandora.

"Because she and I own stock in several companies, and, added to that, her formidable reputation as the black widow, it became easy to make you believe she was behind everything."

"I see. The last few pieces of the puzzle are beginning to fall into place. You used similar tactics to convince my other employees to leave their jobs, didn't you?"

"Yes, and they worked." Monroe glanced at Pandora. "Now let's get down to business. Your daughter is waiting in the conference room, lock, stock and baggage. I'm sure Sasha is happy to see her go."

It was the night before Christmas and Pandora, Julian and Destinee were relaxing around the fireplace, drinking hot apple cider.

"I'm so happy to be home, Mama!" Destinee exclaimed. "You have no idea how happy."

"I think I do."

"Are you and Julian going to talk?"

"Yes, were finally going to talk."

"Do you know whether the baby is a boy or a girl, Mama?"

"It's a boy," Julian answered.

"I'm going to have a brother. That's so cool," she said, looking from Julian to her mother. "I guess you want to be alone?"

"We do need to talk, honey. Do you mind?"

"No, as long as I can take my presents up to my room and open them."

"Go ahead, honey. Something tells me we won't want to hear how loud you intend to play most of them."

After Destinee left, Julian pulled Pandora into his arms.

"Can you ever forgive me for doubting you, baby?"

"I already have. At first, I didn't know if I would be able to, but I love you, Julian. You redeemed yourself in a lot of ways."

"Do you care to enumerate?"

She kissed his forehead. "You helped me get my daughter back."

"That's one. Go on."

"You helped me outmaneuver Monroe. When he finds out I converted Destinee's stock to cash and you set up a portfolio for her in your company with the money, he's going to pitch a hissy fit."

"Three."

"I think you've predicted right, that he'll want to sell PanCo back to me lightening quick once he finds out I've sold you my shares. In reality, he holds only fourteen percent of actual shares, and what with the ones he's sold to Roscoe Phillips, both of them will be stuck with the financial responsibility of running the entire conglomerate. And the beauty of it is that if he decides to keep PanCo, he'll be forced to use his personal capital and, probably, a large portion of Roscoe's. I know Monroe. Trust me, he'll want to wash his hands of my empire fast."

"You are a clever woman, Ms. Cooper. I won't even have to do anything to Phillips because, by throwing in his lot with Monroe, he essentially has already shot himself in the foot. The outcome will probably ruin him. Even though I helped, that is only three of the ways in which I've redeemed myself. I want to hear more praise."

"I should be mad at you for being so quick to believe those lies about me."

Julian looked away, self-disgust marring his features. "I know. And are you?"

"I was at first, but more for Desi's sake than mine."

"You can't know how sorry I feel about what I did to you and Destinee."

"But I do."

"And you forgive me?"

"Yes. As you said a little while ago, you've redeemed yourself." Pandora moved her hand across her stomach. "And you've given me this precious little boy growing inside of me." She kissed Julian deeply and snuggled closer to his body, then she ran her fingers under his sweater and shirt and touched his bare skin.

"I would say we had better hurry up and get married."

"And I would say that's the best thing you've said today. There is one thing you have failed miserably to do."

He kissed her. "What is that?"

"To say three special words. I'm waiting."

"Are you now?"

Pandora playfully punched him on the arm. "Yes, I am."

"I love you, Pan. You're my life, my reason for being. I adore you."

"That's a start."

"Only a start. What else can I do?"

"I'll think of something."

"Can I give you some ideas?"

"Most assuredly. I love you, Julian."

"And I love you," he answered, kissing her tenderly. He at last had his heart's desire.

ABOUT THE AUTHOR

Working in the editorial department of the **L.A. Herald** gave Beverly Clark her first exposure to professional writing. From there she wrote fillers for the newspaper and for magazines such as **Redbook**, **Good Housekeeping**, and **McCalls.** She continued to ply her writing talent, penning and publishing more than 100 short stories with **Sterling/McFadden Magazines**.

Soon, Beverly joined Romantic Writers of America and started attending creative writing classes and other related courses. To date, she had completed eight full-length books. Beverly managed a second-hand bookstore for two years and then went on to work at Waldenbooks for seven years. During this time she also helped her local Friends of the Library group in helping children and adults to read and enjoy books.

Beverly's books with **Genesis Press** include: *Yesterday is Gone, A Love to Cherish, The Price of Love, Bound by Love, Cherish the Flame, A Twist of Fate, Echoes of Yesterday, Beyond the Rapture, and A Perfect Frame.*

Beverly has been, and continues to be, one of our best-loved authors.

2007 Publication Schedule

January

Corporate Seduction
A.C. Arthur
ISBN-13: 978-1-58571-238-0
ISBN-10: 1-58571-238-8
$9.95

A Taste of Temptation
Reneé Alexis
ISBN-13: 978-1-58571-207-6
ISBN-10: 1-58571-207-8
$9.95

February

The Perfect Frame
Beverly Clark
ISBN-13: 978-1-58571-240-3
ISBN-10: 1-58571-240-X
$9.95

Ebony Angel
Deatri King-Bey
ISBN-13: 978-1-58571-239-7
ISBN-10: 1-58571-239-6
$9.95

March

Sweet Sensations
Gwendolyn Bolton
ISBN-13: 978-1-58571-206-9
ISBN-10: 1-58571-206-X
$9.95

Crush
Crystal Hubbard
ISBN-13: 978-1-58571-243-4
ISBN-10: 1-58571-243-4
$9.95

April

Secret Thunder
Annetta P. Lee
ISBN-13: 978-1-58571-204-5
ISBN-10: 1-58571-204-3
$9.95

Blood Seduction
J.M. Jeffries
ISBN-13: 978-1-58571-237-3
ISBN-10: 1-58571-237-X
$9.95

May

Lies Too Long
Pamela Ridley
ISBN-13: 978-1-58571-246-5
ISBN-10: 1-58571-246-9
$13.95

Two Sides to Every Story
Dyanne Davis
ISBN-13: 978-1-58571-248-9
ISBN-10: 1-58571-248-5
$9.95

June

One of These Days
Michele Sudler
ISBN-13: 978-1-58571-249-6
ISBN-10: 1-58571-249-3
$9.95

Who's That Lady?
Andrea Jackson
ISBN-13: 978-1-58571-190-1
ISBN-10: 1-58571-190-X
$9.95

2007 Publication Schedule (continued)

July

Heart of the Phoenix
A.C. Arthur
ISBN-13: 978-1-58571-242-7
ISBN-10: 1-58571-242-6
$9.95

Do Over
Celya Bowers
ISBN-13: 978-1-58571-241-0
ISBN-10: 1-58571-241-8
$9.95

It's Not Over Yet
J.J. Michael
ISBN-13: 978-1-58571-245-8
ISBN-10: 1-58571-245-0
$9.95

August

The Fires Within
Beverly Clark
ISBN-13: 978-1-58571-244-1
ISBN-10: 1-58571-244-2
$9.95

Stolen Kisses
Dominiqua Douglas
ISBN-13: 978-1-58571-247-2
ISBN-10: 1-58571-247-7
$9.95

September

Small Whispers
Annetta P. Lee
ISBN-13: 978-158571-251-9
ISBN-10: 1-58571-251-5
$6.99

Always You
Crystal Hubbard
ISBN-13: 978-158571-252-6
ISBN-10: 1-58571-252-3
$6.99

October

Not His Type
Chamein Canton
ISBN-13: 978-158571-253-3
ISBN-10: 1-58571-253-1
$6.99

Many Shades of Gray
Dyanne Davis
ISBN-13: 978-158571-254-0
ISBN-10: 1-58571-254-X
$6.99

November

When I'm With You
LaConnie Taylor-Jones
ISBN-13: 978-158571-250-2
ISBN-10: 1-58571-250-7
$6.99

The Mission
Pamela Leigh Starr
ISBN-13: 978-158571-255-7
ISBN-10: 1-58571-255-8
$6.99

December

One in A Million
Barbara Keaton
ISBN-13: 978-158571-257-1
ISBN-10: 1-58571-257-4
$6.99

The Foursome
Celya Bowers
ISBN-13: 978-158571-256-4
ISBN-10: 1-58571-256-6
$6.99

Other Genesis Press, Inc. Titles

A Dangerous Deception	J.M. Jeffries	$8.95
A Dangerous Love	J.M. Jeffries	$8.95
A Dangerous Obsession	J.M. Jeffries	$8.95
A Dangerous Woman	J.M. Jeffries	$9.95
A Dead Man Speaks	Lisa Jones Johnson	$12.95
A Drummer's Beat to Mend	Kei Swanson	$9.95
A Happy Life	Charlotte Harris	$9.95
A Heart's Awakening	Veronica Parker	$9.95
A Lark on the Wing	Phyliss Hamilton	$9.95
A Love of Her Own	Cheris F. Hodges	$9.95
A Love to Cherish	Beverly Clark	$8.95
A Lover's Legacy	Veronica Parker	$9.95
A Pefect Place to Pray	I.L. Goodwin	$12.95
A Risk of Rain	Dar Tomlinson	$8.95
A Twist of Fate	Beverly Clark	$8.95
A Will to Love	Angie Daniels	$9.95
Acquisitions	Kimberley White	$8.95
Across	Carol Payne	$12.95
After the Vows (Summer Anthology)	Leslie Esdaile T.T. Henderson Jacqueline Thomas	$10.95
Again My Love	Kayla Perrin	$10.95
Against the Wind	Gwynne Forster	$8.95
All I Ask	Barbara Keaton	$8.95
Ambrosia	T.T. Henderson	$8.95
An Unfinished Love Affair	Barbara Keaton	$8.95
And Then Came You	Dorothy Elizabeth Love	$8.95
Angel's Paradise	Janice Angelique	$9.95
At Last	Lisa G. Riley	$8.95
Best of Friends	Natalie Dunbar	$8.95
Between Tears	Pamela Ridley	$12.95
Beyond the Rapture	Beverly Clark	$9.95
Blaze	Barbara Keaton	$9.95

Other Genesis Press, Inc. Titles (continued)

Blood Lust	J. M. Jeffries	$9.95
Bodyguard	Andrea Jackson	$9.95
Boss of Me	Diana Nyad	$8.95
Bound by Love	Beverly Clark	$8.95
Breeze	Robin Hampton Allen	$10.95
Broken	Dar Tomlinson	$24.95
The Business of Love	Cheris Hodges	$9.95
By Design	Barbara Keaton	$8.95
Cajun Heat	Charlene Berry	$8.95
Careless Whispers	Rochelle Alers	$8.95
Cats & Other Tales	Marilyn Wagner	$8.95
Caught in a Trap	Andre Michelle	$8.95
Caught Up In the Rapture	Lisa G. Riley	$9.95
Cautious Heart	Cheris F Hodges	$8.95
Caught Up	Deatri King Bey	$12.95
Chances	Pamela Leigh Starr	$8.95
Cherish the Flame	Beverly Clark	$8.95
Class Reunion	Irma Jenkins/John Brown	$12.95
Code Name: Diva	J.M. Jeffries	$9.95
Conquering Dr. Wexler's Heart	Kimberley White	$9.95
Cricket's Serenade	Carolita Blythe	$12.95
Crossing Paths, Tempting Memories	Dorothy Elizabeth Love	$9.95
Cupid	Barbara Keaton	$9.95
Cypress Whisperings	Phyllis Hamilton	$8.95
Dark Embrace	Crystal Wilson Harris	$8.95
Dark Storm Rising	Chinelu Moore	$10.95
Daughter of the Wind	Joan Xian	$8.95
Deadly Sacrifice	Jack Kean	$22.95
Designer Passion	Dar Tomlinson	$8.95
Dreamtective	Liz Swados	$5.95
Ebony Butterfly II	Delilah Dawson	$14.95
Ebony Eyes	Kei Swanson	$9.95

Other Genesis Press, Inc. Titles (continued)

Echoes of Yesterday	Beverly Clark	$9.95
Eden's Garden	Elizabeth Rose	$8.95
Enchanted Desire	Wanda Y. Thomas	$9.95
Everlastin' Love	Gay G. Gunn	$8.95
Everlasting Moments	Dorothy Elizabeth Love	$8.95
Everything and More	Sinclair Lebeau	$8.95
Everything but Love	Natalie Dunbar	$8.95
Eve's Prescription	Edwina Martin Arnold	$8.95
Falling	Natalie Dunbar	$9.95
Fate	Pamela Leigh Starr	$8.95
Finding Isabella	A.J. Garrotto	$8.95
Forbidden Quest	Dar Tomlinson	$10.95
Forever Love	Wanda Thomas	$8.95
From the Ashes	Kathleen Suzanne Jeanne Sumerix	$8.95
Gentle Yearning	Rochelle Alers	$10.95
Glory of Love	Sinclair LeBeau	$10.95
Go Gentle into that Good Night	Malcom Boyd	$12.95
Goldengroove	Mary Beth Craft	$16.95
Groove, Bang, and Jive	Steve Cannon	$8.99
Hand in Glove	Andrea Jackson	$9.95
Hard to Love	Kimberley White	$9.95
Hart & Soul	Angie Daniels	$8.95
Havana Sunrise	Kymberly Hunt	$9.95
Heartbeat	Stephanie Bedwell-Grime	$8.95
Hearts Remember	M. Loui Quezada	$8.95
Hidden Memories	Robin Allen	$10.95
Higher Ground	Leah Latimer	$19.95
Hitler, the War, and the Pope	Ronald Rychiak	$26.95
How to Write a Romance	Kathryn Falk	$18.95
I Married a Reclining Chair	Lisa M. Fuhs	$8.95
I'm Gonna Make You Love Me	Gwyneth Bolton	$9.95
Indigo After Dark Vol. I	Nia Dixon/Angelique	$10.95

Other Genesis Press, Inc. Titles (continued)

Indigo After Dark Vol. II	Dolores Bundy/Cole Riley	$10.95
Indigo After Dark Vol. III	Montana Blue/Coco Morena	$10.95
Indigo After Dark Vol. IV	Cassandra Colt/ Diana Richeaux	$14.95
Indigo After Dark Vol. V	Delilah Dawson	$14.95
Icie	Pamela Leigh Starr	$8.95
I'll Be Your Shelter	Giselle Carmichael	$8.95
I'll Paint a Sun	A.J. Garrotto	$9.95
Illusions	Pamela Leigh Starr	$8.95
Indiscretions	Donna Hill	$8.95
Intentional Mistakes	Michele Sudler	$9.95
Interlude	Donna Hill	$8.95
Intimate Intentions	Angie Daniels	$8.95
Ironic	Pamela Leigh Starr	$9.95
Jolie's Surrender	Edwina Martin-Arnold	$8.95
Kiss or Keep	Debra Phillips	$8.95
Lace	Giselle Carmichael	$9.95
Last Train to Memphis	Elsa Cook	$12.95
Lasting Valor	Ken Olsen	$24.95
Let's Get It On	Dyanne Davis	$9.95
Let Us Prey	Hunter Lundy	$25.95
Life Is Never As It Seems	J.J. Michael	$12.95
Lighter Shade of Brown	Vicki Andrews	$8.95
Love Always	Mildred E. Riley	$10.95
Love Doesn't Come Easy	Charlyne Dickerson	$8.95
Love in High Gear	Charlotte Roy	$9.95
Love Lasts Forever	Dominiqua Douglas	$9.95
Love Me Carefully	A.C. Arthur	$9.95
Love Unveiled	Gloria Greene	$10.95
Love's Deception	Charlene Berry	$10.95
Love's Destiny	M. Loui Quezada	$8.95
Mae's Promise	Melody Walcott	$8.95
Magnolia Sunset	Giselle Carmichael	$8.95

Other Genesis Press, Inc. Titles (continued)

Title	Author	Price
Matters of Life and Death	Lesego Malepe, Ph.D.	$15.95
Meant to Be	Jeanne Sumerix	$8.95
Midnight Clear (Anthology)	Leslie Esdaile Gwynne Forster Carmen Green Monica Jackson	$10.95
Midnight Magic	Gwynne Forster	$8.95
Midnight Peril	Vicki Andrews	$10.95
Misconceptions	Pamela Leigh Starr	$9.95
Misty Blue	Dyanne Davis	$9.95
Montgomery's Children	Richard Perry	$14.95
My Buffalo Soldier	Barbara B. K. Reeves	$8.95
Naked Soul	Gwynne Forster	$8.95
Next to Last Chance	Louisa Dixon	$24.95
Nights Over Egypt	Barbara Keaton	$9.95
No Apologies	Seressia Glass	$8.95
No Commitment Required	Seressia Glass	$8.95
No Ordinary Love	Angela Weaver	$9.95
No Regrets	Mildred E. Riley	$8.95
Notes When Summer Ends	Beverly Lauderdale	$12.95
Nowhere to Run	Gay G. Gunn	$10.95
O Bed! O Breakfast!	Rob Kuehnle	$14.95
Object of His Desire	A. C. Arthur	$8.95
Office Policy	A. C. Arthur	$9.95
Once in a Blue Moon	Dorianne Cole	$9.95
One Day at a Time	Bella McFarland	$8.95
Only You	Crystal Hubbard	$9.95
Outside Chance	Louisa Dixon	$24.95
Passion	T.T. Henderson	$10.95
Passion's Blood	Cherif Fortin	$22.95
Passion's Journey	Wanda Thomas	$8.95
Past Promises	Jahmel West	$8.95
Path of Fire	T.T. Henderson	$8.95

Other Genesis Press, Inc. Titles (continued)

Path of Thorns	Annetta P. Lee	$9.95
Peace Be Still	Colette Haywood	$12.95
Picture Perfect	Reon Carter	$8.95
Playing for Keeps	Stephanie Salinas	$8.95
Pride & Joi	Gay G. Gunn	$8.95
Promises to Keep	Alicia Wiggins	$8.95
Quiet Storm	Donna Hill	$10.95
Reckless Surrender	Rochelle Alers	$6.95
Red Polka Dot in a World of Plaid	Varian Johnson	$12.95
Rehoboth Road	Anita Ballard-Jones	$12.95
Reluctant Captive	Joyce Jackson	$8.95
Rendezvous with Fate	Jeanne Sumerix	$8.95
Revelations	Cheris F. Hodges	$8.95
Rise of the Phoenix	Kenneth Whetstone	$12.95
Rivers of the Soul	Leslie Esdaile	$8.95
Rock Star	Rosyln Hardy Holcomb	$9.95
Rocky Mountain Romance	Kathleen Suzanne	$8.95
Rooms of the Heart	Donna Hill	$8.95
Rough on Rats and Tough on Cats	Chris Parker	$12.95
Scent of Rain	Annetta P. Lee	$9.95
Second Chances at Love	Cheris Hodges	$9.95
Secret Library Vol. 1	Nina Sheridan	$18.95
Secret Library Vol. 2	Cassandra Colt	$8.95
Shades of Brown	Denise Becker	$8.95
Shades of Desire	Monica White	$8.95
Shadows in the Moonlight	Jeanne Sumerix	$8.95
Sin	Crystal Rhodes	$8.95
Sin and Surrender	J.M. Jeffries	$9.95
Sinful Intentions	Crystal Rhodes	$12.95
So Amazing	Sinclair LeBeau	$8.95
Somebody's Someone	Sinclair LeBeau	$8.95

Other Genesis Press, Inc. Titles (continued)

Someone to Love	Alicia Wiggins	$8.95
Song in the Park	Martin Brant	$15.95
Soul Eyes	Wayne L. Wilson	$12.95
Soul to Soul	Donna Hill	$8.95
Southern Comfort	J.M. Jeffries	$8.95
Still the Storm	Sharon Robinson	$8.95
Still Waters Run Deep	Leslie Esdaile	$8.95
Stories to Excite You	Anna Forrest/Divine	$14.95
Subtle Secrets	Wanda Y. Thomas	$8.95
Suddenly You	Crystal Hubbard	$9.95
Sweet Repercussions	Kimberley White	$9.95
Sweet Tomorrows	Kimberly White	$8.95
Taken by You	Dorothy Elizabeth Love	$9.95
Tattooed Tears	T. T. Henderson	$8.95
The Color Line	Lizzette Grayson Carter	$9.95
The Color of Trouble	Dyanne Davis	$8.95
The Disappearance of Allison Jones	Kayla Perrin	$5.95
The Honey Dipper's Legacy	Pannell-Allen	$14.95
The Joker's Love Tune	Sidney Rickman	$15.95
The Little Pretender	Barbara Cartland	$10.95
The Love We Had	Natalie Dunbar	$8.95
The Man Who Could Fly	Bob & Milana Beamon	$18.95
The Missing Link	Charlyne Dickerson	$8.95
The Price of Love	Sinclair LeBeau	$8.95
The Smoking Life	Ilene Barth	$29.95
The Words of the Pitcher	Kei Swanson	$8.95
Three Wishes	Seressia Glass	$8.95
Through the Fire	Seressia Glass	$9.95
Ties That Bind	Kathleen Suzanne	$8.95
Tiger Woods	Libby Hughes	$5.95
Time is of the Essence	Angie Daniels	$9.95
Timeless Devotion	Bella McFarland	$9.95
Tomorrow's Promise	Leslie Esdaile	$8.95

Truly Inseparable	Wanda Y. Thomas	$8.95
Unbreak My Heart	Dar Tomlinson	$8.95
Uncommon Prayer	Kenneth Swanson	$9.95
Unconditional	A.C. Arthur	$9.95
Unconditional Love	Alicia Wiggins	$8.95
Under the Cherry Moon	Christal Jordan-Mims	$12.95
Unearthing Passions	Elaine Sims	$9.95
Until Death Do Us Part	Susan Paul	$8.95
Vows of Passion	Bella McFarland	$9.95
Wedding Gown	Dyanne Davis	$8.95
What's Under Benjamin's Bed	Sandra Schaffer	$8.95
When Dreams Float	Dorothy Elizabeth Love	$8.95
Whispers in the Night	Dorothy Elizabeth Love	$8.95
Whispers in the Sand	LaFlorya Gauthier	$10.95
Wild Ravens	Altonya Washington	$9.95
Yesterday Is Gone	Beverly Clark	$10.95
Yesterday's Dreams, Tomorrow's Promises	Reon Laudat	$8.95
Your Precious Love	Sinclair LeBeau	$8.95

Order Form

Mail to: Genesis Press, Inc.
P.O. Box 101
Columbus, MS 39703

Name ____________________
Address ____________________
City/State ____________________ Zip ____________
Telephone ____________________

Ship to (if different from above)
Name ____________________
Address ____________________
City/State ____________________ Zip ____________
Telephone ____________________

Credit Card Information
Credit Card # ____________________ ☐Visa ☐Mastercard
Expiration Date (mm/yy) ____________ ☐AmEx ☐Discover

Qty.	Author	Title	Price	Total

Use this order form, or call 1-888-INDIGO-1

Total for books ____________
Shipping and handling:
$5 first two books,
$1 each additional book ____________
Total S & H ____________
Total amount enclosed ____________

Mississippi residents add 7% sales tax

Visit www.genesis-press.com for latest releases and excerpts.